The Senator's Assignment

God bless.

Joan E. Hesler

The Senator's Assignment

Joan E. Histon

TOP HAT

Winchester, UK
Washington, USA

First published by Top Hat Books, 2018
Top Hat Books is an imprint of John Hunt Publishing Ltd., No. 3 East St., Alresford,
Hampshire SO24 9EE, UK
office1@jhpbooks.net
www.johnhuntpublishing.com
www.tophat-books.com

For distributor details and how to order please visit the 'Ordering' section on our website.

ISBN: 978 1 78535 855 5
978 1 78535 856 2 (ebook)
Library of Congress Control Number: 2017952734

A CIP catalogue record for this book is available from the British Library.

Design: Stuart Davies

Printed and bound by CPI Group (UK) Ltd, Croydon, CR0 4YY, UK

We operate a distinctive and ethical publishing philosophy in
all areas of our business, from our global network of authors to
production and worldwide distribution.

CHAPTER ONE

AD 31 (Winter in Caesarea)

The candle flickered as a gust of wind rattled through the shutters of the fort's window, sending a thin spiral of smoke drifting towards him. Fabius blinked rapidly, and rubbed his eyes; they felt gritty and kept watering but he continued writing, his hand moving in short nervous jerks, his pen scratching across the papyrus as if every urgent thought in his head needed to be expressed before dawn. He blew on his fingers. Despite his woolen gloves, they were cold and ached from gripping the pen.

He dipped it into the small clay inkpot and paused, lifting his grey head briefly to compose the next sentence before bending over the long wooden table again. An icy draught whistled around the great hall. He had tried not to let it distract him, but the excruciating pain in his stiffening legs forced him into make circles with his ankles to stir his circulation.

He paused again, this time frowning over the contents of his letter, concerned that it might sound as though he was simply getting something off his chest or airing a grievance; although there was an element of truth in both, he thought guiltily. His pen hovered, his sore eyes drifted to the opening sentences and as they scanned down the lines he gave a *tut* of annoyance. His handwriting was sloping all over the papyrus, and there were a few sentences that were barely legible. Perhaps he should have taken more time, he thought ruefully. But it was too late to do anything about it now. The courier would be leaving for Rome as soon as it was light. He flinched as he realized he'd been up writing half the night.

A squall of rain battered at the shutters. Fabius lifted his head, watching them rattle without actually realizing that they were doing so. Then bending his head over the parchment again,

1

he signed his name at the bottom; his breath coming in long, heavy judders.

Staff Centurion Fabius Salonianus.

Former Chief of Staff to Procurator Pontius Pilate. Governor of Judea.

Not that he was afraid, he told himself blowing on the wet ink; at least not on his own account. But what if his wife and his children... No; no one would dare...

Deliberately dismissing the stream of negative thoughts building in his head, he rolled the papyrus, firmly reminding himself that this unexpected arrival of an old comrade must surely be the fate of the gods. They would never give him an opportunity like this one again, so he had no option; he had to take it. Tying the letter with a leather cord, he slid it among the pile of wax tablets and parchments sitting on the table, so that it looked as though it was part of the material he used for teaching the new auxiliaries at the fort. Then sliding off his stool to avoid scraping it noisily across the wooden floor he opened the shutters to one of the windows. It let in a blast of cold wet air which blew the candle out, but also let in the first faint rays of dawn.

Fabius walked quietly across the dimly lit hall with his tablets and letter, but then he was a quiet man, in his speech, in his manners, in his actions, and in his dealings with people. He knew that what he had just done was so completely out of character that not even his wife would believe him when he told her. He winced as the wooden door creaked on its hinges. He didn't want to be spotted, not this early in the morning. His usual time of arrival wasn't for another three hours yet.

Making his way to the kitchens he opened the door to a blast of hot air. The two legionaries on breakfast duty glanced up briefly as he entered but they were more engrossed in throwing trays of fresh wheat biscuits into hot ovens for the imminent arrival of hungry auxiliaries than to take notice of him. Fabius was relieved to see that the only other person present was his old comrade. He was seated at a table in the corner with a plate of yesterday's wheat biscuits, a glass of milk and an apple.

'Ah! Fabius my friend. I was hoping I'd see you before I left.'

Fabius made his way over to him. He was in his centurion's uniform ready for his long journey north, his travelling bag and heavy cloak at his side. Like Fabius, he had slipped over the far side of middle age but would have looked younger if a long jagged scar hadn't left one side of head bereft of hair, his cheek mutilated, and if a black patch hadn't covered his eye. Despite his ugliness, the smile was pleasant, the teeth white and even, and there was genuine warmth in his greeting.

The smile faded as he gestured to the stool on the other side of the table. 'What's wrong?'

Fabius sat down. 'I need you to do me a favour,' he said quietly.

'Of course.'

'Do you still have access to the Emperor Tiberius?'

There was a pause. 'Yes.'

Fabius glanced around furtively, but the legionaries appeared to be finding breakfast more interesting than the conversation of two old soldiers. He pulled his letter out from under his tablets and turned the scroll protectively in his hand, looking at it as though it contained every precious thought in his head.

'When I was in Palestine...' he bit his lip. 'While I was there I saw things that...things that made me ashamed to call myself a Roman,' he said quietly. 'I thought I'd forget them when I returned to Caesarea. I thought my wife, my children, working on my land and teaching here at the fort would drive those memories away.' He took a deep breath, which he held for a moment, but when released came out in judders. 'When I saw you arrive yesterday with the fresh intake of auxiliaries it was like a...a sign from the gods telling me I could no longer sit back and do nothing.' He slid his precious letter across the table to his companion. 'Can you get this into the hands of the Emperor Tiberius without anyone knowing?'

The nod of the head was a firm one. 'I can. Tiberius still sees me as the man who brought his son through his first battles even though poor Drusus is now dead. The Emperor enjoys my rare visits. Besides, I have a box of his favourite sweetmeats so I can slip this letter in with them.'

Fabius watched his letter being pushed into the travelling bag as though he was watching one of his children being dragged away from him.

'Don't worry, Fabius.' The pleasant smile, the even white teeth were reassuring. 'I won't let you down.' The stool scraped across the kitchen floor as he stood up. 'Now I must go. I only wish my time here had been longer. We have too many years to catch up on.'

Fabius noticed the hand that reached down to pick up the bag gripped it firmly, and in a manner that suggested nothing was going to be pried out of his fingers. 'Be careful,' he said quietly. 'Be very careful.'

CHAPTER TWO

AD 31 (Late winter, Rome)

Vivius ran his finger pensively over his lower lip as a smattering of applause echoed around the circle of senators sprawled across their wooden benches in the Senate House. It was followed by a mumbled response which to his ears sounded ominously like a low rumble of thunder. Throwing his arm over the back of his bench, he traced his forefinger over the carvings on the top and tuned his ears to the whispered comments from behind.

'Unbelievable! Sejanus was forbidden to marry the mother so he betroths himself to her daughter? Ridiculous! She's only a child.'

'That man will do whatever it takes to ingratiate himself with the Imperial house.'

'And eliminate anyone who gets in his way. He gets more powerful every year.'

'Only because he's the emperor's friend. I've heard...' The voices dropped.

Vivius studied his fellow senators objectively, a tiered regiment of white robes with purple stripes whispering covertly behind their hands. Not being a man to indulge in senseless gossip, Vivius set his jaw in a manner that would discourage conversation. But if anyone had approached him, he would have told them quite abruptly that the Senate was there purely to provide a forum for political discussion, not pander to the latest rumours. Drumming his fingers on the carvings, he waited for a response to the more serious issue that had been raised earlier. Fortunately, he didn't have to wait long.

A moon-faced, middle-aged senator, heavy around the waist, demanded the floor and was recognized by the residing consul.

'Regarding this matter of Prefect Sejanus recalling various

army commanders from their posts in the colonies,' he began. 'May I remind you that Tiberius has left Rome's administration completely in the hands of Sejanus, and if Sejanus believes these army commanders are not proving themselves loyal to Rome, then I propose we support his move to replace them.'

Yes, with men loyal to himself, Vivius thought folding his arms firmly across his chest. A row of eager hands, supporters of Sejanus, Vivius guessed, rose into the air to second the proposal but other senators squirmed on their benches. Obviously he wasn't the only senator uneasy over what was happening in Rome's colonies, he thought with satisfaction. The moon-faced senator's eyes narrowed as he scanned the room for those disagreeing with his proposal. 'So if the motion is carried and if no one has anything to add. I suggest we send our congratulations to Prefect Sejanus on his betrothal to our emperor's granddaughter.'

As the senators around him rose to their feet to applaud, Vivius couldn't contain a snort of disgust. Sliding out of his bench he headed towards the door, noting with interest that he wasn't the only one.

Deliberately avoiding eye contact with any of his fellow senators, he moved swiftly out of the building, pausing briefly at the top of the steps, momentarily dazzled by the late winter sunshine. Pinching between his eyes he mulled over the uneasy mood of the Senate and the tensions which had crept in with Sejanus's rise to power.

It took a while for the lukewarm winter sun to seep through his heavy cloak, and for the loud cries of the traders behind their stalls to draw him into the present. Anxious to rid himself of the unsettling events in the Senate, he looked around. A group of children were absorbed in a game of marbles beside a gurgling fountain in the centre of the square. Behind them two women bartered loudly with a stall-holder over a bale of cloth. Vivius flared his nostrils as a sick smell of rotting vegetables drifted his way from a nearby shop. Glancing towards the Temple of

Jupiter he spotted two of the senators who had left the same time as him, scuttling through the crowds as if they couldn't wait to put as considerable distance as possible between themselves and the Senate House. Vivius curled his lip in disgust, but as he unhurriedly made his way down the steps into the square, the more generous side of his nature concluded they were probably too scared of Sejanus's powerful connections to the senatorial houses to risk offending him; plus they had their families to consider. Whereas he was neither scared of Sejanus nor had a family to worry about. He had the luxury of living as he pleased, and it pleased him to keep people like Sejanus at bay.

'Senator Marcianus.'

Vivius turned to find the powerfully built Prefect Macro, head of Rome's police and fire department, marching purposefully towards him from the direction of Capitoline Hill. Macro's face was broad, his chin creased and his eyes spaced too widely apart to make him a handsome man, but it did leave him with an expression of honesty which Vivius liked. He descended the remaining steps to greet him. Macro waited until a handful of gossiping senators had moved away before approaching. He spoke softly and without preamble.

'The emperor wants to see you, Senator. Would you be at the Port of Ostia early tomorrow morning?'

Vivius raised an eyebrow.

'And it would be advisable if you could keep this visit to yourself.' Macro gave a brief nod as if to emphasise the point. 'Now if you will excuse me, Senator.' He gave a brisk salute before he marched away.

Vivius watched him go, his right hand drifting pensively through the folds of his toga, searching out his jeweled dagger hidden in its fold. As his hand closed around the hilt, his forefinger ran smoothly over the ruby in the centre. He chewed his lip. It was three years since he had last spoken to the emperor, three years. What in the name of all the gods could he want with

7

him now?

* * *

(The Island of Capri)

As the small vessel dipped and then rose, and the high waves thundered up against the side, tossing it like a plaything, Vivius chanced a glance down at his knuckles and realised he was gripping the side of the boat so tightly they had turned white. He licked his lips; they tasted salty from the spray that had been swirling over them since leaving the Port of Ostia. Narrowing his eyes, he focused on the jagged sea stacks on the shores of Capri. The larger they loomed, the more reassured he was that they would soon be on solid ground again.

There was a shout from the captain as the wooden jetty was spotted, but Vivius didn't loosen his grip until they had moved into calmer waters. Even then he waited until he heard the clatter of oars and the vessel had nudged up to the jetty before relinquishing his hold altogether. He flexed his knuckles; a finger cracked in protest.

The captain of the boat, his sleeves rolled over his fat forearms, reached out to help him ashore but Vivius brushed him aside. Stepping unsteadily on to the jetty, he waited for his legs to accustom themselves to solid ground before glancing ruefully back to the dark grey land mass of Italy. He grimaced at the thought that somewhere between here and there lay his breakfast.

Leaving barefooted sailors with shabby tunics to secure ropes, oars and sails, Vivius crunched across the shingled beach towards the cliff steps.

A Praetorian Guard, immaculate in his leather stripped skirt and bronzed helmet with its red flash of horsehair, saluted as he approached. 'Senator Marcianus? Would you follow me, please?'

Vivius grunted his acknowledgment and followed the guard

up the steps. As they ascended the wind tugged at his cloak but he gave it the freedom to be blown, hoping that when he got to the top the smell of vomit over him would be a little less pungent. When they reached the palace entrance, Vivius ran his fingers through his dark, peppered-grey hair and adjusted his cloak before following the guard along a wide marble-floored corridor. Their boots echoed with an irritating lack of rhythm until they reached carved double doors at the end.

Vivius braced himself before entering a room that was sparse, cold and devoid of sunlight. A sun-faded fresco covered the far wall; a bust of Tiberius's stepfather, the Emperor Augustus, hugged an empty corner, and two sizeable potted palms graced the entrance through which he had just walked. The only sign of life came from the elderly Tiberius seated at an ornately carved table in the centre of the room, his white head bowed over a clutter of parchments which fluttered with the cool breeze blowing in from the terrace.

'You wanted to see me, Caesar?' Vivius detected a strong smell of burning oil as though Tiberius had been working at his table all night.

The white head lifted and tired blue eyes regarded Vivius with an air of vagueness. 'I did?' He frowned and there was a long pause before he said, 'Ah! Of course! Yes, I did.'

Tiberius placed a paperweight on his parchments, rose to his feet and as he moved gracefully across the room, Vivius could almost feel the aura of gloom accompanying him. His leather sandals squeaked on the mosaic floor, and Vivius caught a glimpse of thin, blue-veined legs through the slit in his purple toga.

'You had a good journey?' The question was asked in a manner that suggested Tiberius was simply being polite.

'The seas were rough, Caesar.' Vivius was forced to raise his head as the emperor approached. He was one of the few men Vivius was forced to look up at.

9

Tiberius indicated the terrace and then stepped outside. Vivius followed, reluctant to have the grey skies, cold brisk wind and thunder of waves remind him that winter was not yet over.

'I have a matter of importance I wish to discuss with you, Senator.'

Tiberius fingered one of the tightly budded shrubs in a pot before leading him through a line of potted trees and shrubs, interspersed with half-naked statues and decorative bushes. When they reached the end of the terrace Vivius kept his distance. He had no wish to admire the sea view, or discover for himself whether the rumours that Tiberius flung the subjects he was disgruntled with over the cliffs were true – not on an empty stomach.

Tiberius wiped his hand across his wrinkled brow as though he was wiping away a headache. 'I have received a most alarming letter from a retired centurion called Fabius. I gather he was Pontius Pilate's former Chief of Staff. It came to me via a trusted friend to my dear son, Drusus.' Tiberius absently fingered one of the leaves on his potted bushes as though the very mention of his son's name demanded a moment of silent respect.

Vivius waited.

'The letter claims that, er...that, er...I...' The emperor's voice drifted off, his eyes glazed over and his brow knitted in a manner that suggested that he was losing track of what he was saying. 'And, er...' His shoulders sagged, and to Vivius's concern, his eyes began to flash nervously around the terrace as though he expected a demon to materialise from some unseen corner to agitate him. Turning to Vivius, he placed a finger on his lips, and then half stooped, he tiptoed towards the potted bushes and began rummaging through the foliage.

Unsure how to handle this strange behaviour, Vivius decided his best option was to wait to see if Tiberius came out of this deranged episode of his own accord before taking action. He clasped his hands behind his back, disturbed to see for himself that rumours of his great military hero's bouts of insanity were true. The emperor's search extended to the statues; running his long bony fingers over them, looking behind them. Finding nothing he crept to the end of the terrace and peered over the edge until satisfied there was no one there, he straightened up. For a while he looked confused but eventually, his eyes landed on Vivius and a glimmer of recognition dawned.

'What was I saying?' His voice sounded flat, vague.

'You've received a letter from a centurion called Fabius, Caesar.'

'I have?' Tiberius blinked rapidly. 'Ah yes, I have.' He breathed in deeply and then pursing his lips blew out slowly. He did this three or four times before saying, 'Normally I would, er...I would ignore the contents of such a letter but...er, but for reasons I can't...can't disclose...or rather won't go into, I'm led to believe there could be some truth in it.'

Vivius was relieved to see that he was losing his glazed expression. 'And what specifically does the letter say, Caesar?'

'Oh, I can give you plenty of specifics, Senator.' There was a long pause.

'Such as?' Vivius prompted.

'Such as...well for a start, Rome's presence in Palestine appears to be upsetting the Jews by us simply breathing the same air as them.' Tiberius rubbed the bristling hairs on his arms but it didn't seem to occur to him to go inside. 'Why is that, I wonder. Why?'

The pause was again a long one.

Curbing his irritation Vivius asked, 'And how are we upsetting the Jews?'

Tiberius looked up sharply. 'What? Who's upsetting the Jews?' And almost as though he'd forgotten he'd asked the question began rubbing his chin and pacing the terrace seemingly trying to gather his wandering thoughts together.

Vivius blew softly through his lips.

Eventually Tiberius said, 'I expect my governors to govern the regions I hold, not involve me in their problems. I remember one instance where the Jews complained directly to me. Me! Why bother me? I confess I have no love for the Jews but I can't afford a possible uprising in my colonies.' His chin jutted out with a sense of pride. 'I have made Rome the most powerful empire in the world, Senator, and I intend it to stay that way. To do that I intend to keep peace in the lands we've taken. If my governors fail to follow my policies, I see it as a failure for the Empire.' Tiberius stared moodily across the terrace towards his potted plants.

Vivius decided to try a different tactic in an attempt to discover what the emperor was talking about. 'And my role in this is what exactly?' he ventured.

'You're a Roman official; you're here to serve Rome's interests, and you were an army officer in Palestine so you'll be familiar with Jewish customs. I want you in Palestine.'

Vivius's heart sank. 'I was only stationed there for two years, Caesar.'

'Long enough!' Tiberius brushed past him as he made his way indoors. Vivius followed, grateful to be out of the cold, although no warmer and certainly no more informed.

'I chose you for this task because you undertook a political investigation for me when you were in the Praetorian Guards. You showed a loyalty to me then that got you noticed. '

'Thank you, Caesar, but I ought to point out that it was more a case of stumbling on a conspiracy than taking on an official investigation.'

Tiberius dismissed the comment with a wave of his hand. Striding over to the table, he picked up a parchment and held it at arms' length so he could read it without squinting. 'According to your record, Senator Marcianus, you not only have military experience, but as a magistrate, you're familiar with treason laws and Roman policies in foreign lands.' He threw the parchment on the table. 'I need someone familiar with Roman policies in my colonies. Your records also show you to be a brave man, Senator, and I need a man who is not afraid of weathering the political storms in Rome at this time.' Tiberius gave him a knowledgeable smirk. 'Ah yes, I may spend all my days on Capri, but I'm well aware of the internal wrangling going on in the Senate. Why they should complain I have no idea. I've given Rome years of stability; there are no expensive wars; I have good men governing my provinces and loyal commanders in my army. But now, for reasons best known to themselves, the Senate hate my new laws and my people hate me for my tax reforms.' He waited, as if expecting a denial. Vivius made no comment.

'On top of which,' Tiberius continued. 'I have members of my family fighting to replace me as Caesar when I am gone. They buzz around me like bees dripping honeyed words into my ear. But I know what they're up to, forcing their scrawny offspring on to me as the next potential heir. Now if my dear son Drusus was still alive...' The emperor's tirade stopped midsentence.

Feeling obliged to make a comment, Vivius said, 'Drusus was a fine man, Caesar, a great loss to Rome.'

'Yes indeed,' Tiberius said softly. He ran his fingers aimlessly across the wax tablets on the table, and then lifting his head regarded Vivius squarely and without even a hint of his previous vagueness. 'There is trouble brewing in Rome, Senator Marcianus,' he said quietly. 'And there are plots being hatched against me. I need a man I can trust.' He eyed Vivius covertly through half-lowered lids. 'I need to know who my enemies are. Mark my words, I will have enemies; members of the Senate perhaps, my family or...or...' He glanced down at the parchment in his hand. 'Or someone closer, someone I trust.'

Sejanus sprang easily to Vivius's mind which is why he said, 'Then perhaps I would serve you better in Rome, Caesar?'

The emperor's words were measured when he said, 'Haven't you been listening to a word I've been saying? I want you in

Palestine. I want you to find out what's going on in that colony. But no one is to know what you're doing.'

'Of course,' Vivius said hastily, but making one final attempt to avert this seemingly impossible assignment, added, 'I do, however, feel it my duty to point out that as a senator I am obliged to remain in Rome to attend the Senate, so I would need a good reason to justify my absence.'

Tiberius's face darkened. 'Then find one and stop making excuses, Senator Marcianus,' he snapped. 'This is a sensitive situation. Sejanus is my friend; a close friend. I rely heavily on him to deal with administrative matters in Rome now that my dear Drusus...' He paused. 'Sejanus chose Pilate for this post of Governor of Judea, and now Sejanus is betrothed to my granddaughter. As he's soon to be part of the Imperial household I wouldn't want to offend him.' Tiberius wagged a finger at him. 'And there's to be no going to the Jewish authorities either; I don't want them to think we're incapable of solving our own problems. This is strictly among ourselves. No one must know what's going on, *no one*. Do you understand?'

I don't even know what's going on, Vivius thought ironically, but all he said was 'Yes, Caesar. In that case may I have the letter?'

'No you may not.' Tiberius barked. 'This is the only proof I have that there are plots against me. I'm not letting it out of my sight.'

Vivius cleared his throat. 'So...if I'm to keep this confidential, and I can't speak to the Jews or know the contents of the letter, how exactly am I to start my investigation, and...what specifically am I investigating, Caesar?'

Tiberius stared at him in a manner that suggested he was puzzled by the question. 'What do you mean, what are you investigating? You're going to Palestine to assess the mood of the Jews and to investigate the Governor of Judea, Pontius Pilate. Is he following Roman policies? If not, why not.'

'Investigate Pilate? But...'

'You have a problem with that?'

Deciding an honest answer might not be in his own best interests Vivius kept silent, his heart sinking deeper into his chest at each depressive beat.

Rummaging through the pile of wax tablets on his table, Tiberius brought out a small tablet and stylus and began writing. 'This is the name of the man who wrote the letter. He lives somewhere in Caesarea. You'll have to find out where.'

'And when do you want me to go?'

'Within the week. The Jews have their Passover festival in early spring. It's a good time to go. Pilate has to oversee the event in Jerusalem, but you're to report back to me, only me, understand?' There was the slightest hesitation. 'Not to Sejanus; only me,' he added and with a glare fierce enough to convince Vivius that there would be dire consequences if he was disobeyed. 'And I want you back in Rome for the start of the summer festival, regardless of what you've found out.'

'That will only leave me two, perhaps three weeks in which…' Catching the glare Vivius bowed his head. 'I shall do as you say, Caesar,' he said quietly.

* * *

Vivius's boots splashed through the puddles, splattering his toga and cloak, as he hurried down the cliff steps towards the jetty, but he barely noticed. He hated confusion, and there was no doubt his usual clear and analytical mind was confused over what he considered to be a bizarre assignment. Was the emperor hinting he mistrusted Sejanus? And investigate Pontius Pilate? Investigate what? His policies, his actions, his conduct, his handling of the Jews? And how in the name of Jupiter was he supposed to assess the mood of the Jews if he wasn't allowed to speak to them. As for how he was supposed to find a letter writer in a city the size of Caesarea…

He glanced up apprehensively as a low rumble of thunder echoed across the leaden skies. Anxious to reach the mainland before the storm broke, he stopped momentarily to check the jetty to see if his boat was ready, and was relieved to see bare-footed sailors scurrying around the vessel fixing sails and preparing for a prompt departure. He noticed another boat drawing alongside. The sailors in that one securing their flapping sails and oars ready for landing.

Vivius sucked in sharply through his teeth when caught sight of their passenger. With his hand resting on the mast, his cloak blowing in the breeze, the bull-necked, beefy figure of Prefect Lucius Aelius Sejanus, Commander of the Praetorian Guards, made an impressive figure in his Praetorian uniform.

Realising there was little chance of avoiding him, Vivius continued his descent down the steps, his mind methodically ticking off the options for a feasible excuse as to why Sejanus would find him on the Isle of Capri.

It was the sound of angry voices being carried over the pounding of waves and up the shingled beach that made him stop mid-flight. He glanced towards the rocking boat. Sejanus's legs were splayed like tree stumps, his frenzied arms waving in the air. Vivius narrowed his eyes, trying to identify whom he was angry with. It appeared to be the captain. His back was turned, and his hands were making slow steady downward movements as if he was trying to calm the situation or explain his point of view; a point that was clearly not getting over to Sejanus. The sailors, having secured their vessel, hovered on the shingled shore, listening, watching, unsure what to do.

The blow, when it came, was sudden, sharp, delivered from the back of Sejanus's hand, and from what Vivius could see, quite unprovoked. The captain fell, his cloak billowing out across the deck of the boat like a fallen flag. His anger still not abated, Sejanus kicked out with his full weight behind his boot.

Vivius realised there was little else he could do but stand and watch. He'd seen too many senators thrown into the Mamertine Prison, or known of members in the wealthy equestrian class who had disappeared altogether because they had stepped out of line with Sejanus.

To be on the safe side, Vivius stepped back under the shadow of the cliff, relieved to be wearing his dark cloak. He held the cloak tightly to stop it from blowing and watched the captain pull himself to his feet. He was bent double and holding his ribs. It was obvious he was in extreme pain, but he managed to stagger across the deck and down to the hold.

Sejanus stepped on to the jetty; he looked towards the steps but Vivius was reasonably confident that the shadows of the jagged cliffs were keeping him hidden. Nevertheless, he remained perfectly still until Sejanus had begun crunching his way along the shore. Only then did he feel confident enough to continue his decline. They reached the bottom of the steps together.

'Senator Marcianus?' Sejanus's smile was wide and welcoming, but Vivius noticed it didn't reach his eyes. They had narrowed suspiciously. He gestured to the jetty. 'You're heading back to Rome?' His ruddy apple complexion was sweaty but Vivius suspected that came more from Sejanus's love of wine, rather than healthy living.

'I am.'

'You've been to see the emperor?' His voice rose in surprise.

Vivius remained on the higher step. He had no intention of standing next to a man who, in his opinion, was nothing more than a jumped-up policeman and therefore his social inferior.

'I have.' Vivius struggled to force something resembling a smile on to his face. 'He talked of your betrothal to his granddaughter. May I offer my congratulations?'

'Yes, yes, yes, thank you. Did he ask to see you or...'

'He spoke highly of you.'

'He did?' Sejanus gave a short proud laugh, his open mouth

showing a row of yellow uneven teeth. 'Yes, well, I am the emperor's closest friend and advisor, Senator Marcianus. While Tiberius fights with shadows here on the Isle of Capri, he trusts me to deal with administrative matters in Rome. Was it an administrative matter he wanted to see you about?'

'No.' Vivius cleared his throat. 'As you say, he leaves all administrative matters in your capable hands, Sejanus.' His mind scrambled around for another diverting topic and found one. 'I see you've made further changes to the Praetorian Guards.'

Sejanus's chin jutted out, clearly delighted to be invited to talk about his favourite subject. 'Ah! Yes, as a former Praetorian Guard yourself, you'll no doubt be delighted with the way I've reformed them.'

Vivius made no comment.

'They're more than mere bodyguards for the emperor now. I've turned them into a powerful and influential branch of the government who are more than capable of taking an active role in security and political affairs.'

Vivius wasn't too sure he liked the idea of the already powerful Praetorian Guards receiving even more power but just then his concerns were more with the waves pounding up the beach and the high wind rolling the seas. The last thing he wanted was be stuck on the Isle of Capri all night with a mad emperor and a bully.'So tell me, Senator; did the emperor want you for anything important?'

Vivius listened to his instincts for caution. 'I found him nervous; he believes he has enemies.'

Sejanus snorted through his nose. 'Enemies? You've seen how well guarded he is. I personally have eliminated any political opponents the emperor may have. I've even replaced the army commanders in our colonies if I suspect them of being disloyal.' He paused, and in a manner that suggested he wanted to share a confidence leant forward and added, 'I confess I'm concerned for our emperor's health, Senator. In fact, nothing would please me more than to see him live out his days on Capri, free from political affairs and the calls of public life.'

'I expect you would,' Vivius murmured.

'He dwells on topical issues and then builds them up in his mind until they have little bearing on the actual truth. Paranoia is like that, you know.' Sejanus moved in closer and Vivius's nostrils flared as a whiff of stale wine drifted in front of him. 'In fact, in a few months he'll have forgotten that you were on Capri, and er...a word of advice, Senator.' His voice dropped to almost a whisper. 'So should you.'

Vivius felt the hairs on the back of his neck stiffen.

CHAPTER THREE

(Rome)

Vivius closed his eyes as he breathed in the early morning air, but the fresh smell of dank earth and the woody scent of his olive grove did nothing to clear his head. Sinking down on to his haunches, he rubbed the gnarled and twisted trunk of the nearest tree as if he was trying to erase all memory of the emperor's insanity yesterday, and his own confusion over the assignment. If there was one thing he detested, he brooded, it was confusion. He liked things neat and orderly, each aspect of his life in a separate compartment, like the trees in his olive grove, spaced regimentally the same distance apart.

'The winter frosts haven't done no harm to the trees, master. And if we can keep them black bugs at bay this year I reckon them olives will be at their best come harvesting time.'

The silvery green leaves seemed to whisper a greeting as Vivius's Greek manager approached with an easy and familiar gait through the olive grove. Phaedo was a loose-boned, placid, sleepy-looking man with a round weathered face that crinkled easily into a smile and made him comfortable to be around. Vivius raised his head and watched him examining the buds on one of the higher branches.

'I reckon there'll be no more frosts this winter. Perhaps we ought to plant those young trees now; that is, if you're still thinking of extending?'

Vivius, still on his haunches, had an unexpected image of gazing up at Phaedo as a child and being told by his father that he must listen to this new slave; because despite his youth, Phaedo could teach him all there was to know about growing olives.

'I am, Phaedo. I think we could soon have one of the most

prosperous olive groves in Rome; far better than...' Vivius snapped a dead twig off one of the lower branches with such force that it shook the tree.

There was a pause before Phaedo softly said, 'It's already more prosperous than in your father's day, master.'

Vivius bent his head, concentrating on snapping the twig into pieces with short sharp movements while he wondered why, in the name of all the gods, he was thinking about his father? He hadn't given the man a thought in years.

He stood up slowly, allowing his gaze to drift up the hill towards the old stone farmhouse. The building was half concealed behind the sizeable extension taking place to his own modest villa. The roof of the old farmhouse was sagging, the timber beams rotting, and the shutters were hanging off, leaving it with a neglected and decayed appearance. That was why his father had come to mind, he thought irritably. It was having to make a decision about demolishing a building that had been in the Marcianus family for four generations.

'Should I demolish it or use it for storage?'

'The old family farmhouse?' Phaedo asked, and when Vivius didn't respond added, 'You never liked it, did you?' He paused a beat. 'Why don't you demolish it and extend the long shed. If we're extending the olive grove it makes sense to extend our existing storage facilities.'

Vivius's gaze drifted over the landscape to the long shed which was exactly one hundred and twenty-six child's paces from the old farmhouse. He knew that for a fact; he'd paced it often enough when he'd wanted to escape a beating from his father. Inside stood the massive stone wheels that crushed the olives to pulp, the heavy wooden presses, the winter fire which kept the olives at the right temperature and the big clay pots for storing oil. His face softened into a half smile when he remembered how Phaedo used to scold him for hiding in the empty clay pots when he was small in case he got stuck, yet had been quick enough to

hide him inside one when his father was drunk and looking to
beat him up. His eyes drifted back to the farmhouse.

Strangely enough, it was the smell of the dank earth as he
had crouched under the olive trees that came to mind first; the
squeaky noise the roof of his mouth had made as he had sucked
his thumb; Fabiana, their house slave, standing at the door, her
curls blowing in the breeze, her hand provocatively rubbing his
father's thigh; his father bending down from his horse to whisper
into her ear; the cold air on his white and flat thumb as he had
pulled it out of his mouth.

His father had urged his mount forward. He had leapt from
his hiding place. 'Father! Wait! Wait!'

Reining in his horse his father had waited, the nerve in his
jaw twitching impatiently.

'Don't go, please don't go father. Please stay. Fabiana...she
beats me when you leave.'

His father had glowered down at him. 'Nonsense! If Fabiana
beats you, you must have done something wrong.'

'No, no, no. I'm good.' Vivius had grabbed the horse's mane.
' If you go Brutus will leave the slaves quarters and come into
the house. He drinks your wine and siphons off your olive oil.'

His heart had sank when he saw the disbelief written all over
his father's face. But then Vivius was used to it. There'd never
been any expression of kindness there; at least not since his
mother died. Things had changed when she died.

'Please, Father! Please! Brutus and Fabiana make grunting
noises like animals in your bed when you're away. I've seen
them...and...and Fabiana says she'll thrash me if I tell you.'

His father had leant forward, and for one wild moment,
Vivius had thought he was going to be swung up on to the horse
like when he was little and his mother was alive. But the action
was simply to unclench Vivius's fingers clutching the animal's
mane.

Then he had unhooked his whip.

Even now, as an adult, Vivius winced at the sight of the whip. It had stung his back, flaying his child's skin but he hadn't cried out. His father saw crying as a weakness and weakness wasn't allowed, not in the Marcianus household. His father was a strict disciplinarian to the point of cruelty. He was a soldier and that was his way, Phaedo had once said.

'Now, move boy.' His father had turned the whip on his horse's rump, and the startled animal had lurched sideways knocking Vivius to the ground. His father had ridden off and never even looked back.

Briskly rubbing the bark off his hands, Vivius cleared his throat. 'Right Phaedo, so extending the long shed, finishing the extension to my villa and demolishing the old farmhouse; those are the building projects. As for the olive grove, you'll need to clear those rocks from the hillside before you can plant the new trees.' He looked anxiously at his manager. 'I hadn't anticipated being away right now.'

'I can manage, master. I know what you want.'

'I should only be away a few weeks but don't hesitate to hire more slaves if you need them.'

'And your wedding, master?'

Vivius rubbed his chin, struggling with the image of his betrothed's hazel eyes brimming with tears, and her pert little chin jutting out as she bore the disappointment of having her wedding postponed.

'I've no option. It'll have to be postponed,' he said uneasily. But realising he was bound by the emperor's demands for secrecy set him another problem. What possible story could he give this woman whom he had known since childhood, and who had an uncanny knack of being able to tell when he was lying. He had loved Aurelia all his life, but she appeared to have grown tired of waiting for him while he furthered his career in the army and travelled the provinces of Rome, and to his astonishment, he had returned to find she had married someone else. A disastrous marriage as he had found out later. Despite coming from a wealthy family in the south, her husband, Julius, had turned out to be a rogue and embezzler, and Vivius wasn't sorry when he died in Mamertine Prison, even though he left his wife homeless and penniless. This was one reason why he didn't want to have to lie to Aurelia. or keep her in the dark as that was what her husband had done. Aurelia, he decided as he headed towards his villa, should be protected at all costs – and it was his job to do just that.

* * *

Aurelia knew that if she walked to the end of the street there was the possibility she could catch Vivius on his regular visit to his bookkeeper. A smile crossed her lips at the thought of his surprised expression when he saw her waiting. On the other hand... She grazed her even white teeth over her lower lip, wondering how long she would have to stand in the cold; not too long she hoped, she didn't want to catch another chill, not on her first trip outside. Rising slowly to her feet she called, 'Ruth, bring me my cloak.'

Her tall, shapeless slave with a thick black shining plait reaching to her waist, blue-grey eyes the colour of gull's eggs and a creamy brown complexion drifted gracefully into the living quarters like a swan. She carried two cloaks over her arm.

'There's no need for you to accompany me, Ruth.'

'Are you sure, mistress? You know how poorly...' Her comments faded as Aurelia firmly took the heavy winter cloak out of her hands.

'I shall be quite all right,' she said wrapping it around her shoulders. 'My chill has almost gone,' She focused on fastening the clasp to avoid eye contact with the girl, but was annoyed with herself for being so feeble minded that she felt she needed to explain herself to her slave.

Ruth made no comment but Aurelia was aware of her disapproval as, with her usual stiff solemn air, she glided out of the room.

Aurelia crossed the courtyard, and leaning back against the stone wall, closed her eyes and soaked in the lukewarm rays of the sun. It was purely imagination, she knew that, but it seemed to be promising the early arrival of spring—and then…summer. Summer, and her wedding. A smile played across her lips as she listened to the rumble of traffic from the main highway; the clatter of wheels, braying of donkeys and the friendly banter of drivers. She took a deep breath, realising she didn't even mind the raw stench from the River Tiber today. She loved everything about the city of Rome, everything…except… Her smile wavered. Living in Campus Martius did have it drawbacks. Over a hundred years ago, before the civil war, this marshy stretch of Rome alongside the river had once been a military training ground and pasture for grazing her great-grandfather's horses. Now, since the ruling of the Caesars, the marshland had been drained and impressive new buildings were towering above the decrepit, old stone town house. At least she had a roof over her head, she reassured herself. For that at least she should be grateful. But it was the same every winter; the chills, the colds, and the cough that tied her to the four grey walls of the old Suranus town house. It had deprived her of a social life and friends; not that she had much of either these days, she thought sadly. Not since the money had dried up. She had no callers, no one wrote or…

Opening her eyes, she clenched her teeth and took a firm grip on her depressive thoughts. Once she was married to Vivius and living in the fresh clean air of the hills these winter chills would stop, she told herself. As the wife of a well-respected senator she would make new friends, and this awful sense of isolation would be a thing of the past. Married! She could feel her spirits lifting as she meandered down the street. She even found herself having to resist the urge of breaking into a skip. It was being outside again, she thought. It was giving her a sense of belonging to a wider world, making her feel like a normal person again. She lifted her head, trying to recapture some of the former elegance and poise she used to have.

She'd never been beautiful, she knew that, at least not on the outside. Her ears were too high and her eyes spaced too close together, giving her a lively impish look that made people respond with a smile when they met her. Yet she knew she wasn't unattractive. She was conscious of possessing a warm and ready smile that put people at their ease, and an inner quality that made them feel they were being listened to. And that, she knew, had a magnetic pull of its own, bringing her admiring glances from those who looked beyond the surface.

When she reached the main highway she leant against one of the baker's warm domed clay ovens on the corner, enjoying the warmth on her body and the smell of baking bread.

She covered her mouth with her kerchief as four slow-moving camels trudged gracefully by leaving an exotic aroma of spices behind them. They were closely followed by two rattling wagons piled high with wool and colourful Spanish cloth. She felt a quiver of excitement at the thought of new dresses for the weeks following her wedding. Money was not to be an issue, Dorio had told her before he had left with the Roman Army cavalry. She must get what she wanted. She gave a half smile. Her brother was a dear, always so generous, letting her live in his house, giving her an allowance and even though he and Vivius had never cared for each other, Dorio would never show it, at least not in front of her.

A line of uncomplaining bowlegged donkeys laden with honey trudged by. On their heels was a wagon containing casks of wine. Aurelia watched the wagon pass with a greater interest. The best Syrian wine; isn't that what Vivius said he'd had ordered for their wedding celebrations?

Feeling mentally more alive than she had all winter, she lost herself in the bustle of traffic heading for the warehouses or the parking bays alongside the River Tiber. Being familiar with the movement of the city she knew they would be waiting there until the lifting of the curfew at dusk allowed them to deliver their goods into the city.

And then she saw him and her face lit up. He was weaving his way towards her through the heavy volume of traffic. Unnoticed, her eyes lingered lovingly on him as they had done ever since they were children; ever since that dreadful day his father had...her smile wavered but only momentarily. Shocking though that experience had been she always found herself looking back on it with a strange sense of affection because that was the day she had first known she had loved Vivius. She saw a handsome, serious, deep-thinking man who preferred his own company or the company of a few select friends to a gathering of many people.

He spotted her and his face brightened without actually smiling. When he reached her, he took her hands in his and lifting them to his lips briefly kissed them.

'How are you, my love?'

The stiff and formal greeting was done in a manner he might use to any woman of his acquaintance. She wasn't offended; she was used to his ways. But for once, just this once after her long and lonely winter, she wished she could simply drift into him, feel the warmth of him, the smell of him, the firmness of his body, but she knew him well enough to realise that such an outward display of affection in public would be an embarrassment to him so all she said was, 'I'm well, Vivius.'

She didn't miss his sceptical expression as he ran his eyes over her slim figure making her wish she hadn't piled her hair on top of her head in the fashionable style of the day. Since her long winter chill, it had lost its lustrous brown sheen, and she was conscious that this particular style might have accentuated the hollows in her cheeks.

27

'In fact,' she continued, slipping her fingers through the crook of his arm. 'My physician tells me I shall be blooming for our wedding ceremony.'

Vivius patted her hand in an abstract manner as though his thoughts were elsewhere.

'You will stay for lunch, won't you?' She asked as they walked casually back to the Suranus town house.

Vivius shook his head. 'I'd love to, my dear, but I have something I must discuss with you first and then I, er...must see my bookkeeper and...I have things to do.'

She glanced up curiously at this unusual indecisiveness but decided to wait until they had reached the Suranus town house before enquiring further. When they stepped inside, she handed her cloak to her slave.

'Bring us drinks, would you, Ruth?'

The warmth from the iron brazier wrapped itself around her like a musty blanket as she led the way into her living quarters. She avoided glancing towards the colourful tapestries on the walls hoping not to draw attention to the spreading patches of mould beneath them. But she could smell the dampness and knew such things would not go unnoticed by Vivius.

'It's getting worse,' he said pulling down the corner of his mouth.

Aurelia waved her hand dismissively at him. 'It's the winter flooding that causes the damage; my brother can fix it when he returns to Rome. It's his house, let him sort it out. We'll be married by then.'

It was the strained silence that she found most unnerving.

Vivius cleared his throat. 'How is Dorio? Any news of him?'

Drifting across the raffia mats Aurelia sank down on a low couch worn with age. 'Not since the report from Galilee saying his injuries were serious.'

She waited until he had settled on the couch opposite and Ruth had brought in a jug of grape juice before asking, 'So what did you wish to discuss with me, Vivius? Was it the wedding?' Although concentrating on pouring grape juice into the goblets, she could sense the awkwardness in him, and found she was mentally preparing herself for bad news.

'The thing is...' He cleared his throat. 'I may have to postpone the...wedding...' He threw her a fleeting, almost apologetic glance, but a glance was all it was. 'I have to go away, for a few weeks.'

She handed him a goblet, then picking up her own sank back on her couch and tried to keep the disappointment out of her voice when she asked, 'Where to?'

He cleared his throat again. 'It's, er...confidential, my love. Nothing to concern you. Besides, the less you know the safer you'll be.'

'Safe?' Aurelia lingered over the word before nodding her head knowledgeably. 'Ah! Then I assume it has something to do with your visit to the emperor.' And she would have burst out laughing at Vivius's surprise—if she hadn't been so disappointed over the postponement of her wedding. She toyed with the idea of telling him Ruth had seen him getting out of a small boat at the Port of Ostia yesterday when she had been visiting her sick sister, and that knowing there was only one person in the world who could persuade Vivius on to the seas, it wasn't hard to guess he had been to see the emperor. But irritated at being treat like a woman of no consequence, a fragile ornament incapable of handling reality, she found herself reluctant to give him the satisfaction of knowing where she had acquired her information. She waited for him to take her hand, apologise for the postponement, reassure her, even throw her a look of intimacy, but he didn't.

'Will the Senate give you leave to go?'

'Hopefully.'

'And when do I expect you back?' she asked trying to keep the ice out of her voice.

'Before the summer festival.' He leant forward, rubbing his chin the way he usually did when he was pondering over an idea. 'This physician that's been treating you over the winter months Aurelia, is he an army physician?'

'Yes. I'm one of his private patients.'

'Is he influential? I mean, what are the chances of him having Dorio transferred from Galilee to the infirmary in Jerusalem? Fort Antonia is far better equipped than anything they've got in Galilee. '

She frowned at him. 'Why would he do that? Besides, my physician tells me that if Dorio's able to travel the army could send him home.'

'They could, but I guess...I guess I was thinking that, er...if Dorio can be transferred to Jerusalem, then I can bring him back to Rome in time for the wedding. You'd like that, wouldn't you?'

Why was he talking to her as though she was eight years old, she thought irritably. 'Of course I'd like that, Vivius. But my initial response is to ask what you're doing in Jerusalem in the first place. I don't believe for a second that you'd travel all the way to Palestine for Dorio. Besides, Dorio's under army orders. I can't see the military allowing you bring him back to Rome because you want to?'

'It depends how far my influence stretches in Palestine,' Vivius said cautiously, 'And, I suppose, on the severity of his wounds.' And he seemed to be speaking to himself when he added, 'But the trip might look feasible if your army physician were to accompany me.' He looked up at her. 'Has he seen action?'

'Yes, but to go anywhere he would have to get permission from the army,' she reminded him. She paused. 'I assume then that the emperor needs you to go to Palestine, Vivius.' She waited for him to enlighten her, but when he didn't, she continued, 'I confess it would be lovely to have Dorio home for our wedding, but who in their right mind is going to believe a senator from

Rome would travel all the way to Jerusalem for a wounded Decurion? I certainly don't.'

'You don't?'

'No I don't.' She paused a beat and then leant forward. 'Talk to me, Vivius,' she said quietly. 'I can tell you're disturbed about something. What is it?'

He shook his head. 'What's the name of your physician?' he asked avoiding eye contact.

She tried not to show her frustration as she rose to her feet. Silently drifting over to table where she kept her writing materials she picked up a stylus, wrote the address on the tablet but found herself having to resist the urge of throwing it at him.

He took the tablet without looking at her, and she could see he was lost in his own private world again; a world that she had never been allowed to enter. His mind clearly not on her, or her disappointment, or their forthcoming wedding; whenever that was — he hadn't even said.

* * *

Vivius sneezed. Dammit! Did they never clean this place? He rubbed his nose in an attempt to clear away the smell of dust while he examined the floor-to-ceiling shelves of old scrolls and wax tablets in the Hall of Records.

'Reports from Palestine in the last four years you said, Senator?' A weasel-looking bald-headed clerk with the complexion of a candle squinted along a row of ledgers. The only light was coming from a high window.

'Let me see...ah! Here we are.' Pulling a thick volume from one of the shelves, he staggered over to the table with it. More dust rose into the air as he dropped it on the top. 'Is there anything else you need, Senator?'

Vivius opened the volume and grimaced at the hours of reading ahead of him. 'I'll call you if there is.'

He sat down. Deciding that an overall picture of what was going on in Palestine was all he needed at this stage, he turned the parchments over slowly. There was mention of Pilate's introduction of copper coins causing the Sanhedrin, the ruling body and supreme council in Palestine, to send an angry letter of complaint to Rome. It didn't look as though anything had been done about it as there was no reply. There were numerous reports of Jewish demonstrations over the heathen images Pilate had brought into the holy city. It appeared the Sanhedrin had been forced to send in their own police guards for fear of reprisals from the Romans, but there had been reports of skirmishes anyway. Then there were the Zealots, the religious fanatics who opposed with the sword any attempt to bring Jewish land and culture under the dominion of idolatrous Rome. Vivius read these reports with more interest as the Zealots were the party responsible for Dorio's injuries. Finally, Vivius came across a brief report from Pontius Pilate.

...*the demonstration got so out of hand that the only way to restore order was to send in my legions; we killed over two hundred Jews.*

Vivius rubbed his chin. Well he had certainly got his overall picture. Two hundred Jews killed in one demonstration and Pilate thought so little of it, he found it barely worth covering two lines? That at least was worth probing into although probably not serious enough to warrant spending too much time on, and possibly not what Tiberius wanted him to investigate anyway, but it was a start. No mention of Sejanus whatsoever.

Despondent, Vivius closed the volume with a thud sending a cloud of dust into the air. Now all he had to do was convince the Senate that he needed to go to Palestine to gather valuable information on their thriving olive industry with a view to expanding his own estate, and while he was there assess the wounds of his future brother-in-law who had been fighting for the glory of Rome.

* * *

(The Port of Ostia — approximately 15 miles from Rome)
Vivius blew on his frozen knuckles, stamped his feet and viewed the pale blue skyline breaking over the Port of Ostia with some misgivings. No one ventured out on the seas during the winter months, but as this was early spring he had hoped it would be kind to him. It didn't look as if it would. Despite the promise of a fine day, he knew from bitter experience that the brisk wind blowing from the north could make the seas rough.

'Senator Marcianus!' The shout from the top of the gangplank had a ring of impatience to it. 'Will you be long, sir? The boat's loaded and I need to catch the tide.'

Irritated at being dictated to by a mere captain, Vivius flared his nostrils, inhaled lungful's of cold, salty sea air and concentrated on the early morning barge drifting down the River Tiber from Rome. When it docked only a handful of passengers alighted, mainly dockworkers, merchants and a few travellers, no one from the Roman Army that looked remotely like a physician. Vivius hissed impatiently through his lower teeth.

'Senator Marcianus!'

A fresh-faced, skinny young man, Vivius guessed him to be of Greek origin, had alighted. He was racing towards him with a colourful but shabby patchwork travelling bag bouncing off one leg and a smart leather medical case bouncing off the other. In fact, everything about the young man seemed to bounce — the curls in his hair, his running feet — his whole body seemed to be like a bouncing ball.

'Senator Marcianus?' Vivius's name came out in short sharp pants. 'I'm sorry I'm late, Senator. It was all last minute as you can guess.'

Vivius raised an eyebrow. 'I'm all out of guessing, young man. Who are you?'

'Ah, yes. Sorry.' The young man dropped his bags. He spoke

quickly, barely leaving space for a breath. 'The army physician you asked for was called to the hospital last night. Six high-ranking officers have been seriously wounded. He wasn't too pleased about having to stay I can tell you, but the army said the wounded officers took priority.' He gasped his next breath. 'Anyway, he tried arguing but they wouldn't listen; so he sent me in his place.' The young man smiled; a wide, good-natured smile that had the effect of lighting up his face.

'And who are you?'

'My name's Lucanus. I'm a physician.' He struggled to keep the note of pride from his voice. 'The army physician you asked for is my mentor. He took me on to help with his private patients when I qualified last year.'

'Hmm.' Vivius inspected the young man from head to toe. His brown tunic was of poor quality, his untidy brown curls gave him a permanently unkempt look, he needed new sandals and Vivius surmised that his shabby patchwork travelling bag would be an offense to even the poorest of travellers. The only redeeming features about him were that he was clean, he spoke intelligently—if not a little too exuberantly—and at least the leather medical case gave the impression he was serious about his profession.

'Well I'm afraid you've had a wasted trip, er...'

'Lucanus.' The young man paused a beat. 'I know I don't look like much, Senator, but I had the best grades at Tarsus Medical School,' he added persuasively.

'Senator!' The call from the vessel was sharper this time. 'If that's our passenger, then, sir, we really must leave or we'll miss the tide.'

Vivius raised his arm as indication that he'd heard. 'I specifically wanted an army physician. I'm used to travelling with them. If I can't have one then I'd rather travel alone.'

'I would have thought any good physician would do to look after the wounded Decurion?' Lucanus's pleading honeybee

34

eyes reminded Vivius of a puppy waiting to be thrown a bone.

He sighed. The last thing he wanted was a total stranger accompanying him on the long journey to Palestine, but Lucanus did have a point. If he was lumbered with the wounded Dorio for the return journey he'd never get back to Rome. But a naïve young physician?

The captain of the vessel now shouted with a firmness bordering on rudeness. 'Senator, please sir. We're taking up the gangplank this minute. Are you boarding with us or not?'

Vivius cursed the captain and then he cursed the wounded officers that had changed his plans and left him with this puppy of a physician. 'I suppose you better get aboard,' he snapped.

CHAPTER FOUR

(Caesarea)

'Good morning, Senator. What a lovely morning, isn't it? How are you feeling?'

Vivius cringed at the exuberant greeting so early in the day but made no attempt to remove his elbows from the table, his head from his hands or to open his eyes. But he did summon up enough energy to drop the corners of his mouth as a response.

'Ah! You're probably more of a soldier than a seaman,' Lucanus consoled and there was a genuine sympathetic tone in his voice. The chair opposite scraped on the wooden floor as he sat down. 'I guess it's still too early in the spring to expect calm seas, but I had hoped you would have recovered when we reached the inn and you'd had a comfortable night's sleep.' He paused and when there was no response added, 'Obviously not. Do you want something to settle your stomach?'

Vivius grimaced and pushed the plate of bread, the jug of milk and a strong smelling yellow cheese to the far side of the table.

'As your physician I would advise you to eat something.' Lucanus pushed it back in front of him again.

Vivius forced an eyelid open with the intention of glaring at the '*my* physician' remark, but Lucanus had already lost interest in the conversation and was gazing out the window.

'Isn't it wonderful being in Caesarea, Senator? Look at that lovely stone building opposite. Don't you think it equals anything we've got in Rome? I've heard the city has sports arenas and gladiator games. Personally I prefer the theatre. Do you think there'll be time for a visit to the theatre? Of course, I don't know how long your business in Caesarea will take, or indeed how long you intend staying in Jerusalem. In fact, I don't know anything about this trip at all; I simply walked into the army hospital to help out and my mentor...'

Vivius pinched between his eyes.

'...not that I'm complaining. After all that studying I could do with a bit of excitement in my life. I've always wanted to see more of the world so this trip is a wonderful...'

And then he ran his hand down his face.

'But there is one question I would like to ask you senator, if you're up to answering it?'

Vivius forced both eyelids open. 'Not really.'

'My mentor, the army physician, said if he'd been around he could have watched your back. What did he mean?'

Vivius ran his tongue around the inside of his mouth. It was thick, tasted foul and he could still smell his own vomit. He cleared his throat. 'Perhaps he thought that as a senator visiting the colonies I could be in danger.'

'And are you?'

'Not if no one knows I'm here.'

'And do they?'

'No.'

'Hmm. Can I ask another question?'

'If you must.'

'Well, er...my mentor said that while I'm in Caesarea, and if I get the chance, I should visit a Greek physician who's come across a file of ancient parchments on cures for foreign diseases. He's interested to discover whether the Greek's findings would help cure the diseases picked up by Roman legionaries when they're sent to foreign parts. He thinks the information would be of interest to the army hospital. I'd like to visit this chap if there's time. Who knows, if I succeed in bringing back useful information the hospital might even take me on full time.' He smiled crookedly. 'My problem is, that an important physician like this Greek wouldn't want to discuss matters of importance with a nobody like me.'

Vivius had been allowing Lucanus's voice to drift over him but that comment resonated through his foggy brain. He cleared his throat. 'Didn't your mentor give you a letter of introduction?'

'No.'

Leaning forward with a grunt, Vivius picked up a small tablet and a stylus. Writing a few words on the tablet he pushed it across the table. 'This will make sure he sees you. He wouldn't want to ignore a request from a Roman senator.' He paused a beat. 'Why don't you have the letter delivered this morning, and while you're waiting for a reply you could explore the city?'

Lucanus's face lit up but then fell again. 'You...you don't need me to, er...watch your back?'

Vivius raised an eyebrow. 'Do you know how to use a sword?'

The young man flushed. 'Not exactly,'

'What do you mean, "not exactly"? You either do or you don't.'

'Don't.'

'I thought so.' Vivius rubbed his chin and eyed him sideways. 'Why don't you stay on in Caesarea for a day or so, make sure you get everything you need from this Greek physician. Helping our legionaries in this manner is vital to their success on the battlefield. Having been an officer of the legion in foreign climates myself, I know.'

'Really? Won't the Decurion need me?'

'Not immediately. I've arranged for his transfer to the infirmary in Jerusalem. They're far better equipped than anything they've got in Galilee, including physicians.' He glared at Lucanus when he added, 'But only for a day or so, understand? If I chose to leave Jerusalem early, I'll need you around.'

'Yes, of course, Senator, but if you're going to Jerusalem why are staying in Caesarea...?'

Vivius pointed to the door.

Once Lucanus was out of the way, Vivius rubbed his face vigorously with both hands. Knowing he was unlikely to make much headway until he felt more alert, he forced down the bread roll and milk; the cheese he couldn't face. Then throwing his cloak over his shoulder, he left the inn to spend a quiet hour or so at the baths.

Two hours later, refreshed by the steam, the warm water and an excellent masseur, he found himself striding through the prosperous new Roman city of Caesarea in the sunshine. Posted here as a young legionary he found himself fascinated over the changes that had taken place. Where he remembered fields of corn, crumbling wooden houses and plots of overgrown land, there now stood streets of well-designed stone buildings with wide steps and high Doric columns. And where he remembered marshland and vegetation there were houses, squares and fountains surrounded by statues of gods. He found a wall near one of these fountains and sat down, forcing himself to set an action plan with his assignment; the first chance he'd had since leaving Rome without bouts of seasickness disrupting his thought patterns.

So, whatever route he took with this assignment, it was bound to end in trouble, he brooded. What Tiberius's reaction would be if he didn't come up with solid evidence against Pontius Pilate didn't bear thinking about. One the other hand, Sejanus would probably have him thrown in Mamertine Prison if he returned to Rome with irregularities against the man he personally had chosen to be governor of Judea. As for Sejanus himself? Did the emperor suspect him of…something? And the gods alone knew what Pilate's reaction would be if he discovered he was under investigation.

Vivius ran his hand over his clean-shaven chin as if in some vague way it would wipe away his non-too-secure future. What did Tiberius expect him to look for anyway, he brooded? The whole assignment was…vague. Vivius pursed his lips; he didn't like 'vague'.

Pulling the tablet out of his cloak pocket, he stared down

at it miserably. One name, that was all the emperor had given him: Centurion Fabius Salonianus. How in the name of Jupiter was he supposed to find one man in a city the size of...Vivius furrowed his brow as a thought occurred to him. The obvious way forward was to discredit the letter and perhaps even the man himself. Then inform the emperor he'd discovered Fabius to be a disgruntled employee, who bore a grudge or...What had the emperor said before he succumbed to that strange episode on the terrace? Ah, Yes! Fabius was a retired centurion. Perhaps if Fabius was elderly it would be a simple enough matter to make out he was senile, and had been living in a world of fantasy when he wrote that letter. Vivius realised he was smiling. Tiberius would understand a man who was living in a delusional world. At least it would throw doubt over the authenticity of the letter, draw his assignment to a close and give him an excuse to return home.

Encouraged by the development of this thinking process, Vivius rose to his feet. First, he had to find Fabius. He paused. As a retired centurion, he would be required to live within a few miles of a fort in case his services were called upon in an emergency. Therefore, Vivius decided, his first move should be a visit to the fort in Caesarea. They should have a record of him.

Vivius found a lightness in his step as he headed to the fort.

'Yes, we know Fabius well,' he was informed by a Roman officer with a large-featured face. 'He's a quiet, friendly man; teaches the auxiliaries here three mornings a week. He's not in today, but I'll give you directions to his home if you like?'

Slightly uneasy that this description bore no resemblance to the Fabius he had conjured up in his imagination, Vivius marched briskly out of the fort and didn't slacken his pace until he reached the outskirts of the city. The main niggle in his mind was that if Fabius taught auxiliaries at the fort, he was unlikely to be senile. Still, there were other avenues he could take to discredit the man and the letter such as revenge, a grudge, unreliable, he wrote it for financial reward...Vivius made a mental list in his mind as he walked.

Eventually, he reached the crossroads marked on the crudely drawn map given to him by the fort. Here, he found small market gardens, hamlets and fields for farming and cattle. Taking the road on the left by the stables, he turned on to a narrow track overgrown with weeds. It led him to a modest house with pots of half-open flowers under the windows. Making his way up the path, he rapped on the wooden door; it swung open. Two potted palms decorated the square sunlit hall, a little girl's doll lay in a corner, a child's upturned wooden toy cart stood by the door, and colourful glass marbles were strewn across the floor. Vivius screwed up his face as an overpowering smell of oil drifted towards him, but he stepped inside anyway.

It wasn't the smell of oil, or even the open door, but an uneasy instinct born out of years of living in a dangerous political world that warned him something wasn't right; he could sense it. He stood in the doorway, listening. There were toys in the hall but no sound of children. The house was silent, eerily silent. His hand drifted through the folds of his cloak to the jeweled dagger in the belt of his tunic; his thumb running over the smooth ruby in the handle as he tuned his ears to the silence. The palm leaves rustled faintly as a breeze whispered through the open front door; in the distance sheep bleated, birds chirped in the sunshine. Vivius waited, trying to catch the sound of a human whisper, a breath. There were no sounds. The silence was almost as loud as a shout.

Only when he was confident of his present surroundings did he move slowly and quietly across the hall. One hand clutched his dagger, the other lifted the door latch to the living quarters. He opened it, and sucked fiercely in through his teeth.

It was a shambles, overturned tables, chairs and stools, scattered ewers and urns, tapestries torn from the walls, couches and cushions slashed, the stuffing ripped out and lamps broken, leaving an overpowering smell of oil in the room. But the shambles he only vaguely registered. It was a young boy of about fourteen years of age that caught his attention. The boy's face was white, his eyes glared, his hair tousled, and both hands were grasping a raised short sword that was clearly too heavy for him.

'One more step, I warn you,' he growled but Vivius could see the fear behind the threat.

Unhurriedly, Vivius returned his dagger to the sheath in his tunic making sure the boy saw every precise movement.

The boy's eyes wavered, unsure. 'Who are you?'

'My name is Senator Vivius Marcianus, and I'm here to see Centurion Fabius Salonianus.' Vivius raised his hands hoping the boy would understand the gesture.

The boy studied him seriously for a moment before his gaze dropped to Vivius's toga peeping through his cloak. As it drifted up to his face again, the boy's eyes widened.

'You're a senator?'

'Yes.' Vivius was relieved to see the short sword lowering. He wasn't worried about being attacked; he could easily have overcome the lad, but he had no wish to harm him.

'Father said someone would come,' he whispered. 'He said the emperor would send someone of importance.' He swallowed hard and even though he was trembling, Vivius was impressed by the way he lowered his sword and stood to attention like a Roman legionary. 'Forgive me, Senator. My name is Maximus Remus Salonianus.'

Vivius spread his hands. 'What's happened here? Where's your father?'

Maximus cleared his throat. 'My...my father...he's dead.'

Vivius found his heart sinking into his boots. 'When?'

'Last night. I found him in...in a ditch this morning.' The boy's lip quivered. 'He'd been beaten then...stabbed...in the back.'

Vivius nodded, his methodical brain ticking over ways he could turn this tragic event to his advantage. He watched a middle-aged dumpling of a woman, eyes red and puffy, a sleeveless gown thrown over a course dark green dress, and a linen scarf around her head enter cautiously from the garden. Vivius could see the fear in her eyes.

A little girl, Vivius judged her to be around seven or eight years of age, clung to her mother's dress. A tangled mass of brown hair covered her shoulders, her feet were bare, dress buttons undone and her face was streaked from crying. She stared solemnly up at him, then to his dismay, her lower lip quivered, her face crumpled and with a wail she buried her face into her mother's dress.

Vivius wasn't overly fond of children, simply because he didn't know any. But he was disarmed to have this effect on one. Uncomfortably he turned to the boy.

'Mother, this is a senator from Rome.'

'A...a senator?' The woman ran her hands nervously down her gown. 'Forgive us, Senator. You...you gave us a fright, especially after... Please, won't you sit...' She spread her podgy hands in despair at her ruined chairs.

Vivius gestured to the open doors. 'I think it's warm enough to sit outside, don't you?' he said in the hope he could escape from the foul smell of oil.

'Yes, yes of course. Forgive my manners; I don't know what I'm thinking... Sophia, bring us drinks,' she called. The flustered woman led him into a small family garden at the back of the house with a swing, budding flowers, bushes and an array of blue and white hyacinths emitting a more fragrant scent than was in the house. Beyond the garden stood a field of vegetables in various stages of growth. Vivius sat down on a wobbly homemade wooden stool at the side of a marble table.

A girl of around twelve arrived with a tray of drinks which shook as she carried them through from the house. Like her siblings, her feet were bare, hair unkempt and her face was tear stained.

'You must excuse us, Senator.' The woman poured a pale liquid into three beakers. 'As you can see, you have arrived in the middle of a crisis.'

'What happened?' Vivius asked injecting a sympathetic note into his question.

It was Maximus who answered. 'The upset in the house; that happened early this morning while I was with the Vigils. My fa...father...that happened last night,' he said joining them at the table. He swallowed hard. 'My mother and sisters...'

The woman put a restraining hand on his shoulder. 'Maximus feels guilty for not being here, Senator. But in truth I'm glad he wasn't. Two men broke in early this morning while Maximus was talking to the Vigils. Our intruders demanded to know if Fabius had a copy of—the letter he had written to the emperor.' She spread her hands in a gesture of helplessness. 'I...I pleaded ignorance. I thought it might be safer. That was when they tore the house to pieces. We huddled in the corner, the girls and me, listening to them cursing and swearing as they broke up our home. Then they left. They didn't harm us and they didn't take anything but that was why Maximus greeted you with a sword, Senator. He thought they'd returned.' The woman shook her head. 'It was a frightening experience.' She wiped her nose on the corner of her pinafore. 'Maximus arrived back with the Vigils a few hours later with the news that...' Her hand flew to her mouth to contain her sob.

'But they didn't get what they were looking for,' Maximus interjected. 'That's why you're here isn't it senator; you want to know about the letter?'

'Yes, that's why I'm here. What do you know about it?'

'Everything. The information in the letter should be in my father's journals. I can give you them if you want?'

Vivius was startled by the boy's obvious trust in him. 'You

can?' He took a sip of sweet white apple juice that suddenly felt pleasantly refreshing to his taste buds.

Maximus's stool scraped across the ground and he padded over to a corner of the house. Picking up a shovel he said, 'After sending the letter to the emperor, father thought he should hide his journals. He said they contained too much valuable information to leave lying around and he didn't want them falling into the wrong hands.' He swaggered down the garden path towards the field in the manner of one pleased to be doing something of importance for a senator from Rome instead of helping women clean the house.

'It was only after my husband retired from the army that he plucked up the courage to send that letter,' the woman said. 'I'm pleased they've sent someone to investigate. If Fabius had...' She stifled a sob.

Vivius focused on a bee settling on a blue hyacinth and with a buzz bury into its centre. 'Your husband was a brave man for writing it,' he said. He wasn't sure whether that was true or not, but it seemed the right things to say to a grieving widow.

'Do you think so?' Encouraged by the crumb of good opinion he had about the man she loved, she gave a watery smile. 'Do you think you'll get the men responsible for his death?'

Vivius avoided her steady gaze. 'Perhaps.'

They sat in silence watching the boy digging up the leeks.

'Do you know what's in the letter?' Vivius asked.

'Yes.'

Vivius waited.

'Fabius writes about Pontius Pilate's financial indiscretions.' The woman managed a half smile. 'But don't ask me for details. The man to help you there is a Greek called Nikolaos. He was bookkeeper to Pilate until he was dismissed for challenging Pilate over the taxes.'

'So there is proof of tax fraud?'

'Oh yes.'

'Is Nikolaos, the bookkeeper still in Jerusalem?'

The woman shook her head. 'I don't know.' She gave a sad smile. 'I'm sorry, I'm not much help.'

'On the contrary, you're being extremely helpful,' Vivius assured her. He watched Maximus making his way back to them with the shovel slung over his shoulder, a linen bundle in one arm and half a dozen leeks in the other. He deposited the shovel and leeks on the ground, and there was an air of triumph in the way the boy dropped the linen bundle on the table.

Soil scattered as Vivius removed the dirty linen wrappings. When he had peeled the last one off, he found himself staring at an oblong cedar wood box. He tried forcing it open but the lid was stiff; swollen from the damp earth he guessed. Removing his dagger from his tunic, he pried open the lid. Inside were wax tablets and rolls of tightly wrapped parchments, and at the bottom scraps of poor-quality papyrus with scribbled Greek lettering, hieroglyphics and doodling on them. Ignoring these he unrolled a parchment, only to find himself staring at neat but indecipherable notes, most of which was in Fabius's own form of shorthand. Vivius's heart sank as he opened the wax tablets to find the same.

'Can you read these?'

The boy and his mother shook their heads.

Vivius tapped his upper lip, wondering how in the name of all the gods he was supposed to decipher these notes, and why Fabius had used them in the first place. He stopped tapping. Security, he decided. Fabius would use it for security. So, if he taught Roman auxiliaries he obviously had intelligence and the capability for clear thinking which ruled out the question of him being senile. Vivius mentally ran down the rest of his list for discrediting the centurion.

'One question, and forgive me for being blunt,' Vivius said turning to the woman. 'His work at the fort and as a market gardener wouldn't have made him a rich man, but...' Vivius gestured around him. 'Why would he jeopardise all this by sending the emperor a controversial letter on Pontius Pilate? What did he hope to gain from it?'

Mother and son glanced at each other in puzzlement, but then the woman's eyes filled with tears as she realised the implications of his question. 'Fabius didn't want to gain anything, Senator. He sent it because he was a man of integrity, a man of principles. When he retired from the army he used his savings to buy this place, but he always said he should have done something about the cruelties and injustices he'd seen in Jerusalem. He didn't because he had been afraid but he wrote it all down, as you can see. It was his conscience that prompted him to send that letter to the emperor.'

Vivius could feel his plans for discrediting Fabius and his letter diminishing rapidly.

Maximus laid his hand on Vivius's arm. 'Senator, you will do something about my father's letter won't you? You'll get justice for him, won't you?'

Vivius glanced down at the grubby fingernails and was surprised to find himself moved by the boy's obvious love for his father. He moved his arm away, uncomfortably aware that Maximus appeared to have had what he had always dreamed of having from his own father. Vivius pursed his lips. Blast that farmhouse! Ever since he'd decided to pull it down he'd had nothing but vague images and reminders of his father. They kept creeping up on him like wolves stalking their prey, determined to get their claws into the awful memories he had put so firmly behind him.

Returning the wax tablets and parchments to the wooden box, he said, 'Yes.' And as he quietly closed the lid he realised he was surprised to find himself pushing all plans of discrediting the centurion to one side. 'I'll do something about his letter. I'll get justice for your father.'

But the question of how hung over him like a heavy black

cloud.

* * *

Pontius Pilate twisted in his saddle, his round bulbous eyes squinting through the dazzling orange sunrise emerging over the horizon and skimming over the gleaming bronzed helmets of the small force of Roman auxiliary marching behind him. When they settled on his wife trailing at the back he pursed his lips, still irritated over the way she had kept him waiting over a trivial household incident of a slave not packing the right clothes or some such nonsense. He dug the heels of his boots sharply into his dappled mare's flesh to urge the animal forward. She tossed her proud head and snorted in protest, her breath hot and steamy in the cold morning air. Pilate paid her no heed. He had his mind set on lengthening the distance between himself and the legion. It wouldn't increase their pace, he knew that. They were trained to march at a steady rhythm of twenty miles a day and twenty miles they would do until they reached Jerusalem, seventy miles away. But he wanted the extra distance between them to give himself time to think.

To his frustration, galloping hooves informed him his thought process would have to wait. He turned; Claudia was bearing down on him, her purple travelling cloak billowing out behind her, her long auburn curls blowing in the breeze. He watched, admiring her magnificent horsemanship and the way her body swayed provocatively in the saddle but then turned away as she drew alongside him.

'Why are you so far ahead?

'I had intended to be alone to think,' he said pointedly. His voice was silky smooth, cultured, but nasal as if his adenoids were blocked.

'What about?'

'I have problems.'

'Well, I guessed your bad mood was more than having to leave the comforts of Caesarea to attend the Jewish Passover, my love.' Her voice was low, almost teasing.

He glanced at her sharply but not unkindly. He had no illusions as to why a beautiful woman like Claudia had chosen him out of all her admirers. He wasn't the handsomest man in the world, he knew that. His face was too long, his nose too pointed, his eyes bulged like a frog, and his hairline had begun to recede faster than he would have liked. On top of which he was putting on far too much weight. Nevertheless, he saw himself as an intelligent, experienced and ambitious bureaucrat with connections to powerful men like Sejanus; and Claudia was a woman who loved powerful men.

'Do you want to tell me about it?'

He pursed his lips to give the impression he was considering her offer. There had been times when he had found it prudent to confide in Claudia. Coming from a political family, she had a remarkable insight into the world of politics, and there was no doubt her high connections to the Imperial family had been extremely useful to him on occasions.

'Remember Fabius, my former Chief of Staff?' He didn't wait to find out if she did but continued, 'Some weeks ago a centurion appeared at the fort with a fresh intake of new recruits. He turned out to be an old comrade of Fabius's; they'd fought together in Germania, I believe.' Pilate turned his mouth down at the corners. 'Fabius, I never liked the man. He annoyed me, too fastidious, had this disapproving manner about him. He left my employ bearing me a grudge over'—he waved his ringed fingers dismissively in the air—'some incident or other.' He glanced across to make sure he had Claudia's full attention; he had. He never liked his listener's eyes to glaze over while he was talking. 'I became suspicious when I was informed Fabius was at the fort when he shouldn't have been. He had spent the entire night in the great hall writing, and had handed the centurion a letter before he left. But what really concerned me was that on the centurion's return to Rome, he headed straight for the emperor on the Isle of Capri.'

'I saw him, a disfigured centurion with an eye patch and one side of his face... Ugh!'

'Yes! Yes!' Pilate waved his ringed fingers dismissively at her this time, irritated at having his story interrupted by trivialities.

'How do you know he headed straight for the emperor?'

'Because my informant is reliable, Claudia.' Pilate's jaw jutted out in a manner that should deter further questioning on the subject.

'How?' she persisted.

'Because whenever your repulsive centurion is in Rome, he visits Tiberius.'

'I thought Tiberius didn't received visitors?'

'He doesn't,' Pilate said with forced patience. 'Sejanus discourages them, forbids them even, but this centurion is an exception. When Tiberius's son Drusus was alive, the centurion watched over him on the battlefield. Now Drusus is dead, and Tiberius likes to talk about the battles he fought. This is one visitor not even Sejanus can deter.'

'So you think this centurion handed Tiberius the letter?'

'I know he did because...' he paused. 'Some weeks later a senator from Rome landed in Caesarea.' Pilate delivered the news in a slow, smooth silky drawl and noticed with some pleasure that not only did he have Claudia's full attention but he had brought an expression of concern to her face.

'A senator?'

'Exactly! A rare breed this far from Rome. He *must* have been sent by the emperor.'

'You're guessing, but supposing you're right, what will you do?'

'I've done it,' he said in the manner of a man well in control of events. 'As soon as I was informed of the senator's arrival I left orders for Fabius's house to be searched, any copies of his letter destroyed and he was to be given a…a warning. And it's as well I acted quickly. The following day the senator appeared at the fort. And do you know what he was asking for? The whereabouts of Centurion Fabius Salonianus. Still think I'm guessing?' Pilate sniffed through one nostril in an attempt to clear his blocked nose.

Claudia made no comment so they headed south in silence, passing small white houses nestling on steep slopes, clusters of lime and orange groves, merchants with loaded donkeys and proud-necked camels rolling steadily along. Curious shepherds herding sheep stopped to watch the Procurator and his small auxiliary force, occasionally children waved, but the Roman Governor of Judea considered it too far beneath him to acknowledge the people he governed. Besides, he was too wrapped up in his own affairs.

'My only concern now is if the senator materialises in Jerusalem.' Pilate waited until their horses had clopped over a wooden bridge before adding, 'If he does perhaps we should invite him to dine with us, my dear. See what sort of man he is; can he be bought? Presumably, Tiberius will have given him a copy of the letter. I need to see it. I need to know what I'm accused of. I need to stay one step ahead and cover my back.'

Reaching over she lightly touched his arm. 'Don't worry, my love. Between us, we can handle a senator.'

'Worried? I'm not worried,' he shrugged her off, but he chewed his bottom lip in a manner that suggested otherwise. 'Jerusalem during the Jewish Passover is troublesome enough place with the Sanhedrin complaining to me about something or other, the Zealots causing trouble and all the blasted citizens of Jerusalem to contend with. The last thing I want is a nosy senator poking into my affairs.' He paused as a thought occurred to him. His face brightened. 'Yes,' he said smoothly, 'the Zealots can be troublesome—and dangerous.' He smiled, for the first time in days. 'As you say, my love; between us, we can handle a senator.'

CHAPTER FIVE

(Rome)

As Sejanus stormed unannounced into Prefect Macro's office he waved the tablet angrily at him. 'What do you know about this assignment?'

Prefect Macro looked up calmly. His grey wolfhound slunk behind his master's chair, and even though Macro was a sturdy man he was relieved a desk stood between himself and Sejanus.

'What assignment, Commander?'

'Pontius Pilate tells me Tiberius received a letter some weeks ago from a disgruntled employee. He suspects it concerns affairs in Palestine.'

'Really?'

Sejanus hurled the tablet on to Macro's desk. 'Obviously the letter was damning enough for the emperor to send Senator Marcianus to Palestine to investigate.'

Macro paused a beat. 'And what makes you assume I would know anything about that?'

Sejanus pressed his knuckles down on his desk and leant forward so his face was only inches from Macro's. 'Because I was informed that when Senator Marcianus left for the Isle of Capri, it was on one of your vessels.'

'How do you know he went to see Tiberius?'

Sejanus stood up. 'Damn it. I saw the man on the island myself.' He narrowed his eyes so Macro could barely see his pupils. 'What did the emperor want to see him about?'

'How should I know?' Macro said calmly. 'You're the one who has contact with Tiberius.'

'Uh-huh!' Sejanus grunted. He began pacing the floor. The wolfhound, his ears flattened to his head, slunk towards his favourite corner, his eyes warily watching the pacing.

'Damn it! I can't have the emperor upset.' Sejanus swung his boot furiously at the passing hound. The dog yelped and scrambled back under the desk. Macro could feel his thin body shaking with fear. Sejanus pointed a finger at Macro. 'My Praetorian Guards can't be everywhere. I want a handful of your men on the Isle of Capri keeping a close eye on correspondence to and from the emperor.'

'Spy on him you mean?' Prefect Macro rose deliberately to his feet, acutely conscious that the conversation so far had been with Sejanus looking down on him. If he was going to argue back, he would at least feel more comfortable standing up. 'My men are already stretched to the limit with fighting fires, rounding up runaway slaves and keeping law and order in Rome. Surely anything to do with the emperor falls under the jurisdiction of the Praetorian Guards.'

'It does, but as you say, keeping law and order is the job of the Vigils and I sense disorder brewing on Capri.' Sejanus clasped his hands behind his back and strutted across the room like a man beset with worries on every side. But then, he glanced at Macro sideways and in the unexpected manner of one commander of men confiding in another said, 'Between ourselves, Prefect Macro, our emperor is a sick man, a very sick man. He relies on me. He trusts me implicitly to do what is right for Rome and our colonies, and that is a tremendous burden I can tell you.'

Macro found being an unexpected confidant to Sejanus made him even more uneasy.

'Tiberius refers to me as the 'Partner in his labours.' That's how highly he thinks of me. My job is to protect him from the troubles of Rome; that's why I handle all his correspondence.'

Prefect Macro pursed his lips thoughtfully before saying, 'All right, Commander. I shall send a handful of men over to Capri.'

'Good.' Sejanus paced across the floor and back again and Prefect Macro had to endure a longer silence this time. 'My main problem now is the senator. I've no doubt the emperor has sent him to Palestine but to do what?' He paused. 'I don't trust the man.'

'Oh?'

'If he's fallen for some crazy notion of the emperor's, then making enquiries in the wrong places in Palestine could very well disturb the uneasy peace that rests between Roman and Jew. Not to mention disrupt the business ventures Rome has in that colony.'

'I see,' Macro said quietly. 'Why don't you trust him?'

Sejanus glowered at the cowering wolfhound as if he'd like nothing more than to use his boot on him again, but the animal wisely remained where he was, safely ensconced under Macro's chair. 'There was a court case, three or four years ago against Lady Aurelia's first husband. Treason and embezzlement I think were the charges. I'll need to refresh myself with the case. I remember he was imprisoned for embezzlement but the charge of treason was dropped, and do you know why?'

'I have no idea. But what does this have to do with Senator Marcianus?'

Sejanus looked at him steadily. 'Senator Marcianus was the magistrate who had the charges dropped, and now Senator Marcianus is about to wed the widowed lady.' He paused. 'As I say, Senator Marcianus is not a man to be trusted. Was the senator involved in some political or business venture with the Lady Aurelia's first husband?' Sejanus clearly didn't expect an answer because he continued with barely a pause. 'I believe he was.' And Macro had the first hint that trouble was brewing for Vivius Marcianus when Sejanus sauntered across the office and said, 'I think I shall look into this matter more closely.'

* * *

'Mistress, wake up, mistress. You have a visitor. It's Prefect Sejanus.'

Jerked into consciousness by Ruth's urgent shaking, Aurelia sat bolt upright, sucking in sharply through her teeth at the sudden wave of dizziness. Taking a deep breath in an attempt to clear the thick clouds of sleep, she voiced her first thought out loud. 'Prefect Sejanus? Why would he call on me?' But then realising the stupidity of her question to a mere slave, she waved her hand dismissively.

'Shall I invite him in then bring refreshments, mistress?'

'Yes, er...do that.' Aurelia scanned the room; it was cool now the brazier had gone out, too cool, and the room still had a strong smell of smoke to it. Her sewing and threads were strewn across the chair in the corner, and an unwashed cup and plate stood on the table. She gave a tut of annoyance that Ruth hadn't tidied up after her but decided there was little she could do about it now.

Smoothing the creases in her pale yellow dress, she pinched her cheeks to give them colour and tried to recall the last time she had seen Sejanus so she could give herself a talking point. It was certainly when she mixed more sociably, probably when Julius was...her mind flickered uneasily back to her first husband. Folding her fingers neatly in her lap, she pushed him firmly to the back of her mind just as Sejanus walked in.

'Ah! My dear lady.'

She noticed with some foreboding that he was still the same grim, square jawed, heavily set creature that she remembered. If anything, his bushy eyebrows were thicker making him look more formidable than ever. She had a sudden urge to curl back up on her couch as though this visit was nothing more than a bad dream. Fortunately, her former years of entertaining had taught her how to summon up her social graces whether she felt like it or not. Fixing a smile to her face, she rose to her feet and drifted towards him with her arm outstretched. His hand was rough as he grasped her fingers.

'Prefect Sejanus, this is an unexpected pleasure.' She indicated the couch opposite the one she had been sleeping on. 'Please, join me for refreshments?'

Ruth drifted silently across the room and placing a tray on the table between the two couches, poured their drinks and drifted silently out again.

'You have me curious, Prefect. What can I possibly do for you?'

'I understand Senator Marcianus has gone to Palestine?'

Aurelia's stomach did a summersault at the directness of the question. Dampening down concerns that this was information Vivius hadn't wanted even her to know about, she felt she had no other option but to speak the truth. 'Yes,' she said easily and handed him the goblet.

Sejanus leant back on the couch, his face taking on a puzzled expression. 'And what business could the senator possibly have in Palestine?'

Aurelia took a sip of wine to give herself time to think, then taking time to neatly dab the sides of her mouth said, 'He's travelling to Jerusalem to bring my brother home.' She managed to inject a lightness into her voice that she was far from feeling.

Sejanus blinked rapidly. 'Huh? Your brother?'

'Decurion Dorio Suranus. He was wounded by Zealots in Galilee. The army is transferring him to the infirmary in Fort Antonia.'

Disbelief crossed the Prefect's face. 'And the senator is travelling all the way to Jerusalem just to bring your brother back to Rome? Surely the army could send him back?'

'Not in time for my marriage ceremony, Prefect.' She tilted her head as if reflecting further on the subject. 'Vivius also said something about investigating olive groves while he's in Palestine.' Whether that was true or not she had no idea, but knowing Vivius's passion for his olive grove it was a fair assumption to make.

'Olive groves?'

'Yes, he's been talking about extending his for some time

now.'

Sejanus raised a quizzical eyebrow. 'I see; and does the Senate know about this trip?'

'I've no idea, Prefect, but I would imagine so. Vivius always sticks by the rules.'

Sejanus helped himself to a sweetmeat. He chewed noisily and with an open mouth. 'And who looks after his affairs while he's away?' He ran his tongue over the front of his teeth.

'His manager, and I have a cousin who oversees any urgent or financial affairs.'

Sejanus picked at his teeth, removed a crumb and examining the offending object asked, 'What about his friends?'

'Vivius is not a man with a large circle of friends, Prefect.'

'Not even in the Senate?'

'No one that he's mentioned.'

'I see.' Sejanus looked up from his offending piece of food, and Aurelia didn't like the sadistic gleam in his eyes when he asked, 'Do you remember Senator Rebus?'

'I...I don't think so...'

'Oh, I believe you do. Wasn't there a court case between Senator Rebus and your first husband?'

'That was some years ago,' she said stiffly. 'And I'm not sure why you would...'

'Something to do with embezzlement, wasn't it?'

Aurelia clasped her hands together to stop them shaking. 'Julius was in Mamertine Prison for that when he died, Prefect.' She held her head high and tried not to sound pathetic when she added, 'I was forced to sell my home and belongings, but I paid off all his debts; all of them. This house is my brother's town house. If he hadn't opened it up to me I would be completely destitute.' She found her face could still redden at the shame of it all.

'Uh-huh. Wasn't there also a charge of treason hanging over your husband?'

Aurelia ran her hands up her bare arms; they were covered in goose bumps. 'I try not to dwell on the past, Prefect Sejanus,' she said quietly. 'I focus on the future.'

'Uh-huh!'

Aurelia didn't like the way Sejanus smirked, clearly enjoying her discomfort.

'Tell me about Senator Marcianus's relationship with your first husband.'

'There wasn't one; they never particularly liked each other.'

'Really? I find that hard to believe since Senator Marcianus was the magistrate when the case of treason was brought against your husband.'

'The case was dropped for lack of evidence.'

Sejanus gave a forced laugh, his open mouth showing crumbs of sweetmeat stuck to a row of yellow, uneven teeth. 'My dear lady, I have proof that Senator Marcianus concealed incriminating evidence against your husband.'

Aurelia found she was holding her breath. She forced herself to laugh but to her ears it sounded high-pitched, almost manic. 'You're not suggesting Vivius concealed incriminating evidence, are you? Vivius is a man of integrity, Sejanus. He would never do that.' But even as she spoke, she found it difficult to rid herself of that glimmer of unease at how easily Julius had been exonerated.

'Ah! Forgive me, dear lady. I have upset you. As you can imagine I have a difficult job and there are times I need to ask awkward questions to keep this land of ours safe.' He paused. 'So, as far as you are concerned, Senator Marcianus has gone to Palestine to bring your brother home and to, er...inspect olive groves?'

'Yes.'

'He wasn't asked by the emperor to go?'

Aurelia fixed a look of surprise on her face. 'The emperor? Why would the emperor want him to go to Palestine?' She helped herself to a sweetmeat she didn't really want, but it gave her brain time to scramble around for a topic that would enable her to regain control of this conversation. It landed on one. She swallowed hard; the sweetmeat left a sickly sweet taste in her mouth. Forcing a smile across her face, she asked, 'Tell me, Sejanus. How are your children enjoying the ponies you bought from our stables?' She wiped her sticky fingers on the napkin.

'What?'

'Your children's ponies? You bought them from my brother's stables last year...the Suranus stables?' She took a sip of wine to wash away the sweetness, and thought she detected an unstiffening in Sejanus's face.

'Ah! Yes, my children's ponies.' His voice softened momentarily. 'Yes, they love them. My wife, Apicata, keeps them on her property. She lives out of the city now we're divorced.' He wiped the corners of his mouth and for a while his thoughts appeared to be elsewhere. But when he looked up again the human element had disappeared and his eyes had hardened. 'Well, this had been an extremely pleasant interlude, my dear lady.'

Aurelia watched him drain his goblet of wine before he stood up, but finding herself unable to say, 'It was a pleasure to see you,' she simply rose to her feet and smiled sweetly until he had left the room. She waited until the fading crunch of his boots had become at one with the noise of the city traffic before sinking down on the couch and covering her face with her hands.

'Damn you, Vivius! If you'd told me what all this was about I would have been forewarned. Now I've probably said the wrong thing and put you in danger.'

Curling up with her legs under her, she pulled the cushion to her stomach and bit the end of her thumbnail until she felt calmer. After a while, she abandoned the cushion, and uncurling her body wandered over to the open shutters and stared outside. She didn't have much of a view; a few potted plants in a tiny courtyard to give a splash of colour and a high wall covered in green ivy; that was all. She stood here often and sometimes wondered if the smallness of her view was responsible for the narrowing of her vision, or diminishing of her dreams over the last few years. Her lips fell easily into a pout. What sort of a weakling had she turned her into? she brooded. Even now, her only plan of action was to write to Vivius, warn him that Sejanus was accusing him of treachery and bring him back to Rome so he could tell her not to worry and that everything would be all right.

Aurelia was still staring into the courtyard when the thought occurred to her; is that why Vivius keeps things from me, because he sees me as a weakling, a woman who needs to be protected? She pondered on this train of thought as she listened to Ruth clattering dishes in the kitchen. Perhaps that's why Vivius treats me like...like a fragile ornament. She pursed her lips. As for Sejanus, admittedly, he's nothing more than a big bully, but did I make it easy for him? Did he see me as a weak, fragile, incapable woman, easily controlled and even easier to bully? She frowned. And why is Sejanus dragging Vivius into an old case of treason against Julius? She pondered on this final thought a little while longer before taking a deep breath and shouting, 'Ruth!'

Then resolutely sitting down at her writing desk she picked up a stylus and began to write on small tablet. Ruth appeared at the door.

'I've made a decision,' Aurelia said as she continued to write. 'I shall pay Senator Felix Seneca a visit tomorrow. Would you have this sent to him to see if he will be free to see me?'

By the time she had finished her note, Ruth was at her side with her cloak over her shoulders. Aurelia handed the girl the tablet and she left without a word.

The house was quiet without her, but Aurelia was glad of that. She needed time to contemplate what she was getting herself into. So, she mused, Vivius and Felix joined the army at the same time; they were in the Praetorian Guard together; now they were both senators and loyal to the emperor. Plus, he was the only man she knew well enough to trust; and she trusted Felix, implicitly. If anyone could shed light on why Sejanus would want to resurrect this old court case, quell her fears or advise her, it would be Felix, she reasoned.

She bit her thumbnail as the doubts crept in. Although, Vivius and Felix weren't really friends, more acquaintances of long standing. Perhaps she was being presumptuous in expecting Felix to help? And Vivius wasn't going to like her involving Felix in his affairs—especially not Felix. A slow smile spread across Aurelia's face. But then, Vivius knew nothing about her and Felix, and there was no reason why he should. The affair had ended a long time ago. But she was surprised at the way her heart lurched at the prospect of seeing him again.

* * *

Capitoline Hill was busier than she remembered it, noisier, dirtier, more crowded. She kept her kerchief over her mouth, trying not to breathe in the cold mist that had curled between the hills of Rome all day.

Ruth drew alongside her. 'Not far to go now, mistress. Senator Felix Seneca lives around the next corner.'

Aurelia hid a smile. She knew exactly where the senator lived, but she wasn't about to relate information of that nature to her slave. She removed the kerchief from her mouth. 'You might as well go to the market for that material I wanted, Ruth. There's no sense in you waiting around for me. Besides, I've arrived a lot earlier than expected so I may take a short walk.'

With a slight bow of the head that made her plait slide over her shoulder Ruth murmured, 'Yes, mistress,' before heading down Capitoline Hill, with not even the cobbles underfoot diverting the smoothness of her walk.

Aurelia waited until she was out of sight, then, with her heart giving a pleasurable flutter she sauntered the last few yards to Senator Felix Seneca's town house.

Standing behind a leafy shrub across the road, she examined the house and was surprised to find it had hardly changed since her last visit. It was old but well cared for with newly oiled doors and shutters, red and pink geraniums under the windows, neatly trimmed bushes and recently swept steps.

Her fingers played nervously with the cord on her cloak, conscious that although her cloak had been expensive in its day, it was not as fashionable as those worn by the senators' wives and mistresses now. As for her favourite pale blue dress, Aurelia pulled the dark blue ribbon over the tiny hole Ruth had made during the last minute tucks.

She grazed her tongue across her teeth, surprised to find her mouth had turned dry. 'It's months since I've seen him. What if he's shocked by how dreary I've become, in my dress, in my speech, in my company? What if he's not interested in my problems? What if...? What if...?'

The front door opened.

It was an automatic gesture that caused Aurelia to slide behind the shrub. She didn't quite know why she did. Partly, she knew it was because she didn't want to be caught in this momentary lapse of insecurity and partly, to her surprise, an elegantly dressed woman in a fusion of pink and grey had stepped outside. Felix was holding her hand and he looked serious; he was nodding as the woman talked.

Aurelia peered through the branches, trying to make out the woman's face, but she had her back turned. What Aurelia did make out was that her elegance stretched far beyond her attire. She was tall and held her head high, giving her a regal air. Her hair was coiled, neatly styled in the fashion of the day, and adorned with combs. Releasing Felix's hands she pulled up her hood to protect her hair from the dampness, the slow graceful movements of a woman of high breeding. Then with barely a rise of her hand as a gesture of farewell she turned, her cloak billowing out as she sailed across the courtyard.

Felix closed the door.

Aurelia bit her lip, uneasy to find herself in the position of spying, but curiosity urged her to inch forward to see the woman's face. There was something familiar about her, something... Aurelia breathed in sharply as she recalled a gentle woman stroking the horses in the Suranus stables. Apicata! Apicata was the woman Sejanus divorced in the hope of winning a woman of even higher breeding; and it didn't get much higher than the wife of Drusus, heir to the Imperial throne.

Aurelia waited until Apicata was well down Capitoline Hill before discarding her shelter and making her way nervously to Felix's house. She did so conscious of her lack of elegance in dress and manners.

There was no need for her to knock. Felix Seneca wandered easily down the steps to greet her. She noticed there was a broad grin spread across his handsome face and wondered if he had spotted her hiding behind a shrub watching him and Apicata and was amused by the idea. She hesitated halfway across his courtyard but then he held out his arms in greeting.

'My dear Aurelia, what a pleasure to see you.'

She grasped his hands, they were firm, warm and steady. 'Forgive me for being early, Felix, but thank you for agreeing to see me.' She smiled briefly, suddenly unsure of him.

'I was surprised hear from you,' Felix said closing the door behind them. 'And curious; your note sounded urgent?' He gestured towards a long and elegant couch in his living quarters. Aurelia sat down.

A servant hovered, and while Felix issued instructions for refreshments, it gave Aurelia a chance to examine the room. Nothing had changed. It was still elegantly furnished with obscure wall paintings she had never liked but with plastered borders of vine leaves and grapes that she had. Although she found both were hard to make out as the room was dim, the shutters being partially closed to keep out the mist.

Her eyes drifted from the walls and as they landed on Felix, she quivered with pleasure. He was still a winsome man, she decided; immaculate in his dress, had the bearings of a former officer of the legion and Praetorian Guard, light-brown hair, a classic nose and the high intelligent forehead of an aristocrat from the upper social class of Rome. Yet none of these things had attracted her to him in the first place. It had been his kindness and trustworthy face; a face that broke easily into laughter or a smile. She had trusted him implicitly once, but now she had seen Sejanus's former wife in his home ...? He turned, as though he sensed her watching him.

'Refreshments are on the way,' he said with a smile.

She flushed, dropping her gaze on to her clasped fingers. Yes, he had sensed her watching him.

He came to sit next to her, placing his hands over hers, and there was a teasing note in his voice when he said, 'Why do I get the feeling you're not here to resurrect our short but extremely delightful love affair, my dear Aurelia?'

She laughed, but it was more a release of tension than of amusement. 'No, I'm not, Felix. Although I must confess I am tempted; you look extremely good today.'

He squeezed her fingers. 'And you're as beautiful as ever, my love.'

The elegance of his previous guest flashed through her mind. She pulled her fingers away but didn't contradict him because no one had said that to her for a long time, which brought her thoughts back to Vivius and the reason for her visit.

The slave brought in refreshments. She waited until he had served drinks, honey cakes and sweetmeats and had left the room before saying, 'Can I ask you something, Felix?'

He raised his eyebrows at her. 'Of course, my love.'

'What...what was Sejanus's former wife doing here?'

'Apicata?' If he was surprised by her question he didn't show it. He paused thoughtfully before saying, 'She had a problem which she thought I could help her with.'

'Then you and Apicata are not, er...'

Felix threw back his head and laughed. 'Are you serious, Aurelia? Me and Apicata?' But then his smile faded. 'Of course not, but I would appreciate it if you wouldn't mention her visit to anyone.' He paused. 'Now, what is this all about?'

Aurelia looked down at her fingers. 'Seeing her here makes it more difficult for me,' she said awkwardly. 'It's Sejanus I've come to you about.'

Felix took her hands in his. 'Aurelia, there's nothing you can say about Sejanus that Apicata hasn't revealed which is ten times worse.'

Aurelia gave herself a few seconds to bolster up her courage before launching into her story. She left nothing out because she knew that if she wanted Felix's advice she had to be honest; besides, that was the way it had always been between her and Felix, honest and open. Felix listened; he had always been a good listener, she thought, but instead of the teasing gaze which had lingered earlier, his jaw had set as her story unfolded, and she could see she had brought a somber note to her visit.

'I remember the case against your husband well,' he said when she had finished. 'Julius was imprisoned for embezzlement, but the charges of treason were dropped for lack of evidence.' Felix knitted his brow. 'So Sejanus claims Vivius was withholding valuable evidence, did he?' There was a pause. 'Vivius is a man of integrity. Do you believe he withheld evidence?'

'I...' Aurelia looked Felix squarely in the face. 'No, of course not.' And simply saying it out loud helped to allay some of her own hidden fears.

Felix's eyes clouded over. 'The trouble is, Sejanus has brought far too many loyal Romans to trial with false accusations of treason. And from what you say it looks as though he's trying to compile a case against Vivius. But why?' Reaching over Felix handed her a plate of sweetmeats. 'Here, have one of these. You've barely eaten, and I need a chance to think.'

Aurelia helped herself to a sweetmeat she didn't particularly want but which would have been churlish to refuse, then she reclined back on the couch and watched Felix wander over to the window. His eyes wore a glazed expression that told her he wasn't absorbing what was going on outside but concentrating on her problem. Daintily wiping the corners of her mouth, she smiled inwardly at the thought of him finding her worthy of such attention.

Felix had his back to her when he asked, 'So Sejanus questioned you about Vivius's family and friends and his acquaintances at the Senate, did he?'

'I told him Vivius has no family,' she said quietly. 'There's only me.' She daintily dabbed the crumbs on her upper lip with her napkin. 'There's Phaedo, the Greek manager of his olive grove; he trusts him. And I suppose I could include my brother Dorio in the list, although he and Vivius tend to annoy each other more than anything.'

The silence from the window was so prolonged that Aurelia wondered uneasily if she had over-burdened Felix, but then he murmured, 'There's a growing number of people who would like to see Sejanus's tyranny brought to an end, Aurelia.' He clasped his hands behind his back and Aurelia got the impression that he wasn't really talking to her but voicing his thoughts aloud.

'The equestrian order, Tiberius's family, members of the Senate, and now...Apicata.' Felix said her name as though he had found a perfect gem.

'But if Sejanus is brought down, how will Tiberius rule? I thought he was...ill, paranoid?'

Felix nodded. 'He has bouts of madness, which is why the Senate and the equestrians are wary, and why Rome is rife with rumours about...' Felix glanced at her sharply before waving his hand dismissively in the air as though she was incapable of understanding what was really going on. She curbed her annoyance. 'Rumours and more rumours. My point is this, the political climate in Rome is changing rapidly and Sejanus...' But then turning to Aurelia he frowned as though a thought had just occurred to him. 'Palestine, you said? What in the name of all the gods is Vivius doing in Palestine?'

Aurelia shrugged, still slightly peeved at being dismissed for an assumed lack of understanding. That was why she spoke a little more harshly than she intended. 'He didn't say.'

'Hmm.' Felix appeared not to notice, his mind still absorbed with why Vivius was in Palestine. 'Sejanus has been consolidating power in foreign lands over the last year or so by replacing Roman governors and army commanders with men loyal to himself. The Governor of Judea, Pontius Pilate is one of them.'

Felix moved unhurriedly towards her, his hands clasped behind his back, the furrow still on his brow. 'But Sejanus won't have put Pilate in that post unless he wanted something in return. What? If the emperor has sent Vivius to discovers what that is, and he returns with incriminating evidence, we may have further cause for bringing charges against Sejanus.'

Aurelia was about to ask who he meant by 'we' when Felix sat down beside her and picking up her hand kissed her fingers. His lips were warm, soft, slightly damp, and distracted her. She waited, she could tell his thoughts were elsewhere, perhaps even on Apicata. But all he said was, 'I think the best thing Vivius can do is to complete his assignment and get back to Rome in one piece.'

Aurelia felt her hands breaking out into a sweat. 'You think he's in danger?'

Felix squeezed her fingers. 'Don't worry, my dear Aurelia, Vivius has spent a lifetime getting out of scrapes, political and physical.' He paused. His face softened. 'My main concern from now on is keeping you away from Sejanus.'

A chill prickled the back of her neck. 'You think I'm in danger?'

'I don't want to alarm you, but putting pressure on you would be one way of forcing Vivius to hand over whatever incriminating evidence he may unearth in Palestine.' He paused. 'We'll monitor the situation and if you think you're in danger, my love, send me word, day or night. My summer house is but two days' ride out of the city, you can go there.'

'I couldn't do that, Felix. I might put you in danger.'

Felix grinned wickedly at her. 'The only danger I'd be in would be from Vivius when he finds out.'

Aurelia smiled shyly. 'You're a true friend, Felix.' She lightly touched his cheek with her fingers but he kept his hand over hers, and it was warming to sense the attraction for her in his eyes. But then she dropped her gaze as her thoughts drifted back to Vivius, the way they had always done since they were children. 'I must go,' she said softly and although she hated leaving him, she knew it would be unwise to stay.

CHAPTER SIX

(Jerusalem)

Vivius's boots echoed on the stone slabs as he marched down the dimly lit corridor. The escorting sentry, half a step ahead was shorter, taking more steps and irritatingly distorting the rhythm. Vivius watched the oil lamps on the wall twist their shadows into giants as they approached. He had forgotten how gloomy Fort Antonia could be with its thick stone walls, high towers and long corridors. He tried to recall which part of the fort he had been in when he was billeted here as a young officer in the legion; it wasn't down here, that's for sure. So far, the only familiar features had been the steps leading down to the dungeons, and those in the central hall leading up to the dining quarters. What he did recall was his commanding officer telling him that Fort Antonia was so large an entire legion and their auxiliary personnel could be garrisoned here, which was exactly what it looked like now with all the extra soldiers drafted in for the Jewish festival.

The sentry escorting him pointed to a door at the far end of the adjoining corridor. 'The infirmary is down there, Senator.'

Vivius covered the remaining yards to the infirmary alone. Opening the door he found himself in a long and dingy room. The only brightness came from a thin shaft of sunlight forcing its way through a high narrow window, but failing to fall on the twenty or more beds regimentally lined up like legionaries on either side of a parade ground. An overpowering smell of drugs and body odours drifted his way; he grimaced, his scan of the beds for Dorio fleeting. There was no sign of him, but then, as half the occupants were either bandaged like Egyptian mummies, or buried under their blankets he couldn't really tell.

An army medicus stacking the shelves with phials and

surgical instruments glanced up. 'Can I help you?'

'I'm looking for Decurion Dorio Suranus?'

The medicus pointed to the door he'd come through. 'You'll find him across the corridor.'

Vivius nodded curtly, left the room and closed the door behind him. He gave the stench in his nostrils time to disperse before opening the door opposite. He found this room to be barely a quarter of the size of the infirmary, and the narrow window faced north leaving the room cold and the four tightly squashed beds in the gloom. Dorio was in the corner bed, next to a small table with a basin and jug. His face was as white as the basin, and despite the cold air, his dark tousled curls and forehead were wet with sweat. It wasn't hard for Vivius to surmise he had a fever. Like the other three occupants, he was sleeping, a single grey blanket drawn up to his chin.

Vivius narrowed his eyes as he studied the sleeping Decurion. Why in the name of all the gods did he find it so hard to relate to his future brother-in-law, he mused? They tolerated each other for the sake of the one woman they both loved, Aurelia; yet despite having known each other since childhood, that was about all that could be said of their relationship.

As he stood watching him sleeping, Vivius found fleeting memories drifting to the surface. It was Dorio's lifestyle that irritated him, he concluded. The young man enjoyed being surrounded by people, loud people who liked to drink a lot, laugh a lot, party a lot. Vivius pursed his lips. He found such people exhausting; he much preferred his own company. And yet...Vivius frowned as one particular incident surfaced; Dorio standing at the fence on the Suranus estate talking softly to his horses, caressing their silky necks, feeding them, at one with them, and the animals nodding their heads, snorting, nuzzling in response.

Dorio stirred. Vivius took a deep breath, and anxious to get this visit over and done with, reached over and touched the wounded man's shoulder. The eyelids flickered then dragged themselves open as if they had lead weights attached. It took a while for recognition to dawn. When it did, Vivius was greeted with a frown.

'What are you doing here?' Dorio's voice was barely above a whisper.

'I've come to take you back to Rome.'

Dorio licked his cracked lips. 'You're joking, right?'

'No, I've brought a physician with me. He'll be with us in a day or so.'

'*You've* come all this way for...?' A rasping cough shook his whole body.

Vivius averted his head from the spittle. When the spasm had passed, Dorio's right arm emerged from the bedcover.

'There's only one problem.' His fingers grasped the edge of the blanket and threw it back.

Vivius's expression never faltered at the sight of the missing left arm. The stump, above where the elbow should have been, was swathed in bandages and blood was seeping through, leaving a bloody red mark on the sheet. But worse was the foul smell that had emerged when the blanket was thrown back. Vivius had acquired enough medical knowledge on the battlefield to know that smell was more than blood, body odours and drugs.

'When did they do that?'

'Can't remember. They've stuffed me with so much poppy juice I've lost track of time...yesterday, the day before?'

Vivius lifted the blanket further. Dorio's chest was swathed in bandages. He had cuts and bruises on his face and legs but there didn't appear to be any other serious injuries.

'I've...broken a few ribs.'

Vivius suspected that broken ribs were the least of Dorio's worries but he refrained from saying so. Picking up a towel from the bottom of the bed, he dabbed the fevered brow.

'Not so good, eh?' Dorio whispered. 'You know what this

reminds me of?'

'No. What?'

'When we were kids, remember? You always made me play the wounded legionary. I was the youngest, you said. I had to do as I was told, you said. And you always had to be the hero coming to the rescue. So, how will you get me out of this one then, hero?' A hint of a grin struggled to emerge but lost the battle to a spasm of coughing. 'Sorry,' he muttered. 'These drugs...they make me...ramble. '

Vivius pulled the blanket back up to Dorio's chin. 'Well, first of all, I'm going to have a word with the medicus to see if we can make you more comfortable.' He examined the room in disgust. 'This is an awful place. I don't know how you can stand it.'

'I don't have a lot of choice...' The cough that started up this time brought with it a rattle of phlegm. Jerking his body across the bed, Dorio spat into a bowl which Vivius was relieved to see was on the other side of the bed. Exhausted by the exertion, Dorio rolled back on his pillow. There was streak of saliva down his chin.

'My horse, Vivius; they had to destroy my horse. Remember her? The one with the blaze of white on her nose, I reared from being a foal.' His face crumpled at the memory. 'I'm tired...'

Vivius tried not to feel too concerned when leaving the infirmary, but he had seen enough infected wounds in his time to know that unless Dorio's fever dropped he might not make it out of there. And as his boots clattered back down the corridor another thought occurred to him. A dead Dorio would leave him with no excuse to remain in Jerusalem.

* * *

Vivius vigorously rubbed the heels of his hands into his eyes, leaving floating white dots in front of him. Then with a sigh, he lounged back on his seat and drummed the journal on the table with the end of his stylus. As he had suspected, Fabius's notes were undecipherable, and if he didn't make some headway with this assignment soon it looked like his future... Well, there wouldn't be one would there? Flicking over one of the parchments he studied it for the umpteenth time. There were odd words in Latin, but the majority of it was in Fabius's own indecipherable form of shorthand.

'Come on Fabius; help me out here. What are you trying to say?' He ran the stylus over the squiggles on the page.

'...discovered that...are deeply...people...easily...by our...images and effigies on...as...'

Vivius ran the stylus over the words 'images and effigies.' Images and effigies of what, he pondered. Rome was full of images and effigies. They were on everything: buildings, walls, standards, the Roman legion's shields. He paused. Was that it? Could 'Roman shields' be two of the missing words? Deciding he had nothing to lose by assuming they were, he replaced each of the shorthand markings with the letters 'Roman shields.' To his surprise, the missing letters appeared to make words elsewhere. He continued working on the rest of the page.

Two hours later he sat back, satisfied with the results. There were still words missing but the gist of the Fabius's entry on this page, at least, was clear.

'I have discovered that the Jews are a deeply religious people and are easily offended by our idolatrous... They see the images and effigies on our Roman shields as...offensive. Pilate's predecessor had respect for the Jewish culture. He removed all Roman images and effigies before allowing our legion to enter (Jerusalem?). The emperor's policies were right. His methods have kept peace between Roman and Jew.

Since his arrival, Pontius Pilate has shown no such concern for Jewish customs. Six days ago he permitted his legion to carry their standards into the city at night. When the (citizens of Jerusalem?) awoke the following morning and discovered ensigns of Caesar in their holy city they appealed to Pilate to remove them. Pilate refused.

For five days now, the Jews have been demonstrating. At times they have come perilously close to rioting. At one point, Pilate had his soldiers surround the protesters and threaten (them with crucifixion?) *The Jews refused to move—but they didn't riot either. Strange people; they were willing to accept death rather than allow the* (desecration) *of their Mosaic law.*

Day 6: Pontius Pilate has finally been forced to remove the images. He...'

There was a knock on the door. With a *tut* of annoyance, Vivius pushed back his chair, strode across his cramped quarters and flung it open.

'Senator Marcianus?'

The slave making the enquiry had a deep guttural accent, and a mass of black freckles on his thickset nose. His turban, colourful mode of dress and black slanting eyes gave Vivius the impression he came from lands to the east of Rome, but his skin was dark like the inhabitants south of Egypt.

He gave a solemn bow. 'Procurator Pilate wondered if you would care to join him and his wife for dinner this evening, Senator.'

Vivius gave a nod of approval. As a visiting senator from Rome, he'd been waiting for such an invitation. 'Thank the Procurator. Tell him I would be delighted.'

'Yes, senator.'

The slave's gaze drifted over to the box and the journal on the table.

'Was there anything else?'

'No, Senator.'

Vivius closed the door. Wandering back to the table, he tapped his fingers rhythmically on the lid of the box. He wasn't unduly concerned over the slave seeing the box or the journal. He was only a slave and probably illiterate, but someone had been so anxious to get hold of this material that they had ransacked Fabius's house, threatened his family and killed Fabius.

Vivius glanced around his cramped quarters, but one glance was enough to dismiss any thoughts of hiding it here. A table, four chairs and a long couch on the back wall; that was it. As a visiting senator he had expected better accommodation, but then needing space for extra troops for this Jewish Passover appeared to have taken care of those expectations. He wandered into his sleeping quarters: a bed, a chair, shelves for his clothes and a smaller shelf for idols.

Returning to the table he flattened the rolled parchments, stuck them inside the tablet and pushed it into the pocket of his tunic. It was bulkier than he would have liked but he was confident his toga would hide them, at least until he could find a more secure hiding place. Then pushing the journal into the pocket of his tunic, he draped his toga over the top and left his quarters to assess for himself the man he had come to investigate.

* * *

'Senator Marcianus, welcome.'

Vivius found Pilate's greeting silky smooth and given in the manner of a bureaucrat well used to entertaining.

'We rarely receive senators in Jerusalem, so I look forward to hearing what we have that would drag you all the way from Rome.'

A glitter of expensive rings adorning the Procurator's stubby fingers elegantly motioned him towards one of the three couches placed squarely around a low dining table. Vivius settled himself on the central couch and as Pilate gave instructions to his servants, Vivius glanced around him.

The Procurator's quarters were typically Roman with tapestries depicting the colonies of Rome, a bust of Tiberius, a chequered gaming board and marble statues of lions. Shimmering oil lamps lit the room, and the magnificent view outside was of lanterns lighting the wide steps leading up to the temple. There was nothing of a personal nature in the room, but then Vivius guessed that was because Pilate spent most of his time in the affluent city of Caesarea.

'Wine, Senator?' Pilate spoke with a whine, as though he had nasal problems.

Vivius's sweep of the room landed back on his thin-lipped, spotlessly neat host who had one arm slung casually over the back of his couch, and had turned to summon his slave with an impatient twitch of the fingers.

First impression, Vivius decided, was that Pilate was one of those bureaucrats who was overly fond of the sound of his own voice, had got where he was by mixing with the right people, and probably wasn't averse to compromising his integrity by bribing and scheming to get what he wanted either. Vivius pursed his lips. He had never liked the type, but obviously Pilate had impressed Sejanus.

'Ah! And there you are, my dear. Senator Marcianus, may I introduce my wife?'

Vivius turned, and found his pulses quickening as a vision in shimmering deep sea green drifted into the room. The bracelets on her arm jingled a greeting, gold hoop earrings dangled against her cheeks, and her red lips parted in an easy smile showing a row of even white teeth. Placing his goblet on the table, Vivius rose to his feet.

'It's a privilege to welcome you to Jerusalem, Senator.' Her voice was soft and low, she had a pleasing fragrance of roses about her, and he liked the way her green eyes flickered approvingly over him as he took her hand. 'I hope we can make your stay a pleasant one.'

Vivius was sure she could; he wasn't so sure about Pilate. Vivius found his gaze lingering on her low-cut dress as she reclined elegantly on the couch, but as he lounged down beside her he was disturbed by the rustle of the journal in his tunic. If she'd heard, she gave no indication of it.

The slave with the black freckles and colourful turban laid an oblong tray of shellfish, eggs, sauce, raw vegetables and bread on the table.

Claudia reached over, picked up a sliver of fish and dropped it into the neatly rounded O of her lips. 'So tell me, Senator,' she said between mouthfuls. 'What are you doing so far from Rome?'

Vivius sucked a white fish from a shell, breathing in sharply as the bitter tang of salt caught his palate. Reaching out for his goblet of wine, he said, 'I have personal interests here.'

'Personal interests? In Jerusalem?'

'Yes. I own an olive grove in Rome which I plan to extend.' Vivius swished the wine around his mouth before placing the goblet back on the table. 'I've thought for some time now that it would be to my advantage to visit one of Palestine's famous olive groves. The methods of growing, fertilizing and harvesting are basically the same as our own, but there are a few subtle differences which could account for the larger olives or more abundant clusters. So, I decided, while I'm in the area, it would be a good opportunity to extend my knowledge.'

'Ha! We have Roman friends with a sizeable olive grove the other side of Bethany,' Pilate raised his goblet to him. 'I insist my wife show it to you.'

Claudia reached over to help herself to more fish, wafting a pleasing aroma of roses in his direction. 'Yes, Senator. Allow me to take you there.'

Vivius wiped the corners of his mouth as he contemplated the pleasures of an outing with Claudia; the pleasures he didn't contemplate for long, the valuable source of information she could be to him, if handled correctly, he pondered a little longer.

'You had no problems leaving the Senate?' Pilate asked.

Vivius tried not to think of the jars of olive oil he had promised to bribe his way to Palestine. 'The Senate are as anxious as I am to increase our output and trade of oil,' he said, pleased that at least that part was true. 'They agreed there was a valid reason for a business trip to Palestine.' He paused. 'Especially when I told them that my future brother-in-law, Decurion Dorio Suranus, was here and had been badly wounded by Zealots in Galilee. I'm hoping I can take him back to Rome with me.'

'Zealots!' Pilate snorted through his nose. 'Those religious fanatics are a constant irritant to me, Senator. They're dangerous, unorganized, unpredictable, and not beyond stabbing anyone they suspect of anti-Jewish propaganda. They'll even incite their own people into action if it suits their cause. Galilee is where they have their headquarters but despite having placed a heavy Roman presence in the area, we still haven't caught their leaders. No doubt I'll find them in Jerusalem for Passover; recruiting, would you believe. I'd have the whole lot of them crucified on the spot—if I knew who they were.' He paused, as if realizing his tirade was a little too venomous for a quiet dinner party. 'So the Decurion was wounded by them in Galilee, was he?'

'Yes. He was transferred to Fort Antonia to have his arm amputated.'

The breath going through Pilate's nostrils whistled faintly. 'You could have let the army send him back to Rome when he was fit enough.'

Vivius kept his eyes lowered as he dipped his bread into the sauce. 'I could have done, but my bride wanted him at our wedding ceremony this summer.'

Vivius didn't like the way Pilate sniffed through one nostril leaving him with something resembling a sneer.

The slave with the turban brought in a tray of cold game surrounded by steaming vegetables, and tried to remove what remained of the shellfish.

'No, no, Rico, leave it. More wine,' Pilate slammed the empty jug into him with a force that made him grunt. 'Meanwhile it will be our pleasure to entertain you, Senator.' He pulled back his lips in a yellow smile. 'I'm sure the Jewish king would be delighted to welcome you to one of his parties.'

Vivius wiped his hands on a towel to give himself time to think. Herod Antipas's parties were notorious for being wild and politically dangerous events and he was never at his best at these social affairs anyway. In his experience, they were always overrun with foreign dignitaries who ate, drank and made ridiculous deals that were totally forgotten the next day.

'That's extremely kind of you, Procurator, but my stay will be a short one. Just till the Decurion is well enough to travel.'

'Perhaps you should have an escort around Jerusalem, Senator. You know you've arrived at the start of the Jewish Passover, don't you? It's a ritual feast of storytelling of the liberation of Israel from Egypt I don't know how many hundreds of years ago.' He gave a forced laugh. 'As long as it doesn't give these damned Jews any ideas of being liberated from Rome. That's the trouble with these commemorative celebrations.'

Vivius picked up a leg of game. 'The Jews can be troublesome people,' he said casually, turning it over in his fingers, examining where to take his first bite. 'I've no doubt you've had your problems dealing with them.'

'Problems? We've allowed the Jews to rebuild their own temple and worship their own God. We've even allowed the Sanhedrin, as a judicial body, to deal with their own civil and criminal cases, but they're constantly harassing for more freedom. If they would control their own Zealots I might be more amenable to their demands, but they don't. Then there's this new sect that's irritating them, and consequently irritating me.'

'Sect?'

'The sect of the Nazarenes. They're constantly at loggerheads with the Pharisees.' He paused. 'The Pharisees are a religious group, highly educated, well spoken, and widely respected in the Jewish culture,' he explained. 'They claim this sect of the Nazarenes are preaching at variance with the laws and teachings of their God so they're constantly dragging them in for questioning or to give them a good thrashing. It doesn't seem to deter them.'

'Are they as aggressive as the Zealots?'

'Goodness, no. They're not aggressive at all, but the way their numbers have grown in only a year is becoming a concern, so I keep an eye on them.'

Claudia's body moved seductively as she turned to face him. 'The sect started a year ago when we crucified a Jew by the name of Jesus. He was a Nazarene, and claimed to be their long awaited Messiah. In only three years he built up quite a following, but the real trouble came when his followers claimed their God resurrected him from the dead.' She shrugged her shoulders, the strap of her dress sliding an inch down her shoulder. Who knows, it could be true,' she said softly.

'As you can hear this story has caught my wife's imagination,' Pilate sneered.

Deciding to move the conversation on to something more relevant to his assignment, Vivius asked, 'Wasn't there an incident recently, something to do with riots and the massacre of two hundred Jews?'

Pilate considered him guardedly. 'The word "massacre" is questionable, Senator. There were Zealots amongst those citizens and they needed to be controlled. Give the Jews too much freedom and they abuse it.' He popped a sliver of fish into his mouth; his jaws snapped as he chewed. 'The next thing you know the Zealots are gaining the upper hand.'

'How do you deal with them?'

'Crucify them.'

'Who? The Zealots or the common Jew in the street?'

Pilate shrugged before leaning forward to examine the tray of game. 'I have a difficult job, Senator. I'm responsible for taxing these people, and for implementing Rome's judicial functions on them. The Jews don't like paying our taxes and they don't like being ruled by Rome. My discipline has to be harsh to deter troublemakers. Crucifixion; that's the best way.'

Rico cautiously removed the platter of fish from the table.

'And how do you reconcile your actions with the emperor's foreign policy of keeping the Jews' approval by giving them freedom of worship and freedom to keep their own laws?'

Pilate glared at him. 'I do that, Senator; when I can. But there are times when only brute force will control these Jews.'

Vivius sat forward; the inflammatory journal in his tunic rustled but he resisted the urge to check it. 'So what you're saying is, there are times Rome's foreign policies have to be overlooked for the sake of keeping control?'

Pilate's face reddened. 'No, senator. What I'm saying is, Rome's foreign policies don't always work in a country that...'

'Gentleman, please.' Claudia raised her hand in protest. There was a teasing smile across her lips. They were shining and oily with fish, but Vivius didn't miss the flashed warning to her husband. 'Do I have to listen to politics all evening?' She turned to Vivius, her hair shimmering red under the oil lamps. 'I want to hear about Rome, Senator.'

Deciding this was probably as far as he would get in assessing the Procurator and his views this evening, Vivius relaxed back on his couch and flinging his arm over the back smiled at his hostess. 'Well, there's a growing body in Rome with strong republican views. They want freed men to have a voice in the city. They believe the Senate should be in control of Rome, and the Caesars should renounce claims of being divine.' He shrugged. 'They have their point of view, but in my opinion Rome wouldn't be where it is today without the strength of the Caesars.'

Claudia wafted her hand dismissively in the air. 'No, no. I mean what's on at the theatres and the arena? What are the latest fashions? What are they bringing into the slave markets?'

'I'm sure the senator isn't interested in the latest gowns, my dear.'

Vivius gave a short laugh.

'Then tell me about yourself, Senator. We know you own an olive grove, that you're a senator, and that you're to be married in the summer. What else?'

'I'm a Roman official. A magistrate.'

'You deal with criminals?'

Vivius waited until Rico had replenished Pilate's goblet for the third time before answering. 'I don't judge petty crimes. I deal with treason laws and foreign policies.'

'Ah! That explains your interest in how Rome's policies work in Jerusalem.'

'Partly, but as a military man I've always been impressed with Rome's ability to improve the lifestyles of other countries.'

'And do you report your findings back to the emperor?'

Vivius found a disquiet creeping over him. 'No. My work in the Senate means I'm usually based in Rome,' he answered cautiously.

'Ah! Rome! How is Tiberius? Do you see much of him?'

Vivius studied the cracks in the ceiling as if contemplating the question. 'What I do hear is that he still grieves over the death of his son, Drusus.' He looked at her directly. 'Personally, I think grieving is one of the reasons why he stays shut up on the Island of Capri.'

Rico moved silently around the room clearing away the empty dishes. A second slave brought in a platter of apples with raisins, cinnamon and pastry.

'Then we must be grateful that Rome is in the capable hands of Sejanus,' Pilate raised his goblet in the gesture of a salute.

Vivius shook his head when Rico offered to refill his goblet; he needed to keep a clear head. Judging from tonight's conversation it wouldn't do to underestimate the governor – or his wife.

* * *

Vivius lay on the couch in his quarters, his fingers entwined across his chest and wondered for the umpteenth time how in the name of all the gods could he be expected to make any headway with his assignment when he had no idea what he was supposed to be looking for. Pilate might be tough, even cruel at times, but if their conversation over dinner last night was anything to go by, he was only doing his job and there certainly wasn't sufficient evidence to make charges against him. All Pilate had done so far was disrespect the Jewish religion by flaunting heathen symbols, burn a few houses, crucify a few Zealots and use temple treasury money to build an aqueduct. Of course, massacring two hundred Jews when they complained didn't look too good on his record, but a court of law could always argue there were Zealots in the crowd and he was forced to react to keep order. As for Sejanus, all he appears to have done was chose Pilate for the role in the first place. If the emperor was hinting at anything else he was mistaken.

Vivius scratched his head in frustration. As for how he was supposed to judge the mood of the Jews without speaking to them... He pinched between his eyes.

A knock on the door startled him. Swinging his legs off the couch he opened it. A guard handed him a tablet, saluted and moved away. Vivius opened the tablet.

Senator. My work with the physician in Caesarea is complete. I shall be arriving with the next Roman legion bound for Fort Antonia.
—Lucanus.

Vivius gave a grunt of satisfaction; at least something was going right, he brooded. He paced across his quarters, head down, hands clenched behind his back, his thumbs twirling around each other like dancers in the theatre.

The other inconvenience, he mused, was the amputation of Dorio's arm. Naturally it was more inconvenient for Dorio than it was for him, Vivius conceded. But the latest news from the hospital was that Dorio's fever was dropping. If it kept on dropping it might only be days before the medicus decided he was well enough to travel, which meant his time in Jerusalem was limited. He rubbed his chin fiercely. He needed to get busy; he needed to check the records here at the fort, and then he needed to find the whereabouts of Nikolaos, the bookkeeper.

Deciding there was no time like the present to start, Vivius left the confines of his cramped quarters and took the stairs leading down to the administration offices. A clerk stood in the corridor with a dozen or more tablets in his arms.

'Can I help you?'

He was a mouse of a man with flat white hair that looked as if it had been cut around a basin, grey owlish eyes, and a crumpled tunic.

Vivius brought out his social smile. 'I don't think so, unless, er...' An idea occurred to him. 'Unless you know anything about the Hasmonaean princes.'

The owlish eyes blinked rapidly. 'P-Pardon?'

'Hasmonaean princes. I was assigned to Fort Antonia as a young officer of the legion but this part of the fort was out of bounds to me then.' Vivius moved his cloak to make sure his senator's toga could be seen. 'While I'm here I would like to explore what was their palace and their influence in the area. I trust you have no objection if I wander around?'

The clerk shuffled uneasily. 'Er, ...no, Senator, I...of course not, no of course not. Although I should point out that this area is normally reserved for administrative staff but...I suppose... please, explore all you like.' He lifted a finger as though an idea had occurred to him. 'You do know the fort was built directly over subterranean springs, don't you?'

Vivius didn't. 'How interesting.'

'Ah! Yes, isn't it. And you'll find caves on the lower levels where the dungeons are.' He screwed up his face. 'Dreadful place, cold, dark and...'

'Fascinating. And the rooms here are used for...what?'

'Administration.' The clerk pointed to the room he had exited.

'That's where we do the accounts.'

'You're an accountant?'

The clerk gave a chuckle. 'Oh dear, my goodness me no, no, no. What an idea. I have no head for figures, I'm afraid. I keep records of current affairs in Jerusalem.'

'Current affairs?'

'The arrival and departure of our legions, visitors to the fort, conflicts with the Zealots, demonstrations, that sort of thing.' The clerk pointed to a door. 'That's my office. It's nothing special; no influences from the Hasmonaean Princes in there I can tell you, but I do have a few old volumes which may go as far back as their time here. You're welcome to take a look if you want.'

'Are you sure you don't mind?'

The owlish eyes blinked rapidly, as if surprised that anyone would even consider looking as his musty old volumes. 'No, Senator, not at all, not at all.'

The keys on his belt rattled as he unlocked the door. 'It's rather untidy I'm afraid,' he apologised as they entered. 'And I doubt the Hasmonaean Princes used this room to live in; it's far too small. They probably used it as a cupboard.' He gave a chuckle as he dropped his sealed tablets on to the already littered desk.

Vivius rubbed his nose at the musty smell of old parchments and ledgers stored haphazardly on the wall-to-wall shelves.

'We have a Hall of Records in Rome,' Vivius told him. 'If you can find anything in there it's only by intervention of the gods, but the clerks appear to know where everything is.'

'Oh I can assure you, I know where everything is in here, Senator. Over there, for instance...' As the clerk pointed to the various shelves around the room, Vivius made a mental catalogue.

'And you have records going back how long?'

'Years and years and years, Senator.' He pointed to a row of ledgers on the top shelf. 'Those are the earliest records we have. They might go as far back as the Hasmonaean Princes, and they may even cover the years when Herod the Great changed the palace into a citadel.'

'May I examine them?'

'Of course. Please help yourself. Records going back that far aren't confidential.' The clerk dragged a short pair of stepladders over to the shelves and climbing up pulled the ledgers off the shelves one by one. Layers of dust drifted down with them. He sneezed.

Vivius flicked through one of the ledgers. 'I could spend hours absorbing myself in the information recorded here. You've done well in keeping such a meticulous office. The clerks in Rome should take a lesson from your record keeping.'

The clerk flushed with pleasure. 'Thank you, Senator.' He hesitated. 'Actually, Senator, I was about to go to the canteen for my dinner. We're supposed to lock up when we're out, but if you would like to browse while I'm away then I'm sure the Procurator wouldn't mind.'

'I'm sure he wouldn't,' Vivius murmured picking up one of the ledgers and feigning an interest.

The clerk laid the keys on the desk and beamed at him. 'If I leave you for an hour or so, is that all right?'

'Perfect.'

As soon as the clerk had closed the door, Vivius laid the old ledgers to one side and pulled out the latest chronicled records for Jerusalem. Within minutes, he had come across a report from the tribune of Fort Antonia.

Report:

Pilate believes that building a twenty-five-mile aqueduct into Jerusalem will be progress.

I agree. Unfortunately, he chooses to finance his venture with holy money from the Jewish temple. It is my understanding of these people that they will protest so I have expressed my concerns, warning him that this is an infringement on Jewish religion and could cause protests, demonstrations and even riots.

As I predicted, the Jews protested, but it was a peaceful demonstration. I was ordered by Pontius Pilate to place my legionaries strategically amongst the demonstrators in case of trouble. I did. But unknown to me, Pilate had dressed his own men up as Jews and infiltrated them into the crowd. Then, at his given signal, his men randomly attacked and killed the protesters. Over two hundred Jews were killed.

I would, however, stress there could have been Zealots amongst the citizens that I knew nothing about.

Vivius pursed his lips. A different perspective on the same old story of the death of two hundred Jews, but once again, nothing of significance; at least nothing to build a solid case against Pilate.

The sound of footsteps in the corridor warned Vivius that his owlish clerk could be returning from his dinner. Hurriedly pulling the parchment out of the file, he rolled it and pushed it into his tunic pocket. Then replacing the files on current affairs, he opened the dusty old ledgers on the Hasmonaean Princes and feigned an engrossment in the writings.

The little man beamed at him as though he'd bestowed the greatest favour in allowing a senator from Rome the use of his office to pursue his historical hobby. 'Did you find everything you wanted, Senator?'

'I did. Yes, thank you.' Vivius stood up, made his way to the door and was about to leave when a though occurred to him. Turning back to the clerk he asked, 'Do you remember a Greek called Nikolaos? I believe he was Pilate's former bookkeeper?'

The clerks smile brightened. 'Nikolas? Oh yes, I know Nikolaos well, very well. His accounts office was just over the corridor.'

'Do you know where he's living now?'

'Nikolaos? Oh yes...'

Vivius noticed the clerk's gaze had drifted over his shoulder but it was the aroma of roses that warned him they were not alone. He swung around. Claudia was standing in the corridor behind him, wearing a low-cut, dusky pink dress beneath a brown velvet cloak.

'Good morning, Senator.'

Vivius inclined his head wondering if she had overheard him asking for the bookkeeper's address. If she had, she gave no indication of it but threw Vivius a wide-mouthed smile. 'I've been looking for you.'

'You have?' he said pleasantly. 'I was researching the Hasmonaean dynasty.'

'An interest of yours?'

'Not particularly but it fills in the time while I'm waiting for the Decurion to be well enough to travel. What can I do for you?' He gestured to the door indicating they leave the administration quarters.

'You can take me out of Jerusalem tomorrow.' she said pertly, falling into step with him.

'With it being the Jewish Passover the city is unbearably crowded. You said you wanted to visit an olive grove so I've planned a trip.'

Vivius hesitated. 'Ah! I've made arrangements for Dorio to be transferred to my quarters tomorrow.'

Claudia waved her hand dismissively. 'The medicus can do that?'

'And I'm expecting my Greek physician.'

'If he's travelling with the legion from Caesarea, they won't arrive until late afternoon.' She twinkled mischievously at him. 'Are you trying to avoid taking me out, Senator?'

She brushed against him as they climbed the steps; her body was warm and soft.

He paused, but only briefly. 'You win,' he said with a smile. 'Where are you taking me?'

She raised her dress fractionally above her ankles as they took the stairs. 'We're going to visit a Roman who has an olive grove three miles out of Bethany. The countryside en route is beautiful, his villa is beautiful, his olive grove is the best in the area, and the food is unquestionably more appetising than the food here at the fort.'

They stopped when they reached the door of Vivius's quarters. She rested her fingers lightly on his arm, so lightly it tickled the hairs. 'You've barely been out of the fort, Senator. A change will do you good.'

She was right, he mused. A break would do him good. A break from the smell of drugs in the infirmary, from the cramped conditions of his quarters—and from pouring over unreadable parchments and tablets. He grasped the door handle.

'What time should we leave?'

She inched closer, squeezing his arm, drawing his attention to the softness of her body. 'I shall send Rico to your quarters early tomorrow morning,' she said softly.

'I'll be ready.'

She smiled. 'Good.' The ringlet on the back of her head narrowly missed his face as she swung around. He didn't enter his quarters straight away but stood watching her swaying hips gliding down the corridor.

An image of Aurelia flashed briefly in front of him, but it was only briefly.

CHAPTER SEVEN

(The Kidron Valley)

Simon was a beefy, big-shouldered Jew. His appearance was rough, his features course and yet, possibly because of his great size, he moved with a certain grace up the hill. He stopped when he reached a palm tree and leaning against the trunk drifted his dark, liquid brown eyes lazily across the smoking campfires and colourful blankets spread out across the Kidron Valley. *They look like a rainbow of tents,* he thought. The makings of a smile pushed its way through his shaggy beard as he remembered how, when he was young, his parents, uncles, aunts and cousins used to join the thousands of pilgrims converging on Jerusalem to celebrate the Jewish Passover. They knew they would never find accommodation in the city, so would camp here, on the Kidron Valley. The atmosphere was always relaxed; there was always laughter and chatter and cries of excitement as they came across old friends, family members or neighbours who had travelled from other villages.

Simon wafted his hand as smoke from a nearby camp fire drifted towards him. A small clay stove was set on top of the fire and there was a smell of dried fish, which reminded him he was hungry. He looked back towards Jerusalem, and decided if Zachary didn't arrive soon he was heading into the city for food. That was how he spotted the two horses coming through the city gates. They were followed by two Roman legionaries on foot. From this distance he could see that one of the riders was a woman, the other was clearly a Roman.

Simon spat out a gristly lump of saliva, wiped his sleeve across his wet beard and cursed the Romans under his breath. He did that often; he knew he shouldn't. He knew the sect of the Nazarenes would have something to say if they knew how deep his hatred of the Romans ran. They would tell him he wasn't following the teachings of Jesus, that he should have moved on from this intense hatred of them, learned to forgive them, but he knew he hadn't. Hatred clung to him like a leech, its poison festering inside him like a growing boil. The sect of the Nazarenes were right, he thought. This depth of hatred was against everything they believed in but Simon was used to its venom. He told himself it was part of his fiery nature, and had used this an excuse for his flare-ups, his rants, his spitting so often that he had almost come to believe it himself.

'Simon!'

Distracted, Simon looked around. The shout appeared to have come from a wizened old man, leaning heavily on his staff. His face hidden by his hood, but for an old man he was moving towards him with remarkable speed. Simon narrowed his eyes, but when the old man was only feet away he whipped back his hood to reveal an impish face with laughing brown eyes. 'Ha! Scared you, didn't I?'

'Idiot!' In three long strides, Simon had grabbed the young man by the shoulders of his tunic, and hauled him towards the cover of the palm tree as if he was dragging a sack of potatoes. 'What you doing in Jerusalem, lad?' Simon spoke with a thick Capernaum accent.

Zachary's lanky arms waved uncontrollably in the air. 'Get off you big oaf and keep your voice down. Do you want to announce my whereabouts to the entire Roman Empire?' He glanced around uneasily as he straightened his clothes, but then he lifted his head. 'Barabbas sent me,' he said with unmistakable pride. 'I'm to find out how many extra patrols the Romans have brought in for the Passover. With all the visitors we're recruiting, extra patrols are not good news for us Zealots.'

'Barabbas!' Simon spat the name out. 'Even that idiot should have had more sense than to send a mere lad into Jerusalem. He has a price on his head; do you know that? If the Romans associate you with him...' Simon furrowed his brow as though a thought had just occurred to him. 'Why'd you want to see me?'

Zachary glared at him. 'It seemed like a good idea at the time but if you're going to be grumpy...'

Simon's eyes drifted over Zachary's shoulder to the two riders. They had made a detour from the busy Bethany and Bethpage road and had taken a track which would lead them towards him and Zachary. 'Go on then, I know you're dying to tell me. What have you found out in your snooping?'

Zachary's chest puffed out and the lad seemed to stand an inch taller when he said, 'I saw Pilate arrive at Fort Antonia with his fancy lady and her slaves and far too many auxiliaries. Barabbas isn't going to be pleased with that news I can tell you.' He tilted his head to one side. 'And, interestingly enough, while I was watching the troops I saw a Roman senator arrive. We don't get many of those in Jerusalem,' he furrowed his brow. 'Wonder what a senator is doing here? What do you think?'

Simon jerked his head towards the riders. 'Why don't you ask him?'

Zachary spun around.

Simon watched the approach of the riders with growing animosity. Not so much towards the lady—Pilate's lady—he'd seen her before. She'd been at Golgotha a year ago when his friend Jesus had been crucified. He could remember her standing at a distance from the cross, alone, the hood of her cloak over her head as if she had hoped to remain anonymous, but he had recognized her. He narrowed his eyes when they landed on the approaching Roman, a senator judging from his apparel. His back was straight, head held high, handsome but arrogant in his posture, as if he personally had been responsible for overpowering Jerusalem. Simon sucked at the congealed saliva in his mouth, gathered it together, and waiting until the riders were only yards away, turned and spat it out in front of the horses. Then he looked up, his eyes catching those of the

Roman's. There was an expression of disgust in them, as though he was surveying a mangy dog.

Yet the first thought that shot into Simon's mind was, 'He's a soldier, like me.' Although there was nothing about the Roman to indicate that he was right, Simon held a firm belief that there was something about soldiers worldwide that enabled them to identify each other—in or out of uniform. He held the Roman's chiselled gaze as horse and rider passed by.

Simon's hand inched into the folds of his tunic, his fingers encircling the handle of his dagger as he realised he had probably overstepped the mark, and stupidly with young Zachary at his side. Yet pride forbade him from dropping his eyes. Fortunately, excitable children raced in front of the Roman's mount, distracting from his silent battle. He muttered something, then turned to give instructions to the two legionaries behind. One was short and stocky, a veteran judging from his scars, the other was unmistakable for his long, hairy legs and the wisps of bright red hair protruding through his helmet. The veteran moved up to the senator's mount, nodded, saluted and Simon watched him and the redhead retrace their steps back to the city. When he glanced back at the senator again, he was surprised to see the Roman was watching him, curious, almost questioning.

Simon grabbed Zachary's cloak. 'Hood up, head down, and make for the city.'

'What?'

'Do it.'

Only when they were a safe enough distance away did Simon feel he could chance a glance back. He was relieved to see both riders had moved on.

'Madness you coming into Jerusalem, today.' he snapped. 'Madness!'

'I told you. I'm under orders from Barabbas. Barabbas wants to know whether...'

'Barabbas! Barabbas! Never thought you'd have been stupid

enough to join up with a thug like him.'

'Better fighting Romans with him than walking out on the Zealots altogether, like you.' Zachary's eyes narrowed. 'Have you forgotten what the Romans did to us, cousin?'

Simon pursed his lips tightly to prevent an angry retort which meant they continued their walk in silence. But halfway down the hill, Simon's shoulders sagged and he stopped. 'I don't want to argue, Zachary.' The anger had gone out of his voice, but there was a solemn tone to it as he pointed to Jerusalem. 'See that?'

Zachary followed his cousin's pointing finger.

More impressive than the stone palaces and limestone buildings in the city stood the Temple Mount, rebuilt by the Jewish king, Herod the Great. It rose majestically on its plateau, its high white marble pillars towering above the turreted and buttressed walls surrounding the city. Both men knew it well, the eight gates, the wide temple courts, the balustrade. It made them proud to be Jewish. Nothing could compare with it except... Zachary adjusted his gaze when he realised Simon's finger was not pointing towards the temple but the massive building brooding alongside it—Fort Antonia, once the palace of the Hasmonaean Princes, now a Roman fortress and a clear reminder to all Jews of the superior force who dominated their land.

Simon dropped his hand and began walking again but more leisurely this time. 'Every time I look at that fort I'm reminded who was responsible for that...that butchery?' He made no further comment until they were near the city gates.

'It was the boots what gave them away, did I ever tell you that?' Simon said.

'The boots?'

'Ay, I was standing behind your mother and father; don't know where my folks were, nor my brothers. Somewhere in the demonstration that's for sure. I remember it being hot, and me being bored listening to our Sanhedrin droning on. Pilate had his hands on hips, he looked even more bored than me. We were demonstrating over him using our holy temple money to build his aqueduct. That was when I noticed the boots.'

'Whose boots?'

'Them boots what...' The beggars hovering at the entrance looked up at him hopefully. Simon shook his head, touching the coins in his pocket. He'd had no breakfast and he barely had enough coins for lunch. 'I saw that although some of the men in the demonstration were dressed like us Jews, them boots that they wore were Roman legionaries' boots.'

'You've never told me this before.'

"Cos straight after the...massacre you charged off like a mad bull to join the nearest Zealot unit swearing vengeance on every Roman in sight. And where's that got you, lad? Every time you kill a Roman we get reprisals.'

'I don't need a lecture, Simon. Get back to the boots.'

'I pointed the boots out to your father.'

'I was standing next to my father. I didn't notice.'

'No, 'cos you were too engrossed in a girl if I remember rightly.' Simon gave a wry smile but as the scene unfolded in his mind the smile faded. 'I'd barely given your father warning when the command came from Pilate. Next thing I knew, the Romans had flung off their Jewish clothes, drawn their swords and...and our punishment for complaining to Rome was the slaughter of...of *two hundred Jews*.' Simon couldn't stop his voice from shaking.

'I wanted to stay to fight.'

'I know you did, lad. So did I, but what with...bare hands? We were unarmed. Your father pushed you in my direction and shouted, 'Get him out of here! He created space for us, tried to protect us. I had no option. The demonstrators was screaming, running in every direction. It was chaos. We was helpless against armed legionaries. Our parents, our brothers...' Simon shook his head. 'I want rid of the Romans as bad as you, Zachary. Don't you never accuse me otherwise.'

'Then why did you leave the Zealots?'

Simon scratched his shaggy beard. He desperately wanted to protect him, make him understand the dangers of belonging to the Zealots, especially the group led by that thug Barabbas. 'I was fed up. These skirmishes with them Romans wasn't getting us nowhere. There were always reprisals, more killing of innocent Jews. That was when I came across Jesus, the Nazarene. It wasn't just the revolutionary things he said and the things that he did, it was...'

'He's dead, Simon. I'd have thought you'd have been glad to re-join...'

'But his cause lives on and our numbers grow fast,' Simon interrupted. 'All I'm trying to say is, after three years with him I knew I could never go back to the Zealots. Besides, our ways are more peaceful.'

'So was the demonstration over the temple money and look where that got us,' Zachary retorted.

The silence was awkward.

An overweight woman with an overloaded basket of vegetables elbowed him out of the way. Simon blinked rapidly, surprised to find himself in the marketplace. He'd been so engrossed in his discussion with Zachary he couldn't even remember walking through the city. But now he saw that shoppers were buzzing around the market stalls like bees gathering nectar; stall-holders were bargaining loudly with buyers, and women were dragging crying children around in their wake. Simon stepped back as one of them brushed past, only to bump into two fellow Jews with slaughtered lambs slung across their shoulders. They hurried by leaving an overpowering stench of blood in their wake.

Simon pinched his nose and then grabbed Zachary's tunic. 'Come on. Let's get food.'

Buying a loaf of bread, cheese and a handful of figs they slid into the narrow alley behind a fruit and vegetable stall. The stall-holder barely glancing at them. He was too busy haggling with an argumentative woman over the price of his goods.

'Any news from Capernaum?' Simon asked tearing the bread in two and handing half to Zachary.

Zachary's sullen expression softened. 'Only that your sister's given birth to a boy.' The cheeky grin returned as he bit hungrily into his share of the bread.

'A boy, eh?' Simon said between mouthfuls. 'I didn't even know she was expecting a baby.' He handed Zachary half the cheese.

'By the way, while I was watching Pilate's entourage arrive I saw one of your sect getting a beating.'

'Who? What for?'

Zachary shrugged and helped himself to a fig. 'No idea, but I guessed he was one of yours because he was preaching. Herod's guards dragged him away when Pilate and the Romans arrive. We don't want them thinking we can't handle our own internal affairs, do we?'

Simon grunted. 'Our sect have got our authorities worried. We're growing too fast for their liking. It's getting to the stage if you even mention the name of Jesus you're likely to get a whipping.'

'Why?'

'The Pharisees and Sadducees don't like our teaching, do they? Them religious bodies reckon we're at odds with the Mosaic laws.' He paused. 'Where are you staying?' he asked changing the subject. 'Not with Barabbas, I hope.'

'Stop fretting, Simon. You're turning into an old woman. I'm in a safe house, Nathan's place.' Zachary helped himself to another fig and glanced around the marketplace. 'I really ought to go,' he said biting into it. 'If, as you say, there's a price on Barabbas's head, I better not hang around here in case I'm recognized.' Zachary waved his bread in the air. 'Thanks for this.'

Simon grabbed the sleeve of his tunic as he turned to go. 'Spend Passover with me.'

Zachary twisted his face. 'You mean with the Nazarene sect? I don't...'

'I'll meet you here, in the marketplace,' Simon persuaded. 'I reckon it'll do us good not to argue but to remember happier times.'

'Well...' Zachary wavered but then gave a grin. 'Right! I'll meet you here.' And with a final glance around the busy market square he pulled his hood over his head and disappeared into the crowds.

Simon watched him go, an anxious furrow across his brow. So Zachary was staying at Nathan's place, was he? Yes, Nathan was all right. He was a good Zealot. He could trust Nathan to look out for the lad.

His eyes drifted on to two familiar Roman legionaries browsing around the souvenir stall. One was stocky and scarred, a veteran by the looks of him, and the other had long red hair on his legs and arms. Simon stepped back into a doorway and made contact with the dagger under his tunic; it was a comfort having it at his side today.

* * *

As Vivius rode through the city gates with Claudia, he was surprised to see a colourful blanket of tents spread across the Kidron Valley. He could smell cooking in the air, and sensed the Jewish anticipation for their forthcoming celebration so strongly he felt he could almost reach out and touch it.

'Impressive,' he commented.

She didn't answer, but manoeuvring her mount away from the Bethany road, took a track leading around the village.

Two young boys raced across the path in front of them yelling and laughing. Vivius watched them clamber up a palm tree to see who would reach the top first. It was a game, that's all it was, but for no logical reason he found himself disturbed by an unexpected flash of jealousy. He knitted his brow trying to fathom out why. Perhaps it was because he'd never experienced the joy of playing with sheer abandonment? Perhaps it was because he'd never had a close friend his own age to play with? Yes, it could be either of those things, he mused. Even from an early age his father had been a harsh taskmaster. If he wasn't studying, his father had brought in older boys to train him for combat, and what time was left his father insisted he spend with Phaedo learning about olive groves. Although, he conceded, that had never been a hardship but it did mean his father's... Vivius blew softly through pursed lips. His father—again? He wrenched his thoughts back to the present. He was thinking too much, he decided. He needed to give himself a day off from assignments and investigations.

That was when his eye fell on the big Jew. It was the surly glare that caught his attention; the dark piercing eyes that never wavered from his own, eyes that had the unmistakable message, 'Given half the chance I'd kill you.' But he wouldn't; Vivius knew that, not with two legionaries as escort. Nevertheless, Vivius made a point of returning the silent battle with his own superior stare; that is, until the two small boys ran across the road to join their friends, one of them, in his haste, narrowly missing Vivius's mount. The boy let out a cry of alarm when he saw it was a Roman. The horse snorted, startled, and Vivius was forced to relinquish his silent battle to concentrate on calming the animal. One of the legionaries chased the youngsters away with a loud bellow which gave Vivius an uncomfortable feeling of having a nursemaid. Reining in his mount he waved the legionaries forward.

'I don't think there's any need for you to accompany us farther,' he told them. 'You might as well return to the fort. I think they'll have greater need of you than we do.'

'Yes, Senator.'

Vivius allowed his eyes to drift over to the Jew again. He was still glaring in their direction, but then his gaze dropped to the young lad at his side. He hesitated, spoke to him briefly, then clearly not wanting to create an incident, the Jew turned abruptly and followed the legionaries back to the city. Vivius experienced a brief moment of regret. Tiberius had wanted him to assess the mood of the Jews, and he guessed that was one Jew who wouldn't have been afraid to give it to him in a straight talking manner.

As they moved on, leaving the Kidron Valley and its colourful spread of tents, campfires, smell of food and the relaxed and congenial atmosphere, Vivius realised Claudia was skirting the village of Bethany. He glanced across at her. She had been quiet since leaving the city but now they were away from people he noticed she had closed her eyes and tilted her head back to catch the fresh breeze sweeping down from the Judean hillside.

Unobserved, he watched her body swaying easily in the saddle, her cheeks flushing up with the heat in the sun, her auburn hair, not coiled but blowing free. His smile widened; it wasn't hard to guess she was glad to get out of the city.

They were heading east, he noticed; where fresh green crops warmed to Palestine's springtime, fields of yellow wheat waved in the gentle breeze, and splashes of red and blue anemones grew by the wayside. A moving shadow over the field of wheat caught his eye. He shaded his eyes. A hawk circled lazily above them in the cloudless blue sky; a pigeon gave a throaty call of warning from the branches of a palm tree, a dove cooed his unhurried reply, and the flap of tiny wings grew silent as the sparrows hid in the white-blossomed almond tree.

Vivius sampled a lungful of fresh air, holding on to the fragrance of almond blossom for as long as he could. Then following Claudia's example, he closed his eyes and focused on the warmth of the sun on his back, the musical tinkle of the goats' bells in the distance, and the slow steady rhythm of his mount to draw him away from the problem of his assignment.

They skirted Bethany in a wide arc so they could admire the view, but it was only when the village was well behind them that Claudia became more talkative. She told amusing anecdotes about her life in Rome, in Caesarea and in Jerusalem, and Vivius found himself laughing with her over seemingly trivial incidents. Twice he tried to broach the subject of Pilate but each time she cleverly deviated him from anything remotely political.

Eventually, they rode through an arch supported by two stone pillars and Vivius found himself on a long, straight road of well cared for olive trees planted regimentally on either side.

Claudia pointed ahead. 'I told you their villa was beautiful, didn't I?

'A Roman villa in Palestine?' Vivius raised his eyebrows, at the Ionic columns, balconies, the fountains, the Roman statues and garden of palm trees.

When they reached the stables Vivius dismounted, handed his reins to the stable slave and then reached up to lift Claudia down from her mount. As he wrapped his hands around her slender waist, he found her warm body pleasantly disturbing. She leant forward, her hands resting lightly on his shoulders. He was aware of her yellow silk dress slithering through his fingers, the softness of her body pressing up against his as he brought her slowly down from her mount. As her toes reached the ground she tilted her head back to look up at him, her green eyes regarded him steadily, with invitation, he thought, but he wasn't sure. He kept his hands around her waist longer than was necessary, trying to read her mood; the fragrance of roses was heady, her lips shining, wet. His hand moved deliberately from her waist to her back; he pulled her gently closer, she didn't resist.

'Greetings!'

Vivius breathed in sharply, dropped his hand to his side, and exchanging smiles of amusement with Claudia, he stepped back.

The bellowed greeting had come from a rotund Roman who dressed as if he hadn't given any thought to it. He was trundling towards them with a slack stomach rolled over a thick brown belt, a wide grin spread across his red face, and a butterfly of sweat under the armpits of his tunic.

'Senator Marcianus, I am so delighted you could join us.'

Vivius found himself warming to his host's jovial greeting. If he had seen their near embrace, Vivius guessed he was too polite to mention it.

'We rarely get visitors from Rome so I look forward to hearing your news. I am Hortensius and this is my dear wife, Suzanna.' Hortensius flapped his hand at a thin mousey woman who, stirred by his impatience, picked up her skirts and arrived in a flurry of apologies.

Lunch was already laid out when Hortensius led them into the garden, and Vivius found himself wondering how this easy-going couple could have possibly struck up a friendship with an arrogant diplomat like Pontius Pilate. Their lifestyles and characters seemed miles apart.

After lunch, Hortensius suggested they leave the womenfolk to their chatter and he would give Vivius a tour of his olive grove.

Hortensius took him into the big sheds where he kept his oil presses first, then as they sauntered at a leisurely pace through the olive grove, they discussed the harvesting of olives; which soils the trees flourished best in; pruning, fertilising and the different methods of crushing olives to make oil. Vivius told him about his own olive grove, and the problem of the frost, insects, and his plans for extending.

Out of curiosity Vivius asked, 'Tell me, Hortensius; isn't it dangerous for a Roman to have an olive grove so far out of Jerusalem? Aren't the Zealots a threat?'

'Not really,' Hortensius said easily. 'It's well known that I employ local people for my olive grove, especially during harvesting, and the Jews know I will employ them whenever I have an engineering project. I pay well, the Jews are pleased to have the work, so the Zealots leave me alone.'

Vivius raised his eyebrows. 'You're an engineer?'

'Yes, when I'm not tending my olive grove I'm an advisor to the Roman Army. They use me from time to time.'

Vivius found his assignment rushing back to him with renewed interest. 'Did they use you on the aqueduct project?'

Hortensius nodded and then paused as if reluctant to answer the question. 'It was terrible, Senator. Terrible!' he said in a low voice. 'Two hundred Jews killed. I never thought I'd witness such an atrocity. It was a bad...' He stopped abruptly, frowned, and then, as though relieved to have another focus pointed across his olive grove. 'By Jupiter, there's that blasted boy again! I'm sick and tired of telling his father to stop him playing in my trees. If he doesn't give him a good thrashing this time, then I will. Excuse me, Senator, while I deal with this.'

Vivius silently cursed the interruption but felt he had no option but to stand by while Hortensius puffed his way towards two old farmhouses. They're in a worse state than my own, Vivius thought. Their roofs sank in the middle and their wooden beams appeared to be struggling to hold the house together. In fact, it looked as though one heavy storm was all it would take to demolish them.

He turned back to the olive grove. It was the slightest movement that gave the boy's position away. He was sitting under a tree scratching his ear.

It was that gesture, the scratching of the ear, that drew Vivius's finger to the deep scar under his own ear. Strange, he hadn't thought about that incident for years. He stirred uneasily as the awful memory nudged itself forward. Why in the name of Jupiter was he thinking of his childhood again? He'd put all that misery behind him years ago. Perhaps it was the sight of the old farmhouses? Perhaps it was the boy hiding in the... He found himself listening to the familiar shimmer of silver leaves in the olive grove; they seemed to be urging him to remember.

Again it was the small things that came to mind first; the foul smell of Fabiana's sweat as she dragged him out of the olive grove, the image of her towering over him, whip in hand, the dry earth squeezing through his clenched fists as he curled up on the ground.

'I warned you, boy. I warned you what would happen if you went crying to your father.'

The first lash had struck his ear. Wrapping his arms around his head he had tried to protect himself. Fabiana had grabbed the neck of his tunic; he'd gagged. The tunic ripped, and he felt the hot sun on his back. He could still remember the whoosh of air before the sting of the second lash. He cried out, only once. Then silence. The next stroke flayed his shoulders. The next...

'What are you doing, Fabiana?'

The voice had sounded far away.

'Mind your own business, Phaedo.'

Vivius had raised his head, squinting against the dazzling sun to see Phaedo, their quiet, new slave who knew everything there was to know about olives, towering above him.

'Are you all right, young master?'

The voice still sounded distant. Vivius rubbed his ear. It was warm and sticky to the touch. He realised blood was running down his neck. Struggling to his feet, the world around him had reeled and his ripped tunic had slithered to the ground. Alarmed, his bloodied hands had clutched at his loincloth to avoid total humiliation.

'The master's not going to like you undermining me, Phaedo.' Fabiana had spat.

'And I doubt the Master will like the way you treat his son when he's away.'

'I've been caring for the boy since his mother died.'

'And beating him into unconsciousness is your way of doing

that?'

Phaedo had pulled Vivius to his side. 'Leave the boy alone, Fabiana.'

'Or what...what are you going to do?'

A slow smile had crossed Phaedo's lips. 'I'm going to speak to the boy's tutor. He'll not take kindly to the young master being whipped senseless so he couldn't do his lessons. The master sets great store on his learning.'

That was when Vivius had spotted his Greek tutor riding across the field towards them on his knock-kneed donkey. The little girl who skipped alongside him was...Aurelia. Vivius hadn't dared look at her but had dropped his head, intently studying the dust between his toes.

As the old Greek tutor dismounted, he said, 'Aurelia will be studying with us today, Vivius,' He had spoken as though nothing was amiss. 'Go and get dressed will you?'

Vivius continued staring unblinking at the dust between his toes but then Phaedo had given him a gentle push. Still staring at his bare feet he had headed towards the old farmhouse. Aurelia had followed.

On the way to the old farmhouse he had felt his stomach churn, the vomit rise, but as he retched he put both hands up to his mouth, losing his grip on his loincloth. It slithered down his legs and landed around his ankles. Burning with humiliation he covered his private parts with hands streaked with vomit. He had been too embarrassed to see what Aurelia's reaction was but she had digested the incident without a word. Averting her eyes she had bent down, picked up the loincloth and shyly handed it back to him. Then she had taken his filthy hand, led him into the kitchen and filled a bowl with water from the ewer. Gently pushing him down on a stool she had begun dabbing his back with a wet cloth. Vivius sucked in sharply through his teeth as cold water trickled into the open wounds.

'They...they...beat me...Fabiana...my father...They...'

Those were the words he had blurted out and to his surprise, more followed but in a jumble of inconsistencies.

Aurelia had listened, her eyes widening in amazement at his story. Sometimes she would nod or furrow her brow but the fact that she had listened had drawn Vivius into his first real friendship—and with a girl, younger than him who...

'Where is he, Senator? Where is he?'

Vivius turned to find a panting Hortensius and two of his workers bearing down on him; the butterfly of sweat had now spread down the sides of his tunic. 'Where's the vermin gone? I'll give him the thrashing of his life when I catch him.' Hortensius squinted over his olive grove. 'Can you spot him, Senator?'

Vivius cleared his throat and pointed towards the archway. 'I think he headed over there,' he said and couldn't resist a smile of amusement when Hortensius and his men waddled in that direction. The boy crouching in the trees grinned broadly at him.

Towards the end of the afternoon, an elderly, bald, sleepy looking slave wobbled into the garden with a tray of mussels, shellfish and salad which he set out neatly on the table. When they had had their fill, he brought in a larger tray filled with glazed ham, poultry, vegetables and sauces, which Vivius was alarmed to see wobbled even more precariously on its journey to them. It was only when the meal was over and Vivius had indulged in more than his usual intake of wine, that Hortensius brought up their previous conversation.

'Ah! Senator, you were asking about the aqueduct and the death of those Jews.'

Vivius scrambled around his intoxicated brain for a way to deflect this controversial subject with Claudia in their presence, but with a wave of the hand Claudia did it for him.

'Oh Hortensius, please. We're not going to talk about Jews, are we?' she said with a winning smile. 'It's been such a lovely day, and a relief for me to get away from politics. If you must talk about building projects tell the senator about the road you built around Galilee. That was a magnificent feat of Roman engineering, wasn't it?'

Vivius raised an eyebrow. 'You saw it being built, Claudia?'

'Well...I didn't exactly see it being built,' she wavered.

'But you've travelled on it?' His lips twitched.

'Not exactly but I was, er...' and then from under cover of the table, her bare toes ran unhurriedly up the calf of his leg. 'But I was told about it,' she finished; her long eyelashes flickered mischievously at him.

'Galilee? Ah, yes...' Hortensius's gaze drifted. 'Beautiful road that was.'

As their host rambled on about the roads he had built in Palestine, Vivius was aware of Claudia's toes moving gradually up his leg. He saw her lips quivering with amusement, found her mood—intoxicating, or perhaps that was the wine he mused. He hesitated, aware of the dangerous game he was playing, but the hesitation was brief. Lounging back in his chair he stretched out both legs; the beginnings of a smile playing across his lips.

CHAPTER EIGHT

(Jerusalem)

Zachary had planned to meet up with Simon in the marketplace, but when he opened the door of the safe house to leave, the unmistakable red flash of a Roman uniform across the road caught his eye. He slammed the door shut.

'Romans!' he hissed.

The scraping of stools and scrambling for weapons from the half dozen men around the table threw him into confusion. He scanned the room in a frenzied way for his sword. He'd put it down, somewhere? And where was the back entrance? Should they escape that way? Where was Barabbas? Ah! Upstairs with a girl. Zachary waited feverishly for someone to issue orders, like a child waiting for instruction. His teeth started chattering as it dawned on him that if he hadn't got bored with keeping watch, if he hadn't dozed off and...

Someone inched the door open.

'How many?'

'Can't see.' The man at the door turned to him. 'You sure you saw Romans?'

'Yes...I think...'

'You didn't fall asleep, did you?'

'No, but...I...I was tired. I've been out recruiting with Barabbas all day.' Zachary knew he sounded defensive but he couldn't help himself.

'I can't see any Romans out there now, unless...'

That was when they heard the shout, followed by the clatter of many boots down the lane. A chill of fear ran down Zachary's back.

Someone yelled, 'Barabbas! Romans!'

Zachary heard a heavy thud across the roof just as the front door crashed open and a dozen legionaries charged in wielding swords. Zachary never even got the chance to find his.

* * *

Simon belched, dropped his chin into the cup of his hand and stared moodily over a table littered with empty spice bowls, plates and cups. Normally he enjoyed sharing the Passover meal with the Nazarene friends. It gave him a sense of belonging; but not tonight. He couldn't concentrate. Besides, their numbers had grown to such an extent that half the people he didn't know, and the upper room was so full it had made it hot, uncomfortable and noisy. And it wasn't just this house that was bulging, Simon mused. The other homes were the same. Good news in the way the words of Jesus were spreading, but it did meant the Jewish authorities could no longer ignore them. In fact, the Sanhedrin had turned decidedly hostile lately. There'd even been arrests and beatings.

Simon's gaze wandered towards the open window where the temple glowed orange and gold with the setting sun, and the Judean hillside had turned a dark shade of purple. As for the Pharisees, those keepers of religious law, he mused, they seemed determined to bring their sect down by twisting their words and insinuating they were teaching against the laws of Moses.

Rising to his feet, Simon fastened his sword at his side, draped his cloak over his shoulder and opening the door of the upper room stepped out into the cool evening air. He breathed in deeply. The fragrance of almonds drifted up to him from the tree in the courtyard, its white blossom barely moving, the air was so still. A bird sang his evening lullaby in one of the branches, it's trill contented. But then, from somewhere within the house, a door banged, and the startled bird flew off over the roof tops.

Simon pensively rubbed his beard between his finger and thumb as he thought of the two hours he had stood waiting for Zachary in the marketplace. Admittedly, he hadn't seemed overly keen to join him and his companions for the Passover meal, but Zachary wouldn't have deliberately not turned up. He would have sent word. Simon touched the sword at his side. It was no good, he decided. He couldn't concentrate on a Passover celebration until he had found out what had happened to the lad.

On the spur of the moment, he poked his head back around the door. 'I'm going out,' he said to no one in particular. The room was noisy with prayer, conversations and the humming of psalms so he wasn't surprised when no one took any notice. He closed the door.

An aroma of roast lamb and spices hung in the air as he headed through the upper part of the city. Here, the streets were wider to contain the palaces of the rich and noble, and the lavish accommodation of the High Priest. It was only when he came into the lower part of the city with its narrow lanes and tightly packed houses that Simon became more alert for the Romans.

The harmonious singing of a psalm drifted down from one of the windows. It blended in with the hum of prayers and the tinkle of light-hearted laughter from other houses making the whole city sound like a musical composition. Simon knew he would have enjoyed a walk like this if he hadn't been so concerned.

He passed pilgrims huddled in a corner, their dialects indicating they had travelled from Samaria, Perea, Galilee or further afield for this Passover. Their clothing was rough, their food sparse and their wine smelt cheap, but they beamed a festive greeting at him. Simon gave them a brief nod, his hand never leaving the hilt of his sword.

He decided his best option was to go to the safe house he had frequented when he was with the Zealots, Nathan's house. Nathan always knew what was going on in Jerusalem. He would know what, if anything, had happened to Zachary.

Winding his way through the back streets of Jerusalem

he eventually reached the terrace of dilapidated flat-roofed buildings near the city wall. Nathan's house was second from the end, squashed between a slim, two-storey house which was always overcrowded with dubious tenants, and a short squat building which looked as if one good push would demolish it. Zachary was bound to be there, Simon reasoned. The lad had probably just forgotten, and got too caught up with the affairs of the Zealots.

He glanced furtively around to make sure no one was around before tapping on the door.

'Who is it?'

No longer being a member of the regular Zealots, Simon deemed it prudent to answer, 'Zachary Ben Elazar's cousin.'

The door opened, cautiously at first, but on recognition swung wider, and Simon was greeted like a long-lost but well-loved comrade.

'Simon? Come in, come in.'

Nathan was slightly built, slightly bald and wiry with unsettling black eyes. But Simon noticed the only real change in him was the jagged white scar on his leathery complexion which stretched from the corner of the eye to his chin. It gave a rakish edge to his appearance.

'We don't see you for nearly four years and then you arrive at my door as though you have the entire Roman Army after you.' His eyes flashed a look of alarm. 'You don't, do you?'

Simon shook his head as he stepped inside the comfortingly familiar room. It was still sparsely furnished with four roughly made wooden stools, a table, a threadbare couch and wall-to-wall shelves of dishes and bowls. Simon had always wondered how Nathan found time to earn a living selling his pots in the marketplace. Every time he'd come across him he was either giving refuge to Zealots, planning campaigns or fighting Romans.

'Is Zachary here?'

The fallen expression on Nathan face sent what remained of Simon's hopes plummeting into the depths of despair.

'The Romans raided the safe house at the other end of the city earlier today. Barabbas escaped but Zachary and another chap were arrested and taken to the fort.'

Simon sank down on to a stool and screwed the heels of his hands into his eyes. 'He's just a lad,' he muttered.

Nathan rested his hand on his shoulder. 'Yes, but he was found in a house of Zealots.'

Simon ran his fingers through his grizzled hair. The tension in his head was expanding at such a rate that he felt it was ready to snap at any moment. 'My fault,' he muttered angrily. 'I should have taken a firmer line with the lad after he lost his family. I should at least have stopped him joining up with that thug Barabbas. I tried warning him but...' His stool scraped across the wooden floor as he stood up. 'I have to go, Nathan.'

Nathan examined him soberly. 'Well, I'm here if you need me. I don't need to tell you to be careful, do I? The Romans might have eased curfew for the Passover, but they've got more Roman patrols wandering around this part of the city than there are fish in the Sea of Galilee.'

Simon simply uttered a string of obscenities under his breath as he opened the door.

* * *

'Forgive me for asking, Senator, but is anything wrong?' The young centurion warming his hands over one of the glowing iron braziers in the middle of Fort Antonia's courtyard was clearly eager to be of assistance to a senator from Rome.

'Yes,' Vivius said irritably. 'My physician should have arrived with the legion from Caesarea this afternoon but he hasn't, which is highly inconvenient as the infirmary have transferred the Decurion to my quarters. I now have a disgruntled medicus running between my quarters and his infirmary wanting to know why my physician isn't taking care of his patient.'

'Would you like me to make enquiries, Senator?'

Relieved to have someone else pick up his problem, Vivius stretched out his hands to the warmth of the iron brazier. 'Yes, do that. His name is Lucanus, he's Greek.'

Beckoning to a battle-scarred legionary hovering a distance away, the centurion issued him with orders and joined Vivius warming his hands at the brazier.

'My men raided a house of Zealots this afternoon,' he said by way of making conversation.

'Really,' Vivius answered stiffly. He made it a statement rather than a question hoping he wasn't going to be subjected to a running commentary of how it all happened.

The young centurion wafted smoke away from his face as the breeze changed direction. 'Barabbas was seen recruiting in the city so two of my men followed him to a safe house.' He hedged a grin. 'Unfortunately, one of them has the longest legs and brightest red hair you've ever seen. The Zealots couldn't fail to notice they were under surveillance.' There was a hiss as the breeze ignited a fresh log of wood, sending a spurt of flame into the dark night sky. 'Barabbas was in the house, and believe me, Senator, Barabbas is not a man to tangle with, as my men found out. Fortunately Pilate's auxiliaries were close by so they helped in the arrest. We might not have got Barabbas but we did get another Zealot; Zachary something or other...'

Vivius turned as the discrete cough behind warned the veteran soldier had returned. The glow from the fire highlighted his ugly white scars, giving his face a distorted appearance.

'Excuse me, Senator. The guardhouse tells me your physician arrived with the reinforcements from Caesarea, but as no one could find you, and as there was some confusion as to what a Greek was doing at the fort, the guards refused him entry. So the physician left a message to say he's gone to stay with friends in the Grecian quarter of the city for the night.'

'He's gone to do what?'

'To stay with friends in the Grecian quarter, Senator.' The soldier handed him a ragged piece of papyrus with an address scrawled across it. 'That's where he's staying.'

Vivius crumpled the papyrus in annoyance and thrust it into his tunic pocket. 'Well, he better be back first thing tomorrow morning or there'll be trouble,' he said to no one in particular.

'The physician also left this for you, Senator. He said it arrived the morning you left Caesarea.' Handing him a small roll of papyrus, the soldier saluted, and moved away. Vivius pushed it into his tunic pocket along with the crumpled papyrus and with a curt nod made his way into the fort.

The oil lamp on the table was casting uneven shadows across the walls when he crept inside his quarters. He assumed it had been lit by the medicus when he came to check on his patient. Quietly opening the bedroom door he saw Dorio sprawled out on mussed sheets, his breathing heavy, his curls clinging to the sweat on his brow. Kneeling down at the side of the bed, Vivius ran his hand under the mattress and gave a grunt of satisfaction as his fingers lighted on Fabius's journal.

The movement must have disturbed the patient because Dorio groaned and rolled over. Vivius grimaced and averted his head as a stench of drugs and bodily odours drifted his way. Swiftly leaving the bedroom, and closing the door firmly behind him, he flung open the shutters in his living quarters and inhaled lungfuls of cool night air. A pleasant aroma of spices drifted towards him.

Resting his arms on the sill he gazed across the city of Jerusalem. It looked different from the other nights, he mused. Lights shone in homes giving indication of activity; people wandered the streets, their laughter suggesting they were enjoying their celebration, and enjoying the freedom of having had the curfew lifted for the Passover.

He gave a tut of irritation as a groan emerged from the bedroom. In the name of all the gods, was he expected to sleep through that? Of course, he thought irritably, if he'd curbed his dalliance with the delectable Claudia he might have arrived back at the fort in time for Lucanus, who would now be administering some weird herbal concoction to silence his patient. Although...a hint of a smile emerged at the thought of Claudia. It had been an...interesting day, he reflected. Not an opportunity for him and Claudia to make it more interesting—personally—but then... His fingers drifted pensively through the folds of his toga to his dagger, his thumb running smoothly over the ruby in the handle. Why, he wondered, having spent an entire day in the lady's company, had he returned without a single thing of notable interest for his assignment?

His ponderings were distracted by the groans in the bedroom turning into loud rhythmic snores. Closing the shutters with a clatter, Vivius turned to his table and that was when he spotted the tablet. Curious, he opened it.

Senator: When you were exploring the Hasmonaean dynasty you asked me for the address of Nikolaos the bookkeeper. I cannot give you his address but I can tell you how to get to his house. I shall be in my office all day tomorrow.

The bookkeeper! Vivius tried not to build his hopes up in case it turned out to be another dead end. But on the other hand, he reasoned, surely it was about time he had a bit of good luck.

But first, he decided, he needed Lucanus to pick up his duties. Pulling the crumpled scrap of papyrus from his tunic pocket, he studied the address Lucanus had left him. Of course, he could send someone to get the physician but why bother when in all likelihood he would spend the night tossing and turning with the racket from the next room.

His decision made, Vivius turned off the lamp and left his quarters.

He had always enjoyed walking through cities at night, away

from people, away from the clamour of shoppers, the urgency of businessmen, the noise of traders and whinging of children. He found Jerusalem was no different. Occasionally he came across a Jew sauntering home after the celebrations, or the singing of a psalm drifted through an open window, but on the whole the city was quiet. He glanced behind at regular intervals. Not that he believed he was being followed, but being aware of his surroundings was a habit which had kept him safe over the years.

Only once was he forced to ask a Roman patrol for directions. If the officer in charge was puzzled to find a Roman senator wandering through Jerusalem in the dead of night he didn't show it, but pointed him towards the Grecian quarter of the city, a maze of poor houses situated in narrow streets.

Finding the house took him longer than anticipated, but eventually he discovered it was a typically small Judean house with a flat roof and a dozen or more like it in the lane. To his relief a light still burned in the open window, and there was a murmur of voices from inside.

He knocked on the door. The voices dropped, a chair scraped across the floor, footsteps padded towards him, and the door was thrown open by a large unshaven Greek with bulging apple red cheeks, a gut hanging over his belt, and a wide intoxicated smile that said everybody was his friend that night.

Vivius inclined his head as a prelude to introducing himself, but the arms that were flung wide in greeting and the torrent of Greek assured him such courtesies were not needed, not at this house and certainly not tonight. Vivius stepped smartly back, his hands raised, and was relieved to be saved further embarrassment by the arrival of Lucanus.

'Senator?' The physician beamed at him. 'Come and join us.'

'Thank you, Lucanus, but I'm not here to socialise and neither, may I remind you, are you.' Vivius said stiffly. 'I'm here because your services are needed at the fort.' Judging from the fallen faces his arrival had clearly drowned what remained of the celebrating.

'There's no need to be angry, Senator,' Lucanus said defensively. 'I did call at the fort but the guards wouldn't let me in so I came here. These people are friends of mine. I went to medical school with their son.'

Vivius struggled to envisage the drunken Greek swaying in the doorway conceiving an offspring intelligent enough to attend medical school. 'I'm afraid I must steal Lucanus away from your celebrations,' Vivius said changing easily from Latin to Greek. 'I have a wounded man for him to attend to.'

The lopsided grin took a downward spiral. 'Ah! The duties of a physician, eh? But then you must come inside, out of the chill wind my Roman friend while Lucanus collects his belongings.'

Vivius reluctantly stepped inside, but kept his eyes on his boots as a noisy, arm waving, embracing farewell took place. Only when the door had banged behind them, and the quietness of the city had wrapped itself protectively around him again, did he feel at ease.

'You got the letter then, Senator?

'Letter?' Vivius set off at his usual brisk pace, anxious to get back to the fort. 'Oh, you mean the address of your Greek friends? Naturally, how do you think I found you?'

'No, Senator; I mean the letter from Rome. 'I brought it with me from Caesarea. I left it at the fort for you.'

Aware the physician was lagging behind due to being lumbered with a medical case and a shabby, cloth travelling bag, Vivius slowed down. He patted the pocket of his cloak. He had totally forgotten about it. 'I haven't got round to reading it yet.'

Even as he spoke he was conscious of the figure coming towards them. There was something about his sheer bulk, his steady march, like that of a soldier …that reminded Vivius of the Jew he had seen in the Kidron Valley. It was only as the figure drew closer, and the glaring black pools of hatred in his eyes

118

were turned in his direction that Vivius realised it was the same man. His hand strayed through his cloak to his sword—just in case he needed it.

* * *

Simon was returning from Nathan's house when he heard voices; Roman voices, and it wasn't soldiers; he could tell from the high-class accent of one and the Greek accent of the other.

As he rounded the corner he saw that he was right; one was a Greek traveller, he could tell from his tatty cloth travelling bag, but the other—Simon flared his nostrils. The other was the arrogant Roman senator he had seen riding across the Kidron Valley. The hatred bubbled up inside him like a pan of boiling water. He glanced behind; the lane was empty. No one would see if...his fingers gripped the handle of his sword. Of course there was the Greek, he'd have to get rid of...he was only young; not much older than Zachary but... It was the image of Zachary's cheeky face laughing up at him that took his hatred off the boil. Simon knew exactly what the Romans would do if they came across their murdered senator. Reprisals! And Zachary was already in Roman custody. Simon cursed under his breath and walked on by.

CHAPTER NINE

(Jerusalem)

Pontius Pilate paced the floor of his quarters, hands clasped behind his back, head down.

Claudia patted the chair at her side. 'Sit down and relax over breakfast, my love. You know how fretting upsets your delicate constitution.'

Pilate glanced across at the bowl of figs, grapes and dish of honey cakes laid out on the table, and wrinkled his nose at the sweet sickly smell, but the expression only made his face look like a crumpled sheet. 'Sit down! Relax! Don't be ridiculous, Claudia! How can I relax when you calmly inform me the senator's been asking for the bookkeeper's address. You know the trouble I had with that silly little man, always counting his money, always questioning me over every single coin spent. He even had the audacity of accusing me of misappropriating tax monies, but it was him that was incompetent, and I told him so. The gods alone know what he'll say just to get even with me.' Pilate's usually smooth voice grated as though he needed a strong drink to clear it of phlegm. 'And why does the senator want the bookkeeper's address in the first place; that's what I'd like to know. Who put him up to it? It all stems from that letter Fabius sent the emperor. It's a conspiracy. That's what it is, a conspiracy.'

Claudia nibbled daintily at a fig as she listened to her husband's ranting. 'Against who?'

'Me! Me!' Pilate stabbed his chest so hard that acid indigestion rose from his stomach. He grimaced as he belched. Claudia was right, he brooded rubbing his chest. This upheaval was upsetting his delicate constitution. 'And possibly Sejanus,' he added. 'I gather not all the Senate are agreeable of his rise to power.' Frustrated by this latest news he slapped his hand harder than he intended on the cold marble head of Tiberius standing in the corner. It stung, but only momentarily. After a long pause his fingers began drumming over the marble eyebrows. 'But the senator hasn't got the address yet, you say?'

'I shouldn't think so. There wasn't time; he was out with me all day yesterday.'

'Hmm. Perhaps I should have his quarters watched.'

Claudia waved her hand dismissively. 'Forget the senator. We have him under control.'

'You think so, huh?'

'I do.'

'Then where do you think he went after he left you last night?'

'To bed, I assume.'

'Wrong. He took a late night jaunt through the city. Why he should do that I have no idea.' He threw his wife a look of contempt. 'So much for your charms in keeping him out of trouble, my dear.'

Claudia calmly popped a grape into her mouth, removed the pip and added it to the pile on her dish. 'Would you rather I had spent the night with him?' she asked tersely.

The question hung threateningly between them. Wandering over to the window, Pilate opened the partially closed shutters, rested his elbows on the ledge and studied the dark grey clouds overhead. The air that drifted in was thick and warm as though a storm was brewing. He was aware of Claudia's eyes burning into his back but he didn't move. Her question posed new and unchartered territory between them so he allowed his iron silence to speak for itself.

Eventually he said, 'This has been a troublesome visit, Claudia.'

'Has it?' Her voice had an edge to it as though she was still mulling over his previous comments.

'The Jewish Supreme Council has landed me with more problems than usual. They appear to have no understanding whatsoever of a multi-faith society. One God, they insist, and that's it. Why can't they follow the Roman example, that's what I'd like to know? We have less problems with our many gods than these Jews have with only one.'

'Hmm.'

'Even the slightest change we suggest is met with opposition; either from the fanatical Zealots who will defend the Jewish way of life even if it kills them, or from the Jewish council. Do you know what they're doing now?'

'No, dear.'

'They're using the same tactic as they did with that Nazarene fellow; you know, the one we crucified last year.'

'You mean Jesus of Nazareth?'

'That's the one. They're insisting his followers are a threat to Rome in what they preach. But I know what the Jewish council are up to. They want rid of this sect so they're calling it blasphemy and a threat against Rome so we'll crucify them. Damned impertinence!'

'Hmm, well.' Claudia wiped her sticky fingers, 'I shall leave you to your Jewish problems and I shall see what I can do to amuse the senator today, shall I?'

Pilate made no comment; he didn't even turn when he heard the rustle of her dress as she left the table or clatter of the latch as she left the room. In fact he was still staring out of the window when Rico entered to clear the table. But it was only when his slave cleared his throat as indication of his presence that the Procurator realised he was there.

'I thought you might like some wine, excellency?'

'You thought right,' Pilate waved his hand towards a goblet on the table and listened to the trickle of wine as Ricco poured from the jug. Pilate ran his tongue around his lips. 'This has been a troublesome visit, Rico.'

'Yes, excellency.'

'Made more so by the arrival of the senator.'

'Yes, excellency.' Rico handed him a full goblet.

The pause was a long one.

'It would make my life far less troublesome if I knew what he was up to, where he was going and who he was seeing. The Lady Claudia can't keep him under observation all the time.' He paused. 'In fact, it would reduce my troubles considerably if...if the Zealots disposed of him for me or...or if he simply... disappeared altogether.' Pilate swung round to face his slave; wine slopped over the rim of his goblet at the sudden movement but Pilate's unblinking bulbous eyes never wavered from those of his slave.

Rico hesitated before dropping his eyes and bowing his head. 'Yes, excellency,' he murmured. 'I understand.' And as Pilate returned back to the window, Rico slid out of the room.

* * *

As the thick blanket of sleep lifted, Vivius stretched his full length on the couch only to find as his feet stuck out from under the warmth of the blanket speeding the process up. He sat up slowly and rubbed his face, satisfied that despite having had less than four hours sleep he was remarkably well rested. Whatever foul-smelling herbal concoction Lucanus had poured down his patient's throat on their return to the fort had certainly quietened Dorio down.

Throwing back the blanket, Vivius swung his feet to the ground and turned his attention to Fabius's parchments spread across the table. The down side of hiding them under Dorio's mattress had been the smells. Fortunately, he mused with a touch of satisfaction, he'd had the foresight to air them before retiring last night so he could work on them this morning.

Stabbing an apple in the bowl with his dagger, he sat down at the table and concentrated on the final pages of Fabius's report.

After almost two hours he tossed his pen to one side and

pinching his brow between his thumb and two fingers pondered on how he would get a conviction on Pilate based on the information accumulated so far. The truth was, he wouldn't. There was no real proof that Pilate was acting unjustly towards the Jews, and it was solid proof Tiberius was after. As for Sejanus, there was still no mention of him.

Vivius leant forward, elbows on the table, his fingers forming a steeple as the repercussions of handing over a weak report to the emperor played on his mind. He breathed in deeply and then blew out softly through pursed lips. So, he decided taking his negative thoughts in check; the next step was finding Nikolaos, the bookkeeper; assuming he was willing to talk to a senator from Rome, or indeed had proof of embezzlement, and embezzlement running into a considerable sum of money, not just petty thieving.

Vivius sliced an apple in half with his dagger and crunched into it. Spitting out a pip he rose to his feet and opened the shutters to freshen the stale air in the room. But the air that drifted in was thick and warm, and the sky was dark grey as though a storm was brewing.

There was a knock on the door. Striding across the room Vivius flung it open. It was the medicus; the one that had a tendency to irritate him. Placing a warning finger to his lips Vivius pointed to the bedroom. 'The patient and his physician are sleeping.'

The medicus regarded him coldly. 'That's all very well, Senator, but the physician needs to examine the decurion in the infirmary, *now*.'

Vivius jerked his head towards the bedroom door. 'Then *you* better go and wake him.' He paused. 'Will the administration staff have started work yet?'

The medicus turned up his nose. 'Of course, Senator. We all rise early at the fort.'

Deciding it wasn't worth getting irritated over the haughtiness of his manner, Vivius washed himself in the bowl in the corner, dressed and leaving the medicus to rouse the sleeping patient left his quarters. As he approached the administration offices, he was surprised to find Claudia in the corridor. She was fastening the clasp of her rust brown cloak as though she was on her way out.

'I thought I might ride into Bethany this morning,' she said by way of greeting.

'Alone?'

Her eyes held almost an impish twinkle when she said, 'Not unless you'd like to accompany me. I'd enjoy that.' She paused. 'But you seemed to be on your way to the administration offices.'

Realising he could hardly deny it, Vivius said, 'I was.'

'Not more investigations into the Hasmonaean dynasty, surely? Ah no! Perhaps you were after the bookkeeper's address? Wasn't that what you were after when I found you down there a couple of days ago?' Her brow knitted in mock surprise. 'Why would you want that, Vivius?'

'You were right the first time, Claudia. I was going to read up about the Hasmonaean dynasty.'

'Hmm.' Her green continued twinkling at him. 'Well, I'd hate to disturb your browsing. Perhaps we could make it an afternoon excursion? What do you think?'

Vivius didn't dare to voice what he really thought. One more outing with Claudia would take their relationship on to a completely different level, and tempted though he was to let that happen he was conscious of the dangers and where it would lead.

'I think that sounds like a good idea,' he said carefully.

'Then I shall see you later, Senator.' Flashing him a knowing smile she glided down the corridor like one of the Hasmonaean princesses leaving a delicate aroma of roses behind her.

Vivius took the second flight of steps down to the administration offices and discovered the medicus was right; the clerks in the administrative officers were buzzing around in a manner that suggested the entire Roman presence in Palestine would come to a standstill if it weren't for their records.

Vivius knocked on the office door of the clerk he had met two days ago and entered without waiting for an invitation. 'Good morning.'

The owlish little man was sitting behind a desk piled high with wax tablets.

'Thank you for your note. You have the bookkeeper's address?' Vivius asked.

The clerk's eyes dropped uneasily and he began rummaging through the mess on his desk. 'I can't remember where... exactly but...I've written it down here...somewhere...'

Vivius sat down on a stool.

The shuffling around the desk continued for some time but then it stopped and the clerk's owlish grey eyes blinked nervously at him. 'Senator, may I be permitted to make an observation.'

'You may.'

'I'm not going to ask why you're wanting Nikolaos's address. You're hardly likely to mix in the same circles as him, and I can make a shrewd guess that it has nothing to do with exploring the dynasty of the Hasmonaean princes. So I'm assuming it has something to do with him being Pilate's former bookkeeper.'

'Go on.'

'Nikolaos...' The little clerk sat back in his chair, his fingers playing nervously with a stylus. 'Nikolaos, he's Greek. He left the fort over a year ago, or rather he was forced to leave. He's a good man; a man of integrity. But...' He lifted a wax tablet from under a pile of tablets. 'I've been instructed not to give you this, Senator.' He hesitated before handing it to him.

'Who instructed you?' Vivius reached out and took the tablet.

'I'd rather not say, Senator; if you don't mind. I don't want trouble. But yesterday I took the liberty of telling Nikolaos you'd asked for his address. I hope that was all right. He's nervous about meeting you but...' He leant forward in his chair. 'He won't be harmed, will he, Senator?'

'Not from me he won't.'

The clerk nodded his approval as he pointed to the tablet. 'As you can see I've drawn a map. Nikolaos lives near the Greek quarter of the city, a rough area.' He paused. 'Can I be so bold as to ask you not to mention that I've given you this; not to anyone, and I mean anyone. As I said, I don't want any trouble.'

Vivius pushed the fact that Claudia knew what he was looking for to the back of his mind. 'Absolutely.' He stood up.

Deciding he might have enough time to visit the bookkeeper before his afternoon excursion with Claudia, Vivius left the office and marched swiftly back to his quarters. He flung open the door and breathed in sharply.

'By all the gods...'

The table was overturned, the chair broken, loose pages from Fabius's journal were strewn across the floor soaking up water from the upturned water bowl, and in the middle of the mess was Lucanus, sprawled across the floor.

Vivius hauled the dazed physician into a sitting position. 'What happened?'

'I'm trying to put the pieces together myself, Senator,' Lucanus said faintly. 'I vaguely remember waking up, wandering through here for breakfast and finding a man rifling through your things on the table.'

Vivius stooped down and held up one of the sodden pages of his report. 'Was he reading this?'

'What is it?'

'Never mind. Did you recognize him?'

'How could I possibly recognize anyone, Senator? I only arrived last night, remember?'

'A Roman?'

'I doubt it. He was big and dark skinned. He must have expected your quarters to be empty because when I came out of the bedroom he was startled. He made a run for it but...' The physician attempted a grin but ended up wincing and holding his jaw. 'I stopped him by throwing my medical case at him but...' His face fell when he saw the dint in it. 'Anyway, I threw the chair at him.' He pointed to the broken chair and Vivius caught a note of pride creeping in when he said, 'And then... then I punched him.' He paused. 'Trouble is, I took an oath to heal people, not kill them.'

Vivius retrieved the upturned bowl, filled it with water from the ewer, soaked a towel in it and examined the physician's bloody gash on his jaw.' How did you get that?'

Lucanus sucked in sharply through his teeth as Vivius dabbed the graze. 'He was bigger than me. Ouch!' He glared at him before taking the towel out of his hand and dabbing it gingerly on the wound himself.

Vivius made no comment, but he was surprisingly touched that Lucanus had put up a fight for their belongings. Leaving him to tend to his own wounds, Vivius bent down to retrieve the soggy parchments. Righting the table he placed them on top and examined them. A number of pages were torn, most of them were wet, but none of them appeared to have been stolen. 'Was he reading my report?'

'I shouldn't think so, Senator. He didn't give me the impression he was literate; but he was interested in your letter.'

'Letter? What letter?'

'The one you haven't got round to reading yet.'

Vivius frowned. 'Why would anyone want to read that?'

'I have no idea, Senator. Why don't you read it and find out?'

'Where is it?'

'I wrestled it out of his hand before he ran. That's how I got this.' He pointed to his face before raising a buttock and removing a crumpled piece of parchment. 'I only arrived in Jerusalem yesterday, Senator, but so far I've been turned out of the fort by Romans, glared at by a hostile Jew and fought off a dark-skinned intruder. Can I ask what's going on?'

Vivius took the parchment off his sorry looking physician. 'No.'

'In my opinion, someone saw you leave your quarters earlier, knew Dorio was in the infirmary, but didn't expect to find me here.' Lucanus persisted.

'I need you to keep quiet about this break-in, Lucanus.'

'If you say so, Senator.' Lucanus sucked in through his teeth again.

Vivius glanced at him. 'Thank you for what you did,' he said brusquely.

'Would you do me a favour, Senator?'

'What.'

'Read that blasted letter! If I've put my life at risk, I'd like to know why.'

Vivius gave a distant smile and unrolling the parchment was a little alarmed to see it was from Aurelia.

My dearest Vivius,

I write to warn you.

Sejanus has been to see me. He asked me about your friends, family and acquaintances at the Senate. Then he questioned me about the charges of treason brought against Julius which, as magistrate, you had dropped for lack of evidence. Sejanus is suggesting you concealed evidence. I don't believe you did, my love, but my fear is that Sejanus may have you arrested for treason on your return. Why this unexpected surge of antagonism on his part I can only assume has something to do with your visit to Palestine.

I anxiously await your return—but be careful, my dear love.

Aurelia.

Vivius ran his tongue around the inside of his mouth; it was dry; even drier than on the eve of a battle. 'Pack the bags, Lucanus. We're going back to Rome.'

'What?'

'You heard me.'

'But...hold on senator. Let's be practical. Dorio can't travel, at least, not yet.'

'Then we go without him.'

Lucanus dropped his bloodied towel into the dish of water. 'Can I make a suggestion, Senator.'

'No.'

'Can I suggest you think about this first? It'll take me the rest of the morning to arrange Dorio's transfer back to the infirmary and pack anyway.' The pause was brief. 'And why the sudden haste to return to Rome? Was it something in the letter? If you tell me perhaps I can help. Although I'm not sure what I could do unless it was something medical. But who knows, by sharing the problem I might have a useful suggestion to...'

Lucanus's voice reverberated around Vivius's head like a persistent clanging bell. He could stand it no more. Without a word of explanation, he grabbed his cloak and headed for the door.

* * *

Vivius cursed as an unexpected surge in the crowd knocked him against the wall. Annoyed with himself for not having concentrated on where he was walking, he stepped back into a doorway to take stock of his situation. He ran his finger around his neck and found it uncomfortably damp with sweat. What madness had possessed him to wear his cloak in this humidity, he brooded. But he knew what madness: Aurelia. He hadn't been able to think clearly about anything since reading her letter and leaving the fort.

It was a shout of encouragement from the man in front that drew his attention to the people around him. They were craning their necks, trying to catch a glimpse of some spectacle. He grimaced at the close proximity of their foul-smelling, sweating bodies, and was about to look for the nearest alley to get him away from this chaos when an unexpected gap left him with an unobstructed view of the road. At first, all he saw was a flushed faced Roman centurion cracking his whip, but then he noticed four prisoners dragging their wooden crosses behind them. 'Why in the name of all the gods was he watching this circus?' he thought irritably. He had no interest in the crucifixion of a handful of Jews...and yet...it dawned on him that he'd far rather watch four men staggering to their deaths in Jerusalem than envisage what was happening to Aurelia in Rome.

Vivius ran his hand down his face. He needed to think clearly, logically, he decided. His usually clear and analytical mind seemed to be incapable of functioning but appeared to be governed by irrational fears for Aurelia. Aurelia! He winced. He'd barely given her a thought in days. He'd been so wrapped up in his assignment...and Claudia that... He rubbed the back of his neck, uneasy with the burden of guilt that had landed on his shoulders.

In the distance a low rumble of thunder reverberated across the Judean hillside.

He gave his guilt permission to hover before realising he could do nothing for Aurelia in this emotional state of mind. Taking a few deep breaths to clear his head he made a conscious effort to push his concerns for her to one side.

So, he decided, if he was travelling back to Rome he would need to plan his route, his means of transport and consult with the physician. Despite what he had said to Lucanus earlier he could hardly leave Dorio in Jerusalem. Aurelia would be devastated if he arrived back in Rome without him. As for the emperor, Vivius took another deep breath and tried not to contemplate how he would explain the failure of his investigation to the emperor. That was an entirely different problem, one he would have to work out later. First, he had to get back to the fort.

He stepped out of the doorway, glanced around for an alternative route, and that was when he spotted the hostile Jew who had glared at him — twice.

* * *

Simon trudged through the city gates, his shoulders hunched, his head down, relieved to find that the citizens of Jerusalem, who had jostled him through the narrow streets of Jerusalem, were beginning to fan out across the open spaces either side of the Golgotha road.

He hovered at the side of the road, uncertain what to do next, conscious of the sweat drying on his body. No one took any notice of him; at least, he didn't think they did. Everyone was more interested in the crucifixion.

He waited, wishing he wasn't here yet glad he was; grateful to Nathan's urgent message that told him Zachary had been hauled from his cell for crucifixion early that morning. Simon had run all the way to the prison. At first he thought he might have been able to plead with the authorities, tell them Zachary was only a lad, a messenger, a lookout for the Zealots, nothing more. He'd never killed anyone in his life. But his well-rehearsed speech had remained unspoken, and he had almost wept out loud when he saw the tearstained boy dragging his wooden cross through the streets of the city. Three older men followed with their crosses. That was the moment Simon realised the only thing he could do now was to be with the lad as he died.

So now he waited.

He told himself he knew about death. He'd shed enough Roman blood himself during his time with the Zealots. He'd seen plenty of crucifixions, not least his friend Jesus at last year's Passover. He knew what to expect. This crucifixion was no different from the others. Nevertheless, when he heard the first *thud, thud, thud* of the hammer he couldn't stop himself from shaking.

Digging his nails into the palm of his hands he tried to close his ears to the screams of pain from the prisoners. But his imagination had no mercy, and he saw all too graphically the long nails being hammered into Zachary's fleshy hands and feet, crushing his young bones.

The *thud, thud, thud* of the hammer and the awful screams appeared to go on forever, but when the noise eventually abated the awful silence that fell upon the hillside seemed even louder. That was when Simon forced himself to look up the hill. He vaguely registered that there were a dozen or more empty wooden crosses, but the four occupied ones were silhouetted against a dark grey sky.

Numbed and silent he viewed them.

It was the hint of a breeze through the muggy air that brought him back to something resembling reality. It was heading towards midday. He knew that because he heard the Jews standing nearby say so. They had decided to return to the city for food. He glanced around the crucifixion site, noting the depleting numbers. His shoulders sagged and suddenly he felt weary.

He remained behind the handful of spectators wondering how to get closer, realising that if he aligned himself too closely with Zachary he could be mistaken for another Zealot. There was no point in risking being arrested himself, he thought. He made a careful survey of the area. The Romans from the execution squad had settled on the grass to play dice; their centurion hovered close by engrossed in conversation with another officer. A distance apart from them stood a handful of sombre Jewish officials overlooking the proceedings. Everyone else Simon assumed to be spectators.

He moved casually forward. He wasn't the only one on the move; Golgotha was strewn with spectators. When he reached the first vacant cross he leant against the dried bloodstains; the wood was rough against his fingers. Even at this distance he could smell death, and hear the shallow breathing of the dying men and the weeping of the ladies around one of the crosses. The women didn't look up; they only had eyes for their loved one.

Simon glanced towards the legionaries. Judging from the raised voices there was a dispute over what number was thrown. He waited until the argument was over and they were absorbed in their game again before inching towards the first crucified man. He barely glanced up; it wasn't him Simon was interested in. He moved to the second cross.

'Zachary!' He breathed in fiercely through his nostrils.

The barrage of questions that whirled around his head was enough to make him dizzy. What had possessed the Romans to crucify a mere lad? He hadn't killed anybody, had he? Why today, so soon after his arrest? What about his trial? What about his sentence? Simon licked his lips; they were dry and crusted. He inched forward.

Zachary turned his head as though he sensed his cousin's presence. His face was tearstained, grey, his body bloody, twisted. 'S...i...m...o...n.' His mouth formed his name.

Simon reached out; he wanted to touch him, and stupidly reassure him, but instead they stared at each other wordlessly until Zachary closed his eyes.

Simon choked back a sob. Retreating to the vacant cross he slumped down, his elbows on his knees, his head in his hands and gave permission for his heart to grieve. But added to his grief came the awful realisation that there was no one there to mourn for Zachary, except him. No one knew Zachary was being crucified, only Nathan and he wouldn't dare come. The Romans had given no warning no...

In the distance, a clap of thunder echoed across the Judean hills.

'You there! Are you a family member for one of these criminals?'

Startled, Simon wiped his hand across his wet face and scrambled to his feet. A flushed-faced Roman centurion with a book in his hand was marching in his direction.

'No,' he muttered.

'So you'll have no idea whether the family wants the body of this second to end one? What's his name?' He glanced at his book. 'Zachary Ben Elazar.'

Simon miserably shook his head; torn between risking arrest himself for knowing a Zealot, and being responsible for Zachary's body when it was all over. The centurion moved away. With a groan of disgust over his denial, Simon dropped his head in his hands.

It was this self-absorption; the hurling of recriminations at himself that distracted him from realising he was under observation. When he did eventually sense he was being watched and looked up, it was to lock eyes with the Roman senator. Simon clenched his fists, his hatred flared naturally. The senator was sauntering towards him, his hand resting lightly on his sword.

But then it dawned on Simon that the last thing Zachary would want was to see him arrested; not now, not when he was facing death himself. Gritting his teeth, Simon forced himself to raise his hands as a gesture of 'no trouble', and with his head bowed began backing away.

'You there! I want to speak to you.'

Simon stopped. He glared at the Roman. 'Yeh?' he said, unable to restrain his contempt. 'And I'd like a word with you as well.'

The senator's grip tightened on his sword. 'Go on.'

Simon jerked his head towards Zachary. 'He's not had no trial, Roman. Why?'

'Who?'

'Zachary Ben Elazar.'

'Which one's Zachary Ben Elazar?'

Simon jerked his head towards Zachary again.

'Are you telling me that lad has been crucified without a trial?'

Simon was surprised to find he had the senator's full attention.

'Yes.'

'How do you know?'

'He was only arrested yesterday. There's been no time for a trial.'

'What about these others?'

Simon shrugged. 'Don't know about them.'

The senator frowned. 'Your cousin; he was a freedom fighter and a criminal?'

'A freedom fighter, not a criminal,' Simon corrected. 'But that still entitles him to a trial, doesn't it?'

The Roman senator moved his stance. 'Yes, it does.' He spoke with deliberation, then glanced up at Zachary's cross. 'Well, there's not much we can do about it now. He hasn't got long.'

Simon snorted through his nose. 'I can see that!'

The senator hardened his expression but although his hand remained on his sword his body was more at ease. 'How often does this happen, a crucifixion without a trial?'

'All the time.'

'You have proof?'

Simon detected an interest in the senator's voice that he found confusing. 'No, no proof, but it does.' He realised the senator was studying him carefully.

There was a long pause before he said, 'You clearly care for this lad.'

Simon nodded.

'And you hate Romans.' It wasn't a question more a statement of fact. Simon let his glare speak for itself.

'And you consider this crucifixion to be unjust.'

'Unjust?' Simon snorted through his nose and jerked his thumb towards Zachary. 'This is Roman justice for you. The lad should have at least had a trial.'

'As should any Jew, or Roman, after they've been arrested.'

Simon blinked rapidly.

The senator pursed his lips. He didn't speak for a while but appeared to be trying to make his mind up about something.

Then glancing around and seeing there was no one close enough to overhear, he said, 'I can get justice for the lad if you can take me to a member of the Sanhedrin, one who has access to Jewish records, and one who can keep his mouth shut.'

Simon's mind scrambled around for some hidden agenda the Roman might have for making this request, some cruel trick he wanted to play, or a sadistic move he wanted to make to satisfy his own Roman ego, but he couldn't find one. On the other hand, Simon found that what he wanted more than anything was justice for Zachary. Whether that was to appease his own guilt at having failed the lad he couldn't say. It was hard to work out... but...trust a Roman? 'Why?'

'Do you know such a Jew?'

'I might.'

The silence was an awkward one.

The groan from the cross caused both men to look up. Zachary's pain-fill eyes showed death was approaching rapidly. Simon struggled to keep his emotions in check. He wouldn't show his grief, not in front of a Roman. It took a while before he said, 'I know someone.'

'And you'll take me to him?'

There was the slightest hesitation before Simon nodded. And that was when the first drops of rain splashed on to his cloak and ran uncomfortably down his neck.

CHAPTER TEN

(Rome)

It dawned on Aurelia slowly that the voices drifting through her muggy sleep weren't part of a dream after all. She could feel a draught coming through to her bedroom from an open door, and the sound of voices, urgent voices, then the soft patter of Ruth's feet along the corridor. She sat up alarmed, clutching the blankets to her chest, She glanced at her partially shuttered window and saw from the inky blackness outside that it was the middle of the night.

The knock on her bedroom door was urgent, so was Ruth's hoarse whisper. 'Mistress, mistress, Senator Felix Seneca and a...a lady are here, mistress.'

Aurelia felt her heart pounding in her chest. 'I'm coming.'

Flinging off her bedclothes and grabbing a thick shawl for her shoulders, she tiptoed across the bedroom, her thoughts whirling as to why Felix should be calling on her at this hour of the night—and with a lady? She shivered, whether with fear, or the cold marble tiles penetrating her bare feet, she wasn't sure. She clenched her teeth to stop them from chattering. When she opened the door she found a wide-eyed Ruth standing in the corridor in her nightgown holding an oil lamp high. The flame of her lamp flickered from the draught of the open back door sending uneven shadows across the corridor walls.

'Your...guests arrived at the *back* door, mistress, straight off the river. The lady had fainted; the senator's taken her through to your living quarters. They're both wet through.'

'Off the river? Fainted? What...' Aurelia gnawed nervously at her lip, momentarily confused by the upheaval. 'I suppose...' She ran her fingers over her brow as if it would help get her thoughts operational. 'I suppose...bring them something hot, milk, anything, and towels,' she instructed.

Hurrying into her living quarters her eyes widened when she saw her female guest was none other than Apicata, the former wife of Sejanus. She was shivering uncontrollably, her face white and pinched as she hovered over what little heat remained in the brazier. Her cloak was wet, and the fashionable hairstyle that Aurelia had admired the other day was now devoid of fancy combs and hung in a tangled mass of curls over her shoulders.

Felix rose to his feet as Aurelia entered, his eyes anxiously searching hers for a reaction. His hair was plastered to his head and his cloak hug heavy with dampness.

'Aurelia, my love; I'm sorry about this.' He took her hands in his. They were icy cold. 'I didn't want to involve you but Apicata took ill and we had nowhere else to go where she could be safe. Can she stay till daylight?'

Aurelia's heart summersaulted at the word 'safe', but all she said was, 'You're welcome, both of you. But look at you; you're drenched. You need to get out of those wet clothes.'

Apicata's fingers were trembling as she tried to loosen the clasp of her cloak.

'Here, let me,' Aurelia said gently and was surprised how the simple task of unfastening the clasp and pulling the heavy cloak from her shoulders stopped her own shivering. She noticed the cloak had a smell of salt and sea spray to it. 'I shall get my servant to dry this off by the kitchen fire.' She fingered Apicata's pale cream dress. It was equally damp. 'I'll get her to bring you something of mine,' she added.

Somewhere in her trembling Apicata nodded. Ruth slid in from the kitchen, towels over one arm and a steaming jug of milk in the other.

Felix turned to the girl and with a tone of authority that even had Aurelia quaking snapped, 'If you value your mistress's safety, you'll keep silent about our arrival here.' He pulled off his wet cloak and shook it, sending a spray across the room.

Ruth lowered her eyes and gave the slightest bow. 'Yes, sir.' She handed him a towel, poured the hot milk into the beakers and reached out her hand for Felix's cloak.

He shook his head. 'No. I have to leave.'

Aurelia heart sank. 'Leave?'

Felix waited until Ruth had retreated to the kitchen before saying, 'I have to, my love. I must be seen in the city early tomorrow for a meeting of the Senate. And it must appear as though Apicata has travelled in to Rome to see her children.' He glanced at Apicata's anxious face. 'You understand how important it is that Sejanus lets you take them back to the country with you? No one must know where we've been tonight.'

Apicata nodded; her teeth were still chattering.

Aurelia handed them both a beaker of hot milk. 'And don't worry about me. I certainly won't tell anyone you've been to see the emperor,' she said and was gratified by the look of astonishment on Felix's face.

'How did you...?'

She pointed to his wet cloak. 'It's not raining outside. I would have been able to hear it. Besides, both your clothes have the salty smell of the sea about them, and not even I am stupid enough to believe you'd fancy a nightly row on the sea unless you had to.'

Apicata wrapped her hands around the hot beaker and looked anxiously up at Felix. 'Very good,' he said with a smile and Aurelia found herself blushing at his expression of admiration. 'And you're right. No one must know we've been to see the emperor.'

'Which is why I shall get Ruth to wash Apicata's dress for tomorrow, and why you should do the same, Felix.'

'What? Wash my dress?'

Aurelia shook her head at him, amazed that Felix could still joke and bring a smile to her lips over what appeared to be a serious situation. But then seeing Apicata's anxious furrow had not lifted gently added, 'Don't worry, your secret is safe with me.' She paused, surprised at how calmly she was beginning to take this unexpected crisis and how sharply her mind was working. Turning to Felix she asked, 'I gather you rowed up river from Ostia?'

'Yes. Why?'

'Because you came in through my back door so presumably the boat is still tied near my house?' She lifted her hand reassuringly at Felix's concern. 'Don't worry. I shall get the slave next door to move it. For a few coins he'll do any job I ask.'

'Right.' Felix reached for his purse in the pocket of his cloak and threw a few coins on the table. 'You'll be safe here tonight,' he said turning to Apicata. 'And tomorrow, do as we planned. Go to Sejanus, persuade him to let you take your children home.'

Apicata nodded, albeit nervously. 'Thank you, Felix,' she said. Aurelia realized this was the first time she had heard the woman speak. Her voice was soft, low and cultured.

Felix smiled crookedly at the woman. 'You did well today. That was not an easy interview.'

She looked down into her beaker. 'I know,' she whispered. She paused. 'He will act, won't he?' The worried furrow had returned. 'It's just...he kept saying, "You've no proof! You've no proof! Give me proof."'

Felix hesitated. 'He'll act on it. Anything concerning his son Drusus...' He glanced at Aurelia. 'Have no doubt; he'll act on it.' He flung his wet cloak over his shoulders again. 'Now, get some sleep, both of you. And remember, you must leave first thing in the morning, Apicata. I don't want Aurelia involved in this more than she has to be.' Felix gave a courteous nod to them both before quickly leaving the house.

It seemed unduly quiet in the atrium after he had gone. Apicata was still white, looked exhausted and was clearly not in the mood for talking. So respecting her need for privacy, Aurelia set about finding clean nightclothes and blankets for her guest, then showing her to the guest room allowed her to retire for what remained of the night.

* * *

'You see this, Macro?'

Sejanus flipped a coin in Prefect Macro's direction. The Prefect of the Vigils had just walked into his office for the morning and was sitting at his office desk when Sejanus made his usual unannounced entry. Macro caught the coin neatly in his hand and examined it. His grey wolfhound slid under the desk, his tail between his legs.

'Tiberius has had a second batch minted with my face on them.' Sejanus's chin jutted out in the manner of a man well pleased with himself. 'Ha! What does that tell you, eh?'

'So that's what's put you in such a good mood, is it?'

'It is indeed, and, er...' He leant forward, his knuckles rested on Macro's desk who leant back. The smell of stale wine was strong. 'Have you heard the rumour concerning the emperor naming his heir?'

Macro struggled to keep his gaze remote. 'Naming his heir? Where did you hear that?'

Sejanus stood up straight and waved his hand noncommittally in the air. 'I thought, with your men being on Capri, that they might have picked up the rumour.'

'Well, if they have they haven't reported it back to me.'

'Really?' Sejanus wandered over to the window, hands clasped behind his back but when he turned back again, Macro didn't like the cool smile that had replaced the self-satisfied smug of earlier. 'And it's not the only thing they haven't reported back to you, is it?' he said smoothly.

'Pardon?'

'Senator Felix Seneca? One of my guards saw him leaving the palace on the Isle of Capri and he wasn't alone. There was a lady with him. Obviously they had been to see the emperor. Why have you not reported this to me?'

'Who was the lady?'

'No idea. According to my source she kept her hood up, head down and a scarf covered her face.' He lingered by the window, his hands behind his back, his thumbs dancing nervously around each other. 'You know Felix Seneca; which lady could it be?' he asked in a manner that left Macro time to form his answer.

'Felix Seneca is a man who knows many ladies, Prefect. It could be any one of dozens.'

'Name one.'

'Well I, er...'

'How about the lady Aurelia Suranus, betrothed to Senator Vivius Marcianus?' Sejanus interrupted, glaring at Macro. 'Who was she seen with in social circles before her unfortunate marriage? It was Felix Seneca. Who did she turn to after her husband's death? Felix Seneca. My own enquiries found that much out, and unlike your men, mine were quick to report that the lady visited the same Felix Seneca only the other day.' He stabbed a finger at Macro. 'You should have known that. You should have known Felix Seneca was on Capri but who with, that's what I'd like to know. Was it Aurelia Suranus? Has Vivius Marcianus sent his lady information from Palestine to give to the emperor?' He gave his barrage of questions time to digest before narrowing his eyes. 'I do have your loyalty, don't I, Macro? You wouldn't deliberately keep this to yourself, would you?'

Macro stood up and glowered. 'You ask me a question like that?'

The wolfhound growled softly at the raised voices.

Sejanus gave a 'Huh-huh!' before wandering back to the window.

Macro ran his tongue around the inside of his mouth. It tasted like sawdust, but then it always did when Sejanus was around. 'What are you going to do?'

There was silence from the window.

Macro sat down and placed the coin deliberately on his desk. 'This business of treason with the Lady Aurelia's former husband that you wanted me to look into,' he continued. 'You may be able to make a case of Senator Marcianus being involved. Actually, you could make a case out of anything given the time, but, er...it occurred to me that with the emperor minting these new coins in your honour, and your forthcoming move into the Imperial household, you might not want the hassle of pursuing the matter.'

Sejanus turned angrily. 'Pursue it! Of course, I want to pursue it,' he snapped. 'If the emperor decides to come to Rome to name me as his successor, I can't have the senator or anyone else turning up with false information, can I? Not now, not at a crucial time like this.'

Macro straightened the tablets on his desk. 'Fine. I shall continue looking into it.'

Sejanus narrowed his eyes. 'Uh-Huh! And this matter of your Vigils on Capri not reporting back to you, why would they do that?'

Macro's expression was one of surprise. 'I thought you wanted me to investigate how letters and reports were getting to and from Capri?'

'I did; I do.'

'Then that's what I instructed my men to do. How are they supposed to know who are the emperor's invited guests and who aren't? As I've pointed out to you before, unlike your Praetorian Guards, my men are not political. They simply restore order, fight fires and catch runaway slaves.' He picked up the coin and handed it back to Sejanus. 'As for this matter of Senator Felix Seneca and the mysterious lady, I shall question my men of course, but if, as you say, she had her hood up and didn't want to be recognized, I doubt I'll get far.'

'Uh-huh!' Sejanus examined the coin thoughtfully. 'Good likeness, don't you think?'

'It is, very good.'

'Huh-huh!' Sejanus looked up coldly. 'Meanwhile I think *I* shall pay the lady Aurelia a visit. If she was visiting the emperor yesterday I shall persuade her to tell me why, and I'd be interested to hear whether she's heard from Senator Marcianus in Palestine.'

* * *

Aurelia felt as though her body had barely sunk into the mattress before she was being shaken awake by an unusually panicking Ruth.

'Mistress! Wake up, mistress. Prefect Sejanus is outside.'

Aurelia shot up in bed. The sun had broken through the shuttered windows leaving thin strips of light across the wall. 'What?'

'Prefect Sejanus and two Praetorian—'

'I heard you! I heard you! Where's Apicata?'

'Still in the guest bedroom, mistress.'

Despite the lack of sleep, Aurelia was surprised to find her brain was working with remarkable precision. 'I didn't hear them knock?'

'They haven't. The Senator asked me to stay awake and keep watch while you slept so I saw them arrive.'

'Good. When they knock, take your time in answering then, tell them...tell them I'm sleeping. Give me a chance to hide Apicata.'

'Yes, mistress. Where are you going to hide her, mistress?'

'I don't...I don't know, yet.' Dragging her blanket over her nightgown Aurelia hurried into the guestroom, her thoughts spinning with possible hiding places. Apicata was curled up in the bed, her damp hair still clinging to her head, but her eyes opened immediately when Aurelia entered, almost as if her sleep had been shallow and troubled.

'Sejanus is here,' Aurelia whispered. 'Come, quickly.'

Apicata barely had time to gasp before Aurelia had grabbed her hand and dragged her out of bed. She was pulling her through the atrium when there was a heavy knock on the front door.

Aware there was no time to take her through to the kitchen to hide her in the cupboards, Aurelia looked frantically around her living quarters. 'Quick, under this couch.'

Apicata's eyes widened in alarm at the narrow gap. 'I'll never get under there?'

'You'll have to!' Aurelia hissed and bending down struggled to lift the couch. She managed to raise it a couple of inches from the ground. 'And curl up,' she panted. 'I shall lie on top and my blanket can drape over the edge. Quickly.'

Apicata didn't need any further persuasion. The sound of Sejanus's voice echoed along the corridor as Ruth opened the door. Apicata scrambled under the couch. With a grunt, Aurelia dropped it, flung herself on top, and draped the blanket over the edge. Then closing her eyes, she buried her face in the cushion and concentrated on steadying her erratic breathing. She focused on the smell of lavender, the woolen texture of the blanket over her and tuned her ears to what was going on around her. She heard the murmur of Ruth's quiet voice, then heavy boots stomping through the front door. One, two, three sets of boots… soldier's boots. Her heart fluttered but she retained an easy rhythm of breathing, and hoped Apicata had the sense not to move no matter how cramped she was.

'As I told you, Prefect, my mistress is sleeping.' Ruth's quiet insistence entered with Sejanus and the soldiers. Judging from the position of her voice, she had taken up a stance protectively in front of the couch where Aurelia was lying and under which Apicata was hiding.

Aurelia had a weird sense that Sejanus was watching her, looking for the flicker of an eye, the twitch of a facial muscle, so she kept her breathing regular, her eyelids steady.

'She normally sleeps on her couch, does she?'

There was the slightest hesitation before Ruth said, 'Only when she's had a rough night, as she did last night, sir. It's warmer in here. I keep the brazier on all day at this time of year.'

'Uh-Huh!' There was a short pause before Sejanus barked, 'Search the house.'

Aurelia heard the clatter of boots as Sejanus's Praetorian Guards made themselves familiar with the rooms in the Suranus town house. Sejanus's boots *clonked* on her marble floor as he wandered around the room; he was picking things up...a goblet, a picture. She could tell from where he was standing and the sound of each object as he put them back again.

'Up all night, you say?'

'Yes, sir.'

'She hasn't been out? She hasn't taken any jaunts over to the Isle of Capri, shall we say?'

'No, sir. Not at all, sir.' Ruth sounded shocked. 'My mistress hasn't been well enough to take any jaunts this winter. She was so poorly last night I had to give her some of the medication the physician left. She'll likely be sleeping for hours yet.'

'Huh-huh. Where does she keep her letters?'

There was no reply.

Aurelia heard the rustle of parchments on her desk, the click of tablets being opened and then a 'huff' of annoyance. 'Nothing from Senator Marcianus, I see.' There was a pause. 'Has your mistress had a visitor lately by the name of Senator Felix Seneca?'

Aurelia tried not to hold her breath. She knew her slave well enough to know she would have dropped her eyes to give herself an appearance of subservience.

'My mistress doesn't have many gentlemen callers these days, Prefect, sir.'

'I didn't ask if she'd had many gentlemen callers, I asked if she'd had one particular one,' Sejanus snapped. There was a gasp from Ruth. Aurelia felt the couch shake, as if Sejanus had grabbed the girl by the arm, shaken her and caused her to stagger. 'I want the truth, girl.'

There was silence before Ruth shakily said, 'No sir; I can truthfully say my mistress has had no gentlemen callers...none yesterday, or the day before, or for the last week.'

No! Felix came in the early hours — today!

'But your mistress knows Senator Seneca, doesn't she?'

Again, there was a pause and Ruth sounded frightened when she said, 'I believe so, Prefect, sir.'

'How?'

The pause was longer this time. 'It would be...indiscrete of me to say, sir.'

Sejanus gave a sharp, 'Ha!' that sounded more like a bark than a laugh. 'So it's like that, is it? Your mistress is liaising with dangerous men, girl. Tell her that when she wakes; tell her she needs to be careful who she invites into her bed.'

'Yes, Prefect, sir.'

There was a clatter of boots returning to the room. 'There are three unmade beds, sir.'

'Ah! Are there now? Three?'

'That's easily explained, Prefect, sir.'

'Really?'

'My mistress went to bed as usual, but when I heard her coughing I left my bed and moved into the room next to hers. I can hear her better if she calls. When she took really poorly, I made hot milk and then settled her in here.'

There was silence. 'Huh-huh!' And there was a hint of frustration in Sejanus's voice when he snapped, 'It can wait. I'll speak to her tomorrow.'

Aurelia listened as boots, two, three sets thudded across the small carpet, clattered across her marble floor and had crunched across her courtyard. Only when they had faded into the rumble of early morning traffic noises did she open her eyes. She realised she was shivering with fear and her body felt stiff with tension. Flinging off the blanket she and Ruth lifted the couch and Apicata scrambled from underneath.

'Are you all right, Apicata?'

Apicata nodded and ran her fingers through her tousled hair. 'Except it feels like someone's pounding at my head with a hammer.'

'I'm not surprised.' Aurelia said and touched Apicata's forehead with the back of her hand. 'Hmm. You feel feverish. I'll get Ruth to make you up one of her special herbal concoctions after breakfast.' She turned to her slave. 'Ruth, bring us breakfast, and...well done.'

Ruth dropped her eyes in embarrassment. 'Yes, mistress. Thank you, mistress.'

Apicata waited until Ruth had left the room before saying, 'Felix must be under observation if Sejanus knows he went to Capri with a woman.' Despite the feverish forehead, the hand she laid on Aurelia's arm was cold. 'I'm sorry, he obviously thinks it was you.'

'Don't worry about it.' Aurelia patted the cold hand absently. 'Sejanus is clearly upset by your visit to Capri.'

'And he'd be even more upset if he knew what I'd told the emperor,' Apicata said grimly.

Aurelia glanced at her sideways, trying to discover whether that was a hint for her to ask so Apicata could unburden herself. But deciding she would rather not know said, 'I think I should warn Felix?'

Apicata's eyes widened in alarm. 'You can't leave the house, you...'

Aurelia patted her hand again and continued patting while, having made the decision, she worked out how to implement it. 'If I'm suspected of being Felix's mistress then it'll be no surprise when I visit him. Meanwhile, you do whatever you and Felix planned. Go and see Sejanus, persuade him into letting you take your children home. That was it, wasn't it?'

Apicata nodded. 'I feel...' she bit her lip. 'I feel as if I've landed you in trouble by arriving here and now I'm letting you take all the risks.' She paused. 'Whatever happens, I want you to know that I'm grateful.' Her face hardened. 'Sejanus is an unscrupulous man. What he's done to Rome; what he's done to the Imperial family, to Drusus...' Apicata dropped her head. '"Proof!" That's what Tiberius kept yelling at me. "Where's your proof" He's obsessed by wanting proof but I couldn't give him any. All I have is the word of the woman who...she took a deep breath. 'Well, I've done my best. All I can hope and pray to the gods for now is that Tiberius gets the proof he needs against Sejanus.'

'Yes,' was all Aurelia said, but absently. Her thoughts not on Felix or the dangers of visiting him, but on what decision Vivius would make when he received her letter.

CHAPTER ELEVEN

(Jerusalem)

'A distance, I said,' Simon growled turning his head. 'Keep a good distance behind me. Think I want to be seen walking through the streets with a Roman?'

Vivius breathed in fiercely and wondered how in the name of all the gods anyone could take him for a Roman. With his hood up, cloak wrapped firmly around him and head down to avoid the driving rain he could be any nationality; Jerusalem was swarming with visitors. Nevertheless he dropped back and as he sidestepped a puddle he tried not to contemplate that in meeting up with these Jews he was going against everything his emperor had insisted on about absolute secrecy.

As they neared the temple the Jew ahead came to an abrupt halt. 'That's him,' he murmured. 'He always goes to the temple at this time of day.'

Vivius stopped a few paces behind his guide to watch an aristocratic Jew, on the far side of middling years, coming down the temple steps. His manner was detached, meditative, suggesting an approach would not be welcome. His black beard was short, speckled with grey and neatly trimmed; his fashionable footwear wet and he had his hands tucked into the sleeves of his expensive coat.

'Who is he?'

'His name's Joseph; he's from Arimathea. He's a wealthy businessman and a member of our Sanhedrin.' The aristocratic Jew partially turned his head. 'Let me speak to him first,' Simon said. His boots splashed unconcernedly through the puddles as he made his way toward Joseph.

Vivius was surprised to see how warmly the wealthy Jew greet his uncultured guide as though he was actually pleased to see him. But the smile quickly turned to one of concern during their discussion. Although he was too far away to hear what was being said, Vivius could see from the covert glances in his direction and the occasional nod of the head that Joseph of Arimathea had agreed to speak with him.

Vivius watched the two men walk away from the temple and the prying eyes of the Jewish temple guards and guessed he was supposed to follow, although there had been no indication that he should. He followed them at a distance, equally relieved to be out of sight of Fort Antonia. They walked in this manner towards the shops, stopping eventually at the back of two large, domed bakery ovens on the corner of a busy street. The ovens were hot and a smell of bread lingered in the air.

Vivius approached the two men.

'Good day'—Joseph's black eyes dropped to Vivius's toga under his cloak—'Senator. I am Joseph of Arimathea. I gather you wish to speak to me?' Although his voice was cultured, his manner polite and respectful, Vivius could sense he was wary.

Vivius inclined his head. 'I am Senator Marcianus. I apologise for keeping you out in the rain. As your companion here will have told you, four men were crucified today,' Vivius glanced at his guide. 'Your companion here tells...'

'Leave off calling me "companion." I have a name: Simon.'

Vivius pursed his lips. 'Your...Simon, here...tells me one of those men was his cousin, Zachary Ben Elazar.'

'You knew him?'

'No.'

'Then I'm curious to know why the death of a common Jew would interest a senator from Rome?'

'Because Simon informs me Zachary didn't get a trial, and that crucifixion without a trial is common practice here.'

Joseph stroked his silky black beard thoughtfully. 'It is.'

'How long has this practice been going on?'

'It will be in our court files,' Joseph said. 'But if I recollect correctly, it started when Pilate took up the role of Procurator of Judea.' He paused. 'But...I understand the four men crucified today were Zealots.'

'And that makes a difference?'

'Of course.'

'How?'

Joseph's answer was guarded. 'As you may know, we may have our own courts for most crimes, Senator. But when a Jew is arrested on suspicion of treason against Rome, the sentence is invariable death and for that we are subject to Roman law. When that happens there's not always a trial.'

'And the accused man is crucified?'

'Under Roman rule, yes.' Joseph regarded him steadily. 'May I ask why you're wanting this information, Senator?'

Vivius waited until a family with five children had hurried by before saying, 'I'm a magistrate and senator of Rome. I believe, as does the Emperor Tiberius, that everyone is entitled to a fair trial. That principle applies not only to Rome but to all lands under the rule of the Roman Empire.'

'And your reason for wanting to speak to me was...?' Joseph raised his eyebrows.

'Is it possible for you to get me a copy of your files without anyone knowing? The truth, that is all I'm after. The truth,' Vivius added.

'And what will you do with the truth, Senator?'

'If crucifixions are taking place without a trial this will be dealt with at the highest level in Rome I assure you.'

'If I can get that information for you, how would you feel about calling at the home of a Jew to get it?' Joseph asked.

'I would have no problem with calling at the home of a Jew. Would you have a problem receiving a Roman?'

The corner of Joseph's lips twitched and Vivius saw he was regarding him with renewed interest. 'I live near the pools of Bethesda. Perhaps Simon could bring you...'

'Whoa!' Simon raised both hands. 'Are you mad, Joseph?'

Joseph shrugged his shoulders. 'It's up to you, of course, Simon, but wouldn't you appreciate the chance to get justice for Zachary?'

There was an awkward silence.

'Didn't say I wouldn't bring him, did I? Only questioning the wisdom of bringing a Roman to your house.'

'Thank you for your concern, Simon. Will you bring the senator or shall I give him directions?'

'I'll bring him,' Simon said grudgingly, and without even looking at Vivius added, 'I'll be outside the temple early tomorrow.'

Joseph bowed his head. 'Good. That's settled. Until tomorrow then, Senator.'

'Until tomorrow.'

* * *

(Jerusalem)

Vivius rolled his aching shoulders as he walked through the gates of Fort Antonia, and came to the decision that regardless of what he had said to Lucanus earlier, he was now wet, tired, hungry, and the lateness of the hour dictated they wouldn't be heading off to Rome tonight. In fact, he decided, it would make sense to stay in Jerusalem until he'd had a chance to investigate these new leads. He'd be of no help to Aurelia if he got himself arrested as soon as he set foot in Rome.

But when he reached the big wooden doors of the fort, he slumped against the door frame and ran his hand down his face. An overwhelming despair had washed over him; and it wasn't just for Aurelia. The thought of facing the confines of his quarters, the smell of drugs, groans from Dorio and the incessant chatter of his physician was more than he could handle. What he needed, he decided, was thinking time, planning time, time to consider Aurelia's letter in detail. On top of which, he had acted on the spur of the moment when he had asked Simon to take him to a trustworthy member of the Sanhedrin, and spontaneity was not in his makeup. He needed time to assess his actions.

Feeling better for having made a decision, he headed to the smaller of the two dining rooms, the one allocated for officers and visiting dignitaries. To his relief it was almost deserted. It was a pleasantly warm room with pale yellow wall lights which gave the room a cosy glow. Taking off his wet cloak, he chose a secluded corner with a comfortable couch and a low dining table set out in such a manner that he was unlikely to be disturbed. The meal that day was chicken served with sauces, vegetables and a jug of wine, and while he ate he made a conscious effort not to dwell on either the problems in Rome or his investigation.

It was after his dinner, when he was dozing under the heady glow of the wine, that he found Aurelia gliding into the forefront of his mind as if she had been waiting in the wings for her cue. It was a childhood memory that emerged; she was calling his name, searching for him the way she always did after his father and Fabiana had subjected him to one of their beatings. She had always had this...inner sense when something was wrong, he mused. And she had always known where she would find him — hiding in the olive grove. He remembered the way her small hand would slip into his, and they would sit in a comfortable silence under the leaves of the gnarled old olive trees. Her childish love had been his only comfort during those awful years. A childish love; that's what it had been but... Vivius pinched between his eyes, trying to shut off unexplored emotions that threatened to rise to the fore. He had sworn he would never trust another human being again after his father had...but somehow... Aurelia...

The question that landed on him like a heavy object dropped from a great height prompted him to open his eyes, as if the object was physically standing in front of him demanding he listen. He listened. What sort of a man sought after a dalliance with another woman, while the woman he was betrothed to, the woman who had been his dearest childhood friend, could be in danger—because of him?

The answer crept up on him before he had finished asking the questions. If his actions of the last few days were anything to go by, he was a womanizer—*just like his father*. He abandoned people if something more interesting came along—*like his father*. Vivius pushed his empty dinner plate away as it occurred to him he had no idea how to be sensitive, how to be compassionate... or even how to...love—*just like his father*. Sickened by this honest appraisal of himself he grabbed his cloak and headed for his quarters.

* * *

'Ah! You're back!' Lucanus greeted him in a manner that reminded him of a scolding.

'I wasn't aware I had to give *you* an account of my whereabouts?' he said irritably.

Lucanus's face flushed. 'Oh, sorry, you don't. I didn't mean to sound...you know. It's the aftereffects of being hit over the head. I'm not used to it.'

Vivius glanced around the room. Everything was neat and orderly. There was even a new chair to replace the broken one. Lucanus had obviously been busy clearing up after their intruder. Vivius pointed to the bedroom door. 'Is he sleeping?'

'Yes, he spent the morning in the infirmary.'

Vivius lay down on his bed and entwined his fingers behind his head. 'Good,' was all he said and closed his eyes as a hint he wanted privacy. But then he was forced to open them again when the physician plonked the new chair next to his bed in a manner that suggested he was all set for a long conversation.

'So are we returning to Rome or not, Senator?'

'Not.'

'Can I ask why?'

'No.' He yawned and turned to face the wall. 'Goodnight, Lucanus!'

* * *

The following morning, Vivius hovered outside the temple. He could see why Simon had chosen this spot. He would be relatively unnoticed among the swarms of sightseers buzzing around the temple grounds like bees around a honey pot. Any exchange of words would be lost among the cries of admiration at Herod's magnificent temple, or yells from the money changers and merchants under the covered porticoes. Vivius listened to them trying to outdo each other in an attempt to entice customers to their stalls. Then he spotted Simon. He was loitering around the temple doors with the pilgrims and worshippers, watching him.

The Jew's acknowledgment was nothing more than sharp jerk of the head which Vivius took to be an indication to follow. He followed, a dozen or more paces behind as he had the previous day, until they reached the more affluent part of Jerusalem.

They turned off the main road and took a narrow lane, barely wide enough for a cart, with ivy-covered stone walls. Then Simon disappeared into one of the courtyards.

When Vivius followed, he was surprised to find that Joseph of Arimathea's courtyard led into a garden that, despite it being the onset of springtime, had a display of colourful and exotic plants which vaguely reminded Vivius of the summer exhibitions in Rome. The only difference being, Joseph's garden was considerably smaller and delightfully secluded. Birds chirped in the shrubs, a decorative fountain splashed into a pool of reeds, and there was a strong aroma from a bed of hyacinths. With a gesture of his hand, Joseph invited Vivius to join him on a garden seat in the shade of an almond tree. Simon hovered on the other side of the fountain.

Being reasonably familiar with the Jewish practice of hospitality, Vivius was aware they wouldn't get down to business straight away so he made himself comfortable, drank the sweet liquid offered, exchanged pleasantries and came to the pleasing conclusion that he had chosen well. Joseph was a sharp-minded businessman, a Jew of integrity; and a man he felt he could do business with.

Eventually, Joseph picked up a rolled parchment from the marble table and handed it to him. 'I believe this is what you were after, Senator. It's a copy of our courtroom records.'

Unrolling the parchment, Vivius found it contained a list of arrests going back at least two years. Alongside each name and date was the name of the arresting officer, the charge, the presiding judge and the sentence. But he noticed that many names simply had 'Roman crucifixion' written alongside them. The charge, judge and sentence had been omitted.

Vivius pointed to these entries. 'Were these men Zealots?'

'Some of them.' Joseph hesitated. 'Can I speak frankly, Senator?'

'I would appreciate if you would.'

Joseph paused a beat as if choosing his words carefully. 'Most Jews, including myself, object to being ruled by a foreign power, Senator. But even more objectionable is seeing my countrymen arrested on trumped-up charges, frequently for minor offences, and then crucified by Rome without a trial. It is my belief that everyone should be entitled to a trial—even Zealots.' Joseph spoke without rancour but Vivius could see he felt strongly about the subject. 'We have brought this to Procurator Pilate's attention on numerous occasions but as you will appreciate, if he refuses to act we're powerless to do anything about it.' Joseph allowed his words to register with his guest before adding, 'Simon's cousin, Zachary Ben Elazar, is the last name on the list. I believe he was the one you were asking about?'

Vivius studied the last three entries with interest. 'I see he's listed simply as "thief – Roman crucifixion." So Simon was right; there was no trial?'

'That's correct, Senator.'

'Do you know what he was accused of stealing?'

There was a sharp response from the other side of the fountain. 'Swords.'

'I see. What about the names above, the men who died with Zachary Ben Elazar. Were they stealing swords too?'

'No senator,' Joseph answered. 'I discovered that one of them was a baker.'

Vivius glanced up. 'A baker?'

'The man had been a petty thief for years but never a Zealot. Unfortunately, the Romans caught him making a delivery of bread to a house where it was suspected Zealots were being recruited. He was caught up in the arrests.'

Vivius examined the parchment. 'I see there was no trial. But surely he protested his innocence?'

'I have no idea,' Joseph said. 'He wasn't held long enough for enquiries to be made.'

'Why?'

Joseph glanced cautiously at Simon before saying, 'Pilate likes to have more than one crucifixion at a time; it saves on Roman manpower when they're paraded through the streets as a deterrent for going against Rome. I believe Zachary and the baker were dragged from their cells to make up the numbers.' Joseph folded his hands in his lap. 'We've seen too many innocent men crucified without a trial since Pilate became Procurator, Senator.'

Vivius studied the names of the judges at the side of those charged, and that was when his eyes fell on a familiar name. 'What's this?' he asked quietly. He turned the parchment so that Joseph could see where he was pointing.

Joseph craned his neck. 'It's one of many charges brought against the more prominent Jews in our country by the Roman

Prefect Lucius Aelius Sejanus.'

The steady rhythm of Vivius's heart broke into a trot. 'And why would Sejanus be involved in the crucifixion of Jews in Palestine?'

'Only you can answer that one, Senator.' Joseph hesitated before adding, 'I don't believe he cares for our race.'

'Who has he made these charges against? Do you know them?'

Joseph ran his finger down the list. 'As far as I can see most of them are wealthy businessmen, Jews of authority, members of the Sanhedrin, Pharisees or Sadducees.' He shrugged. 'If they don't comply with requests from Rome, or rather from Prefect Sejanus...'

Vivius's eyes hardened. 'Requests from Sejanus?'

Joseph regarded him shrewdly. 'You appear to be showing an undue interest in Sejanus, Senator, which encourages me to suggest you also make enquiries into his financial dealings in Palestine.'

'His financial dealings?' Vivius ended his sentence with an upward inclination.

There was a lengthy pause, during which Vivius suspected the Jew was debating how much he was at liberty to reveal. But then he breathed in deeply and said, 'I shall tell you what I know.' There was a pause. 'Some months ago a...a friend, Benjamin by name, a loyal and respected Jew, a man of integrity and a member of the Sanhedrin, was informed that Pilate was embezzling from the taxes we pay to Rome. But within days of his discrete enquiries, Benjamin was arrested for treason and crucified without a trial.'

'Can I ask who gave Benjamin his information?'

'Someone who was privy to the finances between Palestine and Rome,' Joseph answered cautiously.

'The bookkeeper,' Vivius breathed the word almost silently, but didn't miss Joseph's startled expression.

There was a short silence. 'When are you returning to Rome,

Senator?'

Vivius rolled up the parchment. 'I have one more investigation to follow up, but hopefully tomorrow or the day after. I'm anxious to get back to Rome. Thank you for...' He held up the parchment as he rose to his feet. 'And for your hospitality.'

Joseph stood up. 'It occurs to me, Senator, that if it's discovered what you're up to, you might have opposition when you try to leave.'

'I might.'

'And I might be able to help you. Simon has friends...'

Simon raised his hands. 'Don't ask nothing of me, not for a Roman.'

Joseph smiled and turning back to Vivius said, 'Get word to me if you need help,' he said quietly.

'Thank you.' Vivius raised a hand as Simon made to get up. 'No. I can find my own way back to the fort from here.'

* * *

Simon waited until he was sure the Roman had left before saying, 'You trust him?'

Joseph's head was bowed in contemplation but he looked up when Simon spoke. 'Mmm? Oh, of course.'

'And you believe he'll get justice for Zachary?'

'I do,'

'Why?'

'Why would he want the information in the first place, unless he was going to do something with it? He's a good man, Simon. I believe he wants justice, but that's not what bothers me.' Joseph stroked his beard thoughtfully. 'Remember the senator's comment when I told him about our friend Benjamin?'

'Not really.'

'When I told him Benjamin got his information from someone who was privy to the finances between Palestine and Rome, the senator muttered, "the bookkeeper".'

'So?'

'The only person privy to Roman and Jewish taxes at a high level was Nikolaos, the Greek bookkeeper who asked Benjamin for help.'

Simon's eyebrows furrowed. 'And what bothers me is why a *Roman* senator would put himself in danger from the *Roman* Governor Pilate for us Jews? I'm not simple minded enough to believe the Roman's motives are that honourable even if you do.'

Joseph pursed his lips. 'I think we should keep our eye on our Senator Marcianus. The more we know what he's up to the better. Follow him, Simon.'

Simon gave him a stiff look. 'What? You think I want to spend the rest of the day following a Roman?'

'He found the time to enquire about Zachary.'

'Why me? If you want him followed, send someone else.'

'Who? You know him; no one else does.' Joseph leant back in his chair. 'Don't you want justice for Zachary?'

'Of course I do, but...' Scratching his beard with a fierceness that made his jaw sting he finished his sentence with a 'For Zachary's sake, I'll follow him. But just for today.'

CHAPTER TWELVE

(Jerusalem)

When Vivius returned to his quarters he was surprised to find Dorio sitting at the table with a bowl of vegetable soup and a roll of bread in front of him. The Decurion was as pale as his shift; there were hollows under his cheekbones and dark rims around his eyes.

'Out of bed? That's good.'

Dorio glowered at him. 'Depends how you look at it. The good news is my fever's gone. The bad news is, I've only one arm, my horse is dead, my unit has been taken over by a more able bodied Decurion, and none of my men have visited me.'

Lucanus shouted through from the bedroom. 'I told you. They've been transferred. Stop feeling sorry for yourself.'

'I'm not feeling sorry myself, I'm stating facts.'

Vivius flung his cloak on the couch, and then slid into the chair opposite Dorio. For a while, he watched chunks of vegetables splatter back into the bowl whenever the Decurion's shaky hand lifted his spoon to his mouth.

'Lost for words, eh Vivius?' Dorio sneered between mouthfuls. 'Not even you can find a use for a one-armed Decurion, can you?'

Vivius made a steeple with his fingers and thought fondly of his old army physician, Gaius. When any of their men lost limbs in battle, Gaius had always handled their situation far better than he had. The only way he had been able to cope with the loss of a limb had been either to ignore the problem or order the wounded legionary to 'pull himself together!' Vivius found his mind flickering over the faces of his men who had been in Dorio's position. Some had died from their wounds, others had died through lack of treatment or fevers, but many more had simply given up altogether because they had lost their sense of purpose in life. Vivius drummed his fingers together, uncomfortably aware that as their commanding officer he should have shown more compassion; done something to lift their depression or... The drumming stopped as it dawned on him that his hard attitude was like a shell he had built around himself for protection against...

He waited until Dorio had finished his soup before shouting through the open bedroom door, 'How fit is your patient, Lucanus?'

Dorio gave a shrill laugh; it sounded almost manic. 'Fit? It may have escaped your notice but I only have one arm!'

'I can see that. I was talking to your physician.'

Lucanus came through from the bedroom drying his hands on a towel. 'He's eating, and I did wonder whether we could manage a walk around the courtyard later.'

'*You* might be able to manage a walk around the courtyard, but count me out,' Dorio snapped.

'Hmm, so when you asked what use a one-armed Decurion could be, it was a meaningless comment, was it?' Vivius asked.

Dorio scowled at him. Lucanus sat down curiously at the table.

'If I saddled a horse, could you manage a journey through Jerusalem?'

'Why?'

Vivius rested his elbows on the table. 'What I am about to tell you is in the strictest confidence.' It crossed his mind that he was beginning to make a habit of breaking the emperor's strict orders for confidence. 'I'm here under orders from the emperor.'

Lucanus banged his fist on the table. 'I knew it! I knew there had to be more to that break-in than petty thieving.'

Dorio was startled. 'What break-in?'

'Oh, you missed all the fun.' Lucanus said in a tone of self-importance. 'We had an intruder when you were at the infirmary. But I tackled him single-handedly. He was a big man but I wrestled him to the floor, and then I...'

Vivius held up his hand before Lucanus embellished his story further. 'I'm only telling you, Dorio, because I believe you can help.'

'With what?'

'My investigation. It's in the interests of Rome.'

'In the interests of Rome? You must be joking. Do I look in any condition to look after the interests of Rome?'

'Do I look as though I'm joking?' Vivius forced his fierce glare to wipe the sneer from Dorio's face. It did.

Lucanus's eyes widened. 'It's not dangerous, is it?'

'No. I've been given the address of Pilate's former bookkeeper. A Greek by the name of Nikolaos. I'm looking for a discrepancy in the taxes.'

Dorio gave a snort. 'You, looking for a discrepancy in the taxes?'

'Not me personally, no. That's why I want you along?'

Dorio moodily wiped the empty soup bowl with a crust of bread. 'I don't know what use you think I can be, I only have one arm.

'And losing an arm affects your head for figures, does it?'

'That's not funny, Vivius.'

'It's not meant to be. As you sneeringly indicate, I'm no bookkeeper. I pay someone to do my finances. I need someone who knows what to look for and understands what the bookkeeper is talking about. That's why I need you.'

Dorio's laugh was harsh. 'You need me? Since when did you need anyone? You *use* people, Vivius; you don't *need* them.'

Vivius was uncomfortably aware of how close to the truth that jibe was. 'You keep the records for your estate. You'd know what to look for, wouldn't you?' he persisted.

'I might.' Dorio drummed irritatingly on the empty bowl with his spoon. 'For Rome, eh?' He turned to Lucanus. 'What do you think?'

Lucanus shrugged. 'Keep me out of this. I'm Greek, remember, and I'm not too sure I want to be involved in anything dangerous.' He twisted the edge of the towel around his finger. 'Besides,' he added. 'I don't know if you're well enough.'

'I think I should know how well I am, don't you?'

'You can't even make the effort to go out,' Lucanus persisted.

Resting his good arm on the table, Dorio rose unsteadily to his feet, his chair scraping across the wooden floor. 'Help me get dressed, Greek, and I'll show you who's well enough to go out!'

'As your physician I think I should advise against too much physical exertion.'

Dorio limped across to the bedroom. 'Advise all you like. If I want to go out, I'm going!'

Lucanus feigned an exaggerated sigh, but as he followed his patient into the bedroom, he turned to Vivius and winked smugly. Vivius curbed a smile.

It took the best part of an hour for Lucanus to dress his argumentative patient in his uniform, and for both of them to escort him to the stables, and hoist him astride a horse. But once settled on his mount, Vivius didn't miss the excited gleam in the Decurion's eyes.

'Are you sure you can manage?' Lucanus asked anxiously. 'I've brought my medical case, wads of bandages and drugs to kill the pain if you need it.'

'I won't need your wretched medical case, Lucanus. I'm a little unbalanced but that's all.'

Snatching the reins from Vivius with his good right hand he dug his heels into the animal, and with Vivius and Lucanus walking on either side of the mount, set the pace. Both men watched him cautiously for a while, but Dorio's profession as a cavalry Decurion soon shone through as his body settled into a comfortable rhythm of riding.

They only stopped when they reached the crowded marketplace. Vivius noticed the hint of a smile threatening to emerge on Dorio's face when he saw stall-holders waving their arms, loudly promising fine things from bright clothes to leatherwear, polished copper pots, unknown spices, baskets, jewellery and painted pottery jars. His eyes drifted over to a group of attractive women arguing over fresh commodities; others fought for the best produce or chattered with neighbours while their children played in the market square.

Vivius watched him breathe in deeply as if absorbing the mix of smells from the food stalls: chicken braising, lamb roasting, fish and vegetables grilling. A trader roasting sparrows on a stick eyed them hopefully. 'Two for a copper,' he bellowed. 'Special deal, five for two coppers.'

'Senator,' Lucanus moved in front of the horse, his face averted from Dorio. 'I think we're being followed,' he whispered.

Vivius turned full circle. 'Where?'

'I can't say exactly. Of course I could be imagining it, all this talk of assignments and danger, and then having a break-in. It's all pretty upsetting for a simple-minded Greek like me. I'm not used to that type of lifestyle.' He gave Vivius a sideways glance. 'If you don't mind me saying so, Senator, being around you can be rather intense.'

'You told me you wanted adventure?'

'I'm rapidly going off the idea.'

'Don't worry; we're only going to see a bookkeeper. There's nothing dangerous in examining a book of figures, is there? Not in the middle of the afternoon, and not in the middle of a city.'

'I hope you're right, Senator.' Lucanus didn't appear to be convinced.

'I'm a senator. I'm always right, trust me.'

When Vivius judged Dorio had exhausted watching the activities in the market, he turned off the main highway and following the clerk's rough map, led them through a maze of narrow streets. When they reached the Greek quarter of the city, they found the row of squalid dwellings. Barefooted children using sticks as swords stopped in surprise to ogle at them. Vivius asked them in Greek where Nikolaos lived, and it took a while before one small boy overcame his nervousness of Romans to point to a house squashed in the middle of five brick-and-mud dwellings with thistles growing out of the walls.

As they made their way towards it, Vivius grimaced at the thought of anyone living in such squalor. He knocked firmly on the door, although he considered one good push might save the occupant the bother of answering it.

The most outstanding characteristic of the weedy little man who inched it open was the startling blue saucer eyes, like pools, which regarded his visitors with fear rather than pleasure. His receding hairline gave the appearance of intelligence, and his grey tunic barely covered his thin bandy legs.

Vivius stepped forward, and forcing a smile attempted to put the little man at his ease. 'We have a mutual friend in the clerk at the fort, I believe. He said you might be able to help me with my enquiries. My name is Senator Vivius Marcianus. This is Decurion Dorio Suranus and his Greek physician, Lucanus.'

The little man glanced nervously up and down the lane before opening the door wider; it shuddered on the floor. 'Forgive me. I need to be cautious. Yes, I'm Nikolaos. I was told you might call. Come in. You are welcome.'

Vivius entered living quarters that were shabby, clean but smelled of poverty. Looking around he judged from the quality of the threadbare couch Dorio was settled on, and the contents of the house, that Nikolaos hadn't always been poor. An exquisitely shaped pot stood on a hand-made shelf, four goblets, and a matching jug on the table, and a woman's hand had embroidered cushions with colourful silks which had faded with age. All were a reminder of a former life more comfortable than this one.

While pouring his guests refreshments Nikolaos conversed with Lucanus in their native tongue. But when Vivius asked about his former occupation as bookkeeper, Nikolaos moved easily back to Latin.

'I trained as a bookkeeper when I was a young man,' Nikolaos told them wriggling on his hard wooden stool to make himself comfortable. 'Like many Greeks, after twenty-five years of service to Rome I was given Roman citizenship. A few years ago I was transferred to Jerusalem and assigned as bookkeeper to the Procurator of Judea. That was when my troubles started.' He clasped his hands tightly together. 'I was aware from the onset that Pilate's records were not as they should be. There were errors; nothing tied up, monies went missing, on paper and in coins. I tried broaching the subject with him. At first he dismissed my findings as errors on my part, but when I persisted he got angry. That was when he tried to bribe me. When he realised he couldn't he began making false accusations against me. Incompetent he called me; incompetent, a bad bookkeeper. Then came the threats.' Nikolaos dropped his head and other than the sound of children playing outside there was silence. 'The stress was too much for my dear wife,' he said quietly. 'After she died I was forced to send my son, his wife and my grandchildren back to Greece for their own safety.' The Greek bookkeeper paused to address Vivius. 'May I ask; why do you want to know all this?'

'I'm…investigating a case of embezzlement.'

Nikolaos regarded him strangely before rising to his feet to refill their goblets. 'When I first suspected fraud in the Treasury Office I decided to keep my own records. I began listing monies received from tax collectors, the percentage that should have been sent to Rome, against the amount that was actually sent. I listed Pilate's expenditures…' Nikolaos shrugged. 'Everything.'

'Do you still have these records?' Vivius didn't wait for a reply but added, 'Of course you do. The clerk wouldn't have insisted I bring a bookkeeper with me if you didn't.'

Nikolaos's gaze drifted over to Dorio. 'Wait here.'

He disappeared through an archway with a curtain draped

in front and Vivius heard what sounded like floorboards being removed, but higher, below ceiling level. A minute or so later, Nikolaos emerged with two ledgers and an armful of rolled of parchments which he dropped on to the table. 'I don't normally keep them here. I had them brought when I was told of your visit.'

Vivius got to his feet and opening the first ledger rested his hands on either side of it and studied the contents. As expected, it was simply a jumble of figures to him. Picking it up he laid it on Dorio's lap and watched him run his finger down the pages.

Nikolaos joined him on the couch and Vivius listened while he explained where the discrepancies and falsifications had occurred on the original ledger. Without having the ledger in front of him the explanations sounded complicated so Vivius was left drumming his fingers on the edge of the couch. He only stopped drumming when Dorio asked, 'What's this third column marked "S" for?'

'It is money going to Prefect Sejanus,' Nikolaos said quietly. 'The Procurator siphons off this amount for him each month.' Nikolaos's finger pointed to a set of figures. 'And this,' his hand swept across the page. 'He siphons off for himself.'

'Why didn't you report what was going on?' Vivius asked.

'And who would I report it to, Senator? My superiors were the guilty ones. And remember, to the Jews I may be a Greek national but I have Roman citizenship and I work for Rome. Besides, I also had an ailing wife and a son and his family to consider. I didn't want trouble.' Nikolaos spread his hands. 'Don't think me a coward, Senator. I was in a difficult position. After my wife died and my son had left for Greece, I tried again. This time I broached a member of the Sanhedrin; Benjamin they called him, a trustworthy man. I thought the Sanhedrin might put pressure on Pilate, or report the discrepancies directly to Rome. But within days of involving Benjamin, accusations of treason were brought against him and he was crucified.' Nikolaos shook his head. 'I couldn't bear being responsible for the death of another Jew after that. Besides, who would listen? Shortly after that I was, shall we say, *forced* to retire because I'd made the wrong noises.'

'Why didn't you join your son in Greece?'

'Travelling costs money, Senator. I'd already used my savings for medication for my wife, and I'd sold what valuables I had to send my son and his family back to Greece.'

'If they crucified this Jew, er...Benjamin, why not you?' Vivius asked.

Nikolaos hedged a smile. 'I'm only alive because Pilate knows that if anything happens to me, proof of his embezzlement will be sent to Rome. You can call it blackmail if you like. I see it as a way of protecting myself. These ledgers are my protection. Pilate wouldn't want to upset Sejanus; he was only made governor because of him, and he certainly wouldn't want to upset the emperor.' Nikolaos shook his head. 'Pilate keeps an eye on me. His men regularly search my premises but they never find anything because'—he pointed to the ledgers—'they're usually in the safekeeping of...friends. I'm taking a risk talking to you, Senator, and I'm only doing it because you're the only one who can help.'

'Can't these friends help? '

Nikolaos hesitated. 'They help me financially and they hide my ledgers. But as long as Pilate lives in Caesarea, and as long as I keep my mouth shut, Pilate will leave me alone. It's an uneasy peace you might say.'

'I see.' Vivius made a steeple of his fingers as he pondered the next step. 'Would you consider returning to Rome with me, bringing your ledgers, giving evidence in our courts? I guarantee you'd be well paid and I could promise you safe passage to your son in Greece afterwards.'

Nikolaos's expression momentarily lit up, but then fell again. 'There may be more freedom to move around the empire these days, Senator, but all Pilate has to do is denounce me as a troublemaker and I'd be arrested as soon as I tried leaving Jerusalem, even if it is with a senator.'

Vivius already knew what the answer would be to his next question, but he asked it anyway. 'Then can we take your ledgers when we return to Rome?'

Nikolaos shook his head. 'As I said, they're insurance against anything happening to me.'

'We could make copies,' Lucanus suggested.

'It'll take days to copy all this,' Dorio said. 'Do we have days?'

'No.' Vivius took the ledger from Dorio and pursed his lips at the thought of this valuable information slipping out of his control. 'You said you wanted my help, then how if you won't let me take you or the ledgers to Rome?'

Nikolaos gently removed the ledger from his hands. 'I thought perhaps I could make a note of the relevant dates the treasury should investigate. That's the best I can do I'm afraid.'

'So you've given up trying to get justice?'

Nikolaos shook his head. 'No, but...' he clasped the ledger to his chest and dropped his eyes, and Vivius could see it was useless pushing him further; this was a broken man.

It was early evening by the time they took their leave of the bookkeeper without anything being fully resolved other than they would call again for a list of the relevant dates the treasury in Rome should investigate. Vivius's depression over the outcome of the visit was not helped by Lucanus complaining that they'd stayed too long, and could he not see, the Decurion was perspiring with weariness? Being in no frame of mind to argue, Vivius assisted Dorio on to his horse and led the way down the lane. He found it uncannily quiet without the noise of the children playing, and although faces peered curiously out of windows at them, no one passed by.

But then, at the junction, three armed men stepped deliberately into their path.

Vivius heard a squeak of alarm from Lucanus; Dorio brought his horse up sharply, and Vivius made contact with his sword. The men were dark skinned, wore dark clothing, had turbans concealing their faces, and carried clubs and short swords. Vivius gave a brief recognisance of their battleground. The lane was narrow; too narrow for their assailants to spread out. He decided to take advantage of that.

'Uh! There's another two behind us, Senator,' Lucanus murmured.

Vivius deliberately withdrew his sword. One sword against five; he didn't need to be told the odds were not in their favour. With a slight movement of the head he murmured, 'Dorio, at my command, I want you to charge straight through them; get back to the fort.'

'Forget it,'

'Damn it, Dorio! Do as I tell you. That's an order.'

'You're not in the army now, Vivius.'

'Can you two argue some other…? Aahh!' Lucanus gave a cry of alarm as the three men ahead of them charged forward.

Dorio backed his horse, leaving Vivius room to strike at their first assailant. Their swords clashed. The second assailant edged forward, his body alert, waiting for the space to attack. Withdrawing his dagger, Vivius slashed it in his direction, keeping him at bay. Still he pressed forward, dodging the dagger. He was so close Vivius could smell his foul breath. Seeing an opening Vivius thrust his sword at the first assailant. Slightly wounded the man backed off, giving Vivius the chance to swipe at assailant two with sword and dagger. The sword sliced the man's arm leaving a crimson streak; he staggered back, dropping his weapon. Assailant three picked it up and armed with two swords, he advanced.

That was when Vivius heard the rallying call to arms from behind; it was Dorio. The shout was closely followed by a clatter of hooves. Vivius knew instinctively what Dorio was up to.

Timing his move with the approach of the horse, he pressed himself back against the wall as Dorio charged past.

Using the strength of his legs, the Decurion delivered a sharp kick with the toe of his boot to the head of one of the assailants. There was a crunch; the man seemed to rise into the air before landing with a thud on his back. Vivius glimpsed the opponent with the two swords being knocked off balance by the charging animal. A loud bellow resounded from up the lane. In the split second given him, Vivius checked their rear.

These two assailants were being attacked by an unarmed physician with only yells, foul language and his medical case as weapons. Even Vivius winced as the leather case came into contact with the assailant's jaw. The man stumbled back against the wall. But Vivius was aware Lucanus would be no match for these thugs; he winced again as the physician received a resounding thud across the head with a club and slumped to the ground.

Knowing there was little he could do to help him, Vivius turned back to Dorio. The Decurion was struggling to keep his seat as he manoeuvred his horse in the narrow lane. But cavalryman that he was, he kept upright, and as he urged the animal back into the fray. Vivius moved into the attack, forcing attacker one into the line of the charging horse. He heard a crack as Dorio's boot came into contact with the man's skull.

Dorio took longer to line up his horse for a third charge. Exhaustion was making it difficult for him to stay astride his mount. Working on the same tactic as before, Vivius forced his assailant into the line of the charging horse. A quick glance behind told Vivius that Lucanus was still out cold and that although they had injured two of their assailants, three remained standing.

That one brief glance; that momentary lapse of concern for Lucanus on Vivius's part, was enough to give the enemy the advantage. Vivius gritted his teeth as a knife pierced his shoulder; then grunted as a heavy club struck the side of his head. Clutching his shoulder he staggered back against the wall. His attackers, not wanting to lose their momentum, pressed forward.

Vivius wasn't afraid to die; he had never been afraid to die, but he knew this wasn't the way he wanted to go. Not here in a dingy back lane in Jerusalem at the mercy of thugs. Weakened though he was he kicked out, his attacker doubled over as Vivius's foot landed in his groin. The effort was too much. Still dizzy from the blow to the head, Vivius's fingers tried to stem the flow of warm blood from his shoulder wound. He was aware his strength was ebbing. He faced his two, or was it three assailants? He couldn't see; the blood trickling down from the blow to his head had gone into his eyes. He wiped them. The assailants advanced.

And that was when, through blurred vision, Vivius glimpsed a figure charging down the lane towards them with his sword raised. Without slowing his pace the figure leapt in front of him, and delivered a punch to the jaw of one of his assailants. There was a clash of steel as the other assailant's advance was stopped and a sword was thrust into his stomach. He fell to his knees. Vivius wiped his sleeve over his eyes. Simon? Simon the Jew?

A warning cry from Dorio distracted him. One of their attackers had squeezed past his horse, but Simon had already seen him. He turned and met the man's onslaught full on. The assailant who had been attacked by Lucanus's medical case, hovered, uncertain whether he wanted to take on another swordsman when he already sported a bloody gash across his head. Dorio made his mind up for him. With one swipe of his boot, he kicked the sword out of his hand. The man backed away.

Only Simon now stood between Vivius and the remaining assailants. The first one lunged forward, but Simon side-stepped him, plunging his sword into the man's hip. Vivius heard the crunch of bone.

Gripping his sword, Vivius forced himself to Simon's side.

Their attackers hovered, uncertain, and then, as if by unspoken agreement, they retreated. Vivius glanced up the lane and was relieved to see Lucanus struggling to his feet, still clutching his medical case.

Breathless, Vivius turned to the Jew. 'Thank you.'

He shouldn't have been surprised that Simon refused to make eye contact, but he was. The Jew simply gave a curt nod, pushed his bloodied sword into his belt and with a final glance around their battlefield, marched swiftly down the lane.

'Wait!'

Simon ignored him.

Vivius flinched as warm blood pulsated through his shoulder. He leant back against the wall and closed his eyes. Despite the wound to his head the cogs of his brain started up readily enough. He furrowed his brow, his first thought being, 'What was the Jew doing in this vicinity? And why would he bother helping…?' Opening his eyes he decided now was not the time for questions. He stumbled towards Dorio. The Decurion was bent over his horse's neck, his good arm clutching his side. Blood was seeping through the bandages of his stump and his boots were bloody.

Vivius grabbed the reigns. 'Next time I give you an order…'

Dorio raised his head; there was almost a smile on his face despite the beads of sweat falling on the horse's mane. 'Did you see me?' His voice was barely above a whisper. 'I can still fight. I kept at least two of them at bay, didn't I?'

Vivius wearily dropped his forehead on to the animal's neck. 'Yes, I saw you.'

'Thank you for what you said.'

'About what?'

'About needing me.'

'It was true.'

'A random attack, do you think?'

'I doubt it. It was too organised for that.'

'Then someone sent them. Who?'

Vivius didn't answer. There were only two people who knew where he was going; one was the clerk at the fort, and the other was…Claudia!

CHAPTER THIRTEEN

(Jerusalem)

Vivius discovered that being admitted into Pilate's private quarters was almost as difficult as securing an audience with the emperor. Rico guarded his master's privacy with the ferociousness of a guard dog. In fact, if Pilate hadn't woken from his nap and heard his voice Vivius doubted whether he would have gained admittance at all. Rico announced him sullenly and then rapidly disappeared, but not before Vivius had noticed deep purple bruising on his neck.

It was a flushed-cheeked, bleary eyed and rumpled Pilate that greeted him. He ran his fingers through his dishevelled hair in embarrassment. 'Forgive me for being asleep when you called, Senator. The Jewish authorities had me awake at some ungodly hour yesterday morning and their demands upon my time never stopped all day. It was the late hours of the evening before I retired.' His bleary bulbous eyes fell on Vivius bandaged shoulder. 'But please sit down; join me for breakfast. I'd like to hear about this scandalous attack made upon you yesterday. I received the report late last night. Were you badly injured?'

'A scratch, nothing more.' Vivius lightly touched the thick wad of bandages. 'My physician tends to be over zealous in his profession, I'm afraid. As for joining you for breakfast, thank you, but I must return to my quarters to pack.' Nevertheless, the ache in his shoulder dictated he sat down.

'You're leaving? When?'

'Tomorrow.'

'Tomorrow? So soon? I hope that unfortunate incident wasn't responsible for your decision to leave, Senator?'

'Not at all. I only intended staying until the Decurion was well enough to travel. Now he is, so I plan to sail from Caesarea.

My physician has unfinished business in that city. Something
to do with a new medication for the Army Hospital in Rome,
believe.' Curious as to whether Claudia was lurking in another
room, he added, 'I simply called to thank you both for your
hospitality. The excursion to the olive grove with your wife was
exceptionally helpful.'

'Ah, yes, my wife. Unfortunately she's gone out for the day.'

'Hmm,' was Vivius's only response but he couldn't help
wondering if Claudia was deliberately keeping out of his way
after yesterday's attack. 'I also thought I ought to report I'd had
an intruder in my quarters.'

'What?'

Vivius watched Pilate's reaction carefully. His surprise
seemed genuine enough but it was hard to tell.

'Was anything stolen?'

'Nothing. A letter was torn but that was all.'

'A letter, was it important?'

'Goodness no, my betrothed giving me a progress report on
my new villa, that's all.'

'About your intruder...'

'Fortunately my physician scared him away.'

'I'm most disturbed by this, Senator. You've had a troublesome
visit with us I'm afraid. Rest assured I shall be making enquiries.'

Vivius waved a hand dismissively. 'Please, there's no need to
bother on my account.

'If you say so, Senator. As for your travelling arrangements
to Caesarea, perhaps a small auxiliary force could accompany
you?'

Vivius shook his head. 'No, but thank you for the offer. I dare
say our travelling will be too slow for them. The Decurion hasn't
quite recovered from his wounds yet.' He rose slowly to his feet,
wincing as a stab of pain shot through his shoulder. 'But now
you must excuse me. I've neglected my physician and his patient
long enough.'

The formalities over and done with, Vivius left Pontius Pilate's quarters with a sense of relief but also a sense of frustration at not being able to confront Claudia over his attack.

* * *

As soon as the door had closed behind his guest, Pontius Pilate poured himself a drink. 'Rico!'

The door barely clicked as Rico entered.

'The senator tells me he's leaving tomorrow, sailing from Caesarea, and he leaves straight after his visit to the bookkeeper.' Pilate's first mouthful of wine for the day he rolled around his palate, savouring the smooth silky liquid and rich fruity body. He swallowed with an 'Ah!' Then licked his lips. 'You saw the bookkeeper?'

'Yes, master. We searched the house after the senator left but there was no sign of the ledgers.'

'So the senator has them?'

'I don't think so, master. I didn't see him bring them into the fort.'

'Then where in the name of all the gods are they?' Pilate's dark bulbous eyes hardened. 'If the senator thinks he can simply walk out of here with information belonging to Palestine he's mistaken.' His eyes drifted over to his slave. 'But he isn't out of Palestine yet, is he Rico?'

* * *

The owlish clerk with the flat white hair was sitting behind his desk when Vivius entered the administration officers. He greeted him with a wide, self-satisfied grin. 'So you got my message then, Senator?'

Vivius flicked open the tablet and read, *'Senator; I have information on the Hasmonaean princes that might interested you.'*

He snapped the tablet shut. 'So what's all that about?'

The owlish clerk didn't answer straight away but rolled his stylus around his fingers, leaving black ink stains on the tips which he appeared not to notice. 'I heard about your attack, Senator. Terrible! Absolutely terrible! I was shocked. Who do you think would hire assassins to kill you? I don't believe it was a random attack by thugs. I don't believe that for one instant.'

Vivius followed the ray of morning sunshine through the open window. It landed on a shield in the corner sending a rainbow of colours across the walls towards a wooden chair.

'Only two people knew I was going to see the bookkeeper,' he said settling himself on the chair. 'You were one of them.'

'I didn't tell a soul, Senator. You have my word on that,' the clerk said vehemently. 'But, er...there was someone else in the room when you were asking for Nikolaos's address. I believe she may have overheard you.'

'Is that what you wanted to see me about?'

'No, no, no, Senator. I have information that might interest you.'

'Not on the Hasmonaean princes I take it?'

The clerk gave a chuckle. 'Oh goodness me, no, Senator; not at all, not at all.' He bent down and withdrew three rolled parchments from a drawer. Making a space between a neat line of scrolls and a tidy pile of tablets he methodically unrolled each one and placed it on his desk. 'When you return to Rome, I wonder if you would take these with you?'

'What are they?'

The clerk ran his inky fingertip over the top of the first parchment. 'This one is a detailed report written by the tribune of Fort Antonia. It covers a peaceful demonstration by the Jews who were objecting to Pilate using their holy temple money to build his aqueduct. Pilate has always claimed there were Zealots amongst the demonstrators so he was forced to act. This report shows the tribune has a different story to tell. Whoever was right, the end result was that over two hundred Jews were massacred that day.'

Vivius injected caution into his response. 'And why would you assume this information would be of interest to me?'

The clerk dropped his eyes. 'If I may be so bold as to say, Senator; you arrive in Jerusalem asking questions; the sort of questions Fabius used to ask.' The corners of his mouth drooped. 'Ah! Poor Fabius. The auxiliaries from Caesarea told us he'd been murdered.' There was a moment of respectful silence before he lifted his head and regarded Vivius with curiosity. 'When you asked me for the address of Nikolaos the Greek bookkeeper, I asked myself, Why would a visiting senator want the address of a former bookkeeper? Then I found out you were asking questions of Simon the Jew.'

Vivius narrowed his eyes. 'How do you know that?'

'I belong to the sect of the Nazarenes,' he said quietly.

'What has that got to do with anything?'

'The people you've been talking to, Simon the Jew, Joseph of Arimathea and Nikolaos, we're all followers of Jesus of Nazareth.'

'I see,' Vivius said stiffly.

'Then there was the day I left you browsing over files from the Hasmonaean Dynasty, but on my return discovered the current report files had been put back in the wrong order. So, I'm hoping my suspicions are justified, Senator, as I might get into trouble for, er...shall we say, mislaying the information I'm giving you today.'

The breath going through Vivius nostrils whistled faintly. 'Go on.'

The clerk's forefinger tapped the second parchment. 'This is the parchment which I think might interest you the most.'

'Why?'

'Compare the second and third parchments, Senator.' Picking one of them up, he reached across his desk and handed it to him.

There was silence while Vivius's eyes scrolled rapidly down each parchment. It was a list of Roman policies signed at the bottom by Tiberius. Vivius was familiar with such documents mainly because he, along with Tiberius and a team of senators, had been instrumental in forming Rome's policies for their colonies. 'So?'

'Governor Pilate's predecessor rigidly followed the policies in the document you're reading. Now, read this one.' The clerk reached across the desk to hand him the third document.

Once again Vivius's eyes scrolled down the parchment, but more slowly this time. As they did, his mouth hardened into a long straight line.

'It's a list of policies for Palestine, Senator, but the policies differ quite considerably. Look at the signature at the bottom.'

Vivius breathed in sharply. 'Sejanus!' He paused. 'What are you saying?'

'I'm not saying anything, Senator. I'm merely showing you that the emperor's policies for Palestine have been replaced by the harsher, stricter policies of Sejanus. And as you have seen for yourself, he has placed his own man in Palestine to implement them. Is that true of all Rome's colonies, I wonder?'

Vivius didn't answer, aware that the accusations of embezzlement and crucifixions were fading into second place as he studied the documents before him. This was exactly what he was looking for, and probably what the emperor was hoping he would find; proof that Sejanus was implementing his own policies and employing his own men in the colonies. It didn't take a genius to work out that if the emperor was out of the way and Sejanus took over as Caesar, he'd have no opposition from the colonies.

'Thank you.' He slid all three parchments into the pocket of his toga.

'And I hope my entrusting these into your care will assure you I had nothing to do with the attack on you yesterday, Senator.'

'It does.'

The clerk took a deep breath. 'Now, as for Nikolaos.' He raised his ink-stained fingers to his mouth and gave a dry cough. 'I'm sorry to inform you that his house was searched after you left. They didn't find his ledgers but he was badly beaten up.' The clerk waited until Vivius had had a chance to register his information before continuing. 'Romans periodically search his house but they've never gone this far before.' He regarded Vivius steadily. 'Still, his beating has convinced him to return to Rome with you.'

Vivius registered his surprise with a slap on the knee. 'Excellent! And his ledgers?'

The owlish eyes beamed before deliberately travelling up his bookcase to the top shelf.

'You have them here, in the fort?' Vivius asked in astonishment.

'There's no safer place than my office, Senator. I can assure you of that. I shall bring them to you tonight when the fort is quiet. Now, can you guarantee Nikolaos's safety to Rome?'

Surprised by this unexpected bonus from this obscure and unforeseen source, Vivius stroked his chin with his finger and thumb while his mind whirled around the problem of getting Nikolaos, his ledgers and these precious parchments back to Rome; his only support being a one-armed, wounded Decurion, and a physician whose weapon was his medical bag.

'My main problem will be getting him out of Jerusalem. I gather Pilate is watching him.'

'May I ask when you intend to leave?'

'Tomorrow.'

'So soon?' The clerk bit his lip. 'I have...friends who have ways of...I shall have to speak to...someone first. I shall get back to you. What about the person who knew you were going to see the bookkeeper?'

'Ah!' Vivius tapped the edge of his nose with his finger as he stood up. 'That's the one person I have yet to deal with.'

* * *

Vivius was faced with an angry physician when he entered his quarters.

'Just look at you, Senator. Your shoulder's bleeding again, and you're flushed. I warned you not to exercise after sustaining a deep wound, didn't I? Now, sit down while I change the bandage.'

There was a chuckle from the bedroom. 'That's right, Lucanus, you tell him.'

Vivius jerked his head towards the door. 'He sounds better.'

'I am!' came the response.

Vivius sank down on to the couch, grimacing as Lucanus opened a phial containing a brown foul-smelling concoction which seemed intended for his shoulder wound. He waited until Lucanus had unwrapped his bandages before saying, 'Apparently, the bookkeeper was given a severe beating after our visit yesterday. When we leave tomorrow we're taking him and the ledgers with us, if... Ouch!' He glared at Lucanus.

'Taking him with us? You're not serious? Isn't that dangerous?'

'No.'

'That's what you said yesterday, Senator. Two hours later we were being beaten up.'

Dorio wandered through from the bedroom and leant against the doorpost. 'By Arabs, they looked like Arabs.' Vivius glanced up at the physician. 'Didn't you hurl your medical bag at one of them?'

Lucanus indicated his neck. 'The fastening caught him here.'

Vivius grimaced as he watched Lucanus dab the brown liquid on his wound. 'Would you recognize him again?'

'Absolutely! In fact,' Lucanus withdrew a roll of fresh bandages from his medical bag and began wrapping them around Vivius's shoulder. 'Now I come to think of it, he resembled our intruder. He had heavy black freckles scattered across his face like...like full stops on a tablet.'

Vivius frowned at him. 'I don't remember you telling me about black freckles.'

'I've only just remembered.'

'Hmm. Pilate's slave has black freckles and less than twenty minutes ago I noticed a nasty cut on his neck. I'd avoid that section of the fort if I was you.'

Lucanus gave a wry grin. 'Don't worry, Senator. I've always avoided trouble. It's only since meeting you that it seems to have caught up with me.' He tied the bandage in a neat knot.

Vivius closed his eyes. His head was beginning to pound, his shoulder throb, and he was in no mood to reprimand a cheeky young physician for the way he spoke to a senator. He gave a half smile. Especially not one who had tackled an intruder single-handedly, and fought assailants with only obscene language and a medical bag as weapons.

He lay back on his couch, his thoughts quickly moving on from Lucanus to his visit to the administration offices and this unexpected bonus from... Vivius chewed his lip as it occurred to him he was placing an awful lot of trust in the hands of one little, white-haired, owlish clerk whose name he didn't even know.

* * *

(Jerusalem)

'Are you on your way to prayers, Simon?'

Shading his eyes against the late afternoon sunshine, Simon found Joseph of Arimathea hurrying towards him in an exotic robe of black, white, fawn and grey and headgear that reminded Simon of a hoopoe bird. 'I am.'

'Let me walk with you. There's a favour I have to ask.'

Simon gave him an uneasy glance. 'Seem to remember last time I did you a favour I ended up defending a blasted Roman.'

Joseph patted his shoulder consolingly. 'And this is another costly favour, my friend.'

'You can ask, but I'm not saying I'll do it,' Simon said gruffly.

Joseph slid his hands into the sleeves of his coat. 'The Greek bookkeeper, Nikolaos, is in trouble,' he said soberly. 'He was badly beaten up last night. The Romans want his ledgers. The only good thing to have come out of it is that Nikolaos has decided that Jerusalem is no longer safe. He wants the Roman senator to take him and his ledgers back to Rome and he's willing to testify against Pilate. My source at the fort tells me they leave tomorrow.'

'So what's this got to do with me?'

'Ah yes, well,' Joseph cleared his throat. 'They need your help getting out of Jerusalem.'

Simon stopped abruptly in the middle of the road. 'What! Are you mad? How am I supposed to do that? I can't concoct a plan overnight. It's madness, Joseph.'

'There's also a wounded Roman Decurion and a Greek physician you'll have to get out as well,' Joseph added.

'Why pick on me?'

'Because as a former Zealot you're the only one among the Nazarene people who would know how to do something like this.'

Simon scowled. 'I'm not helping a Roman,' he said flatly.

'I doubt that's the attitude our Lord Jesus would have taken,' Joseph murmured. 'He told us to forgive our enemies.'

'Forgive? You expect me to forgive the Romans for murdering my family?'

The question hung between them like an iron silence.

'Aren't you forgetting something?' Joseph eventually said but in a coercing manner. 'It's Nikolaos that needs your help and Zachary that needs justice. The Roman can deliver both.'

'You believe that do you?'

'I do. Absolutely!'

'Sounds to me like I'm left with little choice?'

'There's always a choice, Simon,' Joseph said pleasantly. 'You should know that.' He held on to his silken headgear as he ducked to avoid trailing ivy over the arch of the courtyard. 'It's making the right one that's important.' He patted Simon's shoulder. 'Come on. Let's join the others for worship.'

Simon glanced sullenly up at the upper room of the house and came to the rapid conclusion he was in no mood to pray. 'You go ahead, Joseph. I need time to think.'

Sinking down on the wooden seat under the almond tree, Simon leaned back heavily against the trunk. A white blossom floated over his head, landing on his tunic. He brushed it off with short angry gestures.

He had hoped the quiet murmur of prayer drifting down from the window of the upper room might have calmed his troubled mind; it didn't. Perhaps that was because he was more of a fighter than a quiet man of prayer, he brooded. He closed his eyes. Yet what he really needed right now was time to gather his shambolic thoughts together and make sense of what was happening.

He stirred uneasily as he tried to remember the last time he had prayed. His memory skimmed back through the days and landed on the morning he had spotted the Roman senator riding across the Kidron Valley. He gave an angry grunt. Romans! And Joseph says forgive them? How could he possibly forgive them? The familiar loathing rose up inside him like a volcanic eruption. He found its familiarity almost comforting, yet... He pinched between his eyes...yet where had all this...loathing got him? Every time he got angry he felt like he was shovelling fuel onto an already blazing fire. It was burning him up inside. He had no peace; he couldn't pray; he... It dawned on Simon bit by bit that all the hating was doing was destroying *him,* not the Romans.

He opened his eyes and stared miserably up at the almond tree as a second thought occurred to him. If he hated the Romans so much, what insanity had sent him charging down the lane in defence of one? Why hadn't he left the senator to the mercy of those thugs? Why hadn't he stuck a dagger in the Roman's back himself? After all, that's what the Zealots had trained him to do. The Romans had invaded his country, murdered his family, crucified Zachary. Yes, the Zealots were right. They were at war with Rome, perhaps he should go back to them, revenge was...

The Zealots!

The thought burst into his head like a flash of sunlight through the branches of the almond tree. Simon leant forward, his arms resting on his knees. Nathan! Nathan knew ways of getting out of the city. He kept a record of Roman timetables; he knew how to create a diversion. If anyone could get the Greek bookkeeper and his ledgers out of the city, Nathan could if... Simon pursed his lips. If he could be persuaded to help a Roman that is.

Simon sat for a while longer, finding himself torn between his need for revenge on the Romans, and asking himself why he should help this particular one. But at the end of each struggle the same answer came back to him. Regardless of being Roman, Greek or Jew; regardless of class, wealth or even religion; he was in the middle of a fight against injustice and intolerance, a fight against evil. Fighting evil; that's what Jesus of Nazareth lived and preached and what he, Simon, had come to believe he was called to do, not just by prayer but by action.

He rose to his feet, brushing the blossoms off his tunic but less angrily now that he had made his decision. Making his way up the stairs to the upper room he crept inside, closing the door quietly behind him so as not to interrupt the praying. He glanced around for Joseph. The sect of the Nazarene had grown to such an extent that he didn't recognize half of them. They were squashed together on their knees, their heads bowed over folded hands. He spotted Joseph's colourful and expensive attire almost immediately. It stood out against the simple coats and tunics around him. He was kneeling on the floor near the front. Simon groaned inwardly, knowing he'd get no thanks from the leaders for disturbing this quiet hour of prayer.

Taking a deep breath he made his way to the front, conscious of the clatter of his boots on the wooden floor. One or two looked up curiously as he passed, others gave a *tut* of annoyance, but mostly he was ignored.

He touched Joseph on the shoulder, and kneeling down beside him, whispered, 'Did you say there was a wounded Decurion in the party?'

'Yes.'

Simon could almost feel the angry glare from one of the leaders. He ignored him.

'Can you get word to the clerk at the fort that we'll need a cart for the wounded Decurion—and for Nikolaos. By the way, where is Nikolaos?'

Joseph pointed to the far side of the room. 'What are you going to do?'

Conscious of the fact that his untimely interruption was beginning to try the patience of those leading tonight's worship, Simon whispered, 'Tell you later.' Rising to his feet he self-consciously clomped his way back to the door.

Once outside he made his way swiftly towards the Greek quarter of the city, and the terrace of dilapidated flat-roofed buildings. He found Nathan sitting in the semi shade of his front door, hands thick with slimy brown clay, making pots to sell in the market. He glanced up briefly, raised his brows when he saw it was Simon, then focused back on his work.

'This is a surprise; two visits in a three days.' He stood up, viewed the simple round pot on the table objectively, then with a grunt of satisfaction rinsed his hands in a bowl of water. 'What can I do for you?'

'I need your help.'

'Oh yes? To do what?'

Simon took a deep breath, inwardly uttering his first prayer for days, which is why he was surprised when the first words that burst out of his mouth were, 'No one can hate the Romans more than me, Nathan. You know that.'

Nathan wiped his hands on a towel. 'So?'

'They murdered my family, and they crucified Zachary. If I wasn't going against the teachings of Jesus of Nazareth I'd wipe every Roman off the face of this damned earth.' Simon was surprised to find that despite the strength of his words the hatred inside him was a long way from erupting. 'Every Roman, except one,' he added.

Nathan sat down on his stool and regarded him curiously. 'Go on.'

'This one Roman; and make no mistake, Nathan, I loathe him with every bone in my body; he has the power to get justice for the families what were massacred by Pilate. He can also get justice for Jews that were crucified by Pilate without a trial.' Simon paused. 'This Roman; he's a senator, a magistrate and he carries valuable information from our own people to the emperor; information what can have Pilate recalled to Rome.'

Simon found Nathan regarding him with suspicion. 'And why do you want me?'

'I need help getting him and his companions out of Jerusalem and back to Rome.'

'His companions?'

'A Greek physician who hasn't a clue how to wield a sword, an elderly Greek bookkeeper with information which Pilate will do anything to get his hands on, a one-armed Roman Decurion wounded by Zealots, and the Roman senator.'

Simon watched Nathan tracing the scar down his face with his finger in a thoughtful manner. 'The cause is a good one, Nathan.'

The silence was a long one.

Eventually Nathan said, 'So we get rid of Pilate, his replacement might be worse.'

'Can we get much worse?'

'I need a few days to think about it, speak to the Zealots, plan and so on. When do you need to know?'

Simon hesitated before he said, 'Now. They leave tomorrow morning.'

CHAPTER FOURTEEN

(Rome)

Aurelia rubbed the yellow cloth between her fingers and thumb, her lower lip jutting out as though she was trying to make a decision. The stall-holder hovered, a look of anticipation on his face. She felt sorry for him. She had no intention of buying the material but she was pleased it looked as though she had.

'He's over there, mistress,' Ruth murmured at her side. 'By the leather stall.'

Aurelia found her heart was beating like a drum. 'Are you sure it's him?'

'Yes, mistress. He's carrying a cloak over his shoulder like the Lady Apicata said.'

Aurelia glanced up casually from the yellow cloth, her eyes flickering through the bustling shoppers and landing on a tall neat man of middling years who was looking in their direction. He had a shy, pleasant, sleepy-looking face that she immediately liked, and greying hair set far back on his head. She was close enough to see he had strong blunt hands with grizzled hairs on the back.

Deciding it would be safer not to give any sign of acknowledgment, Aurelia held eye contact with the man longer than was necessary before dropping the yellow cloth and moving casually away from the bales of material. The stall-holder's face fell.

Stopping occasionally to peruse various stalls, and to make sure the man with the strong blunt hands and the pleasant face was following, she made her way unhurriedly through the hot and bustling marketplace. Ruth kept her usual few paces behind as they wound their way back through the city to the Suranus town house.

'He's still with us, mistress.' Ruth's keys jangled as she opened the heavy wooden door. 'And I don't think anyone else followed but I can't be sure.'

'Good. Leave the door ajar for him.'

Aurelia barely had time to remove her cloak before the gentle footfall behind told her the man had entered her house. He closed the door quietly behind him.

'Thank you, mistress.'

Aurelia smiled shyly at him. 'Don't thank me yet. We still haven't got you safely away.'

The pleasant face smiled back sending crinkles of laughter lines around his eyes. 'You have my instructions?'

'Yes. Apicata says you're to wait until it's dark. My back door leads down to the river. You'll find a boat outside. You're to row down river to Ostia where you'll be met by the captain of a fishing vessel. He'll take you over to the Isle of Capri.' She paused. 'Do you think we were followed?'

The man shook his head. 'It's hard to say. I kept a sharp lookout. I wouldn't want you to get into trouble for helping us, but...' the man looked at her soberly before pulling a letter out of his pocket. 'My mistress says it's vital this letter gets to the emperor. If anything should happen to me would you inform her?'

'And your mistress is?'

'My mistress is Julia Antonia Minor, the emperor's sister-in-law. I was her slave until she made me a free man. But I still like to serve her when I can.'

Aurelia tried not to look surprised that such an undescriptive looking man should be in service to such a distinguished lady as Julia Antonia Minor. So she simply nodded, and was relieved when she heard Ruth coming in through the door.

'I have made a meal for our visitor as instructed, mistress.' Turning to the man, still with his cloak slung over his shoulder, she said, 'If you would like to come with me, sir.'

The former slave bowed in a manner that suggested the old habits of slavery were still engrained in him. 'Thank you, thank you, mistress.'

Only when they had left the room did Aurelia feel the need to release the excitement of the afternoon by curling up on her faded couch, pulling a cushion into her stomach.

For a while she chewed her thumb nail, fearful of a knock on the door. Her ears strained for the stomp of Roman boots or any unusual sounds from outside, and when they happened her body tensed. But as the afternoon wore on, and the sun slipped behind the roofs of the houses, and the heavy sounds of traffic eased, she found herself becoming calmer; although she had no inclination to relinquish her cushion, pick up her sewing or stir from her couch. More than once she asked why she had got herself involved, but was too scared to answer her own question.

As dusk approached, Ruth brought her a plate of lentils and meat, but after moving the food disinterestedly around the plate, then forcing herself to sample a few mouthfuls she pushed it to one side.

Ruth drifted in to light the oil lamp when it grew dark. She glanced at her briefly before saying, 'You should take him down to the river soon, mistress.'

Aurelia nodded and for the next half hour occupied her time by watching the flickering flame create shadows on the walls. It had that sickly smell of old oil but she didn't care enough to order it be changed. She rose only once, and that was to close the shutters.

The knock, when it came, startled her. She found her hands were shaking. But when she heard the familiar voice she breathed a sigh of relief. Although when Ruth showed Felix into her living quarters, her relief was short lived. Felix's face was set like marble and his eyes were burning with anger.

'Felix, what are you doing here? You know your house is being watched.'

'I gather you have the courier on your premises?'

'Yes, he's in the kitchen with Ruth. What's wrong?'

'What's wrong? What's wrong? Aurelia, what in the name of Jupiter have you been up to?'

'Nothing. I...Apicata asked me to do a message for her, that's all. She's been staying with me.'

Felix ran his hand down his face. 'What?'

'I invited her to stay. She was upset when Sejanus wouldn't let her take her children back to the countryside. She needed someone to talk to.'

'She's not still here, is she?'

'No, she thought it would be a good idea if she spent the afternoon pestering Sejanus for her children while I brought the courier back here. It gives her an alibi if anything goes wrong. Sejanus...' Aurelia faltered. 'Sejanus hasn't had her arrested, has he?'

Felix shook his head. 'No. He wouldn't do that. He wouldn't want to upset his children.'

'Then why won't he let Apicata take them back to the country with her? It's most unfair.'

Felix pinched between his eyes. 'Because, my dear,' he began in a manner that made her feel he was trying to explain a matter of great importance to a small child—or an idiot. 'Since Tiberius minted coins and erected a statue in Sejanus's honour, Sejanus is even more convinced the emperor is on the verge as naming him as his heir. He's insisting his children remain in Rome because he wants them to share in the grand occasion.'

'Then why is Apicata so afraid for them?'

'Wouldn't you be? If there are objections to the announcement and action is taken against Sejanus, Apicata wants her children safely out of the way.'

'Oh.' Aurelia feigned a surprised expression and was pleased to see that her apparent naivety was softening Felix's stiff marble face. The last thing she wanted to do was upset him; she needed him. Deciding the best way forward was to plead ignorance, she asked, 'Who would take action against Sejanus?'

'Tiberius for one. Apicata brought him information that gave him a terrible shock, but I believe he was already having doubts over Sejanus's loyalty.' Felix narrowed his eyes. 'The trouble is, Tiberius is demanding proof. I only hope the letter the courier holds will be proof enough for him to act.'

'If it's from Julia Antonia Minor it will, won't it? I've heard Tiberius has a high regard for her'. She realised Felix was regarding her closely.

'How do you know who it's from?'

Aurelia hesitated. 'Apicata told me. She approached Julia Antonia for help.'

'You clearly know far more than I gave you credit for, my love,' Felix said dryly.

'What does the Senate think?' She asked rapidly changing his line of discussion. She tilted her head persuasively when he dismissed her question with a wave of his hand. 'Tell me, Felix. You know I won't say anything, and I appear to be in the thick of a conspiracy anyway.'

Felix sat down on the couch and looked at her doubtfully. 'Well ... In public Tiberius appears delighted at the forthcoming marriage between Sejanus and his granddaughter. He's lavishing praise on him, calling him "my Sejanus" "the partner in my labours"; he's minted coins and erected this statue in his honour. But in private, there are certain members of the Senate and the equestrian order receiving a very different message. My guess is, Tiberius is trying to find out how strong a hold Sejanus has on his empire.'

Aurelia found her mouth turning dry. 'So...Vivius will have to walk back into all this?'

Felix gave a half smile. 'Vivius will know what's going on, my dear Aurelia. I believe that's why Tiberius sent him to Palestine in the first place. He wants proof. If Pilate is involved in illegalities, then you can be sure Sejanus will be at the root of it.' Felix took her hand and squeezed her fingers as a gesture that his anger had gone. Then pointedly changing the subject said, 'Now, as for this courier Apicata has foolishly got you mixed up with, I gather the plan is to take him down to the river?'

'Yes, the rowing boat is still there and Apicata has a fishing vessel waiting at Ostia to take him over to Capri.'

Felix glanced through the shutters into the darkness outside. 'Then let's get this man on his way. And then, my dear Aurelia, I think we need to discuss getting you out of Rome.'

'What? I'm not leaving Rome!'

Felix gave her one of his winning smiles. 'Think about it. We'll talk after I've taken Apicata's courier down to the boat.' Releasing her hands he made his way to the kitchen, leaving her to a cascade of jumbled thoughts.

Curling up on her couch and clutching the cushion to her stomach again, she listened to the mumbled conversation from the kitchen, the click of the back door latch as Felix and the courier left her house. She twisted around to watch the lantern's dim light from her back window. It waved to and fro as they made their way down to the river then disappeared altogether. Leaving her couch she waited anxiously by the window for Felix's return, and only breathed easily again when she saw the return of the waving light. It was the click of the latch on the back door that brought her to her decision.

'Well, despite my disapproval, that's a valuable piece of information you've helped get to Tiberius, my darling Aurelia.' Felix flung his cloak over the chair, rubbed his hands briskly to warm them up. 'Now, sit down,' he ordered.

Containing the irritation at being ordered around in her own house she sat down and allowed him to take her hand in his. They were still cold from his being outside.

'Stop looking so worried, Aurelia. I have it all worked out. You're to stay in my summer villa. It's a day's ride from the city, but you'll be safe there until this is all over. It shouldn't be long, a few weeks at most.'

Aurelia dropped her eyes. 'I can't stay in your summer house, Felix. What will people say? What will Vivius say? Besides, why should I leave Rome? Give me one good reason.'

'You want a list? Because, my love, you've been harbouring Sejanus's greatest enemy.'

'I have?'

'You have. Apicata is a bitter woman. She was rejected by Sejanus for a younger woman; a woman from the Imperial household. Apicata will do whatever it takes to bring Sejanus down, and use whoever she needs to do it, which is quite useful to some of us in the Senate.'

Aurelia blinked rapidly. 'I thought...I thought she was my... friend.'

'I know you did, my love.' Felix kissed her fingers. 'Another reason you need to leave Rome is because you are betrothed to Vivius. That makes you a valuable asset. If Sejanus has you, then he believes he'll have whatever information Vivius brings back from Palestine.'

'Vivius would never betray his country,' Aurelia said vehemently. 'Not even for me.'

'Wouldn't he?' Felix paused. 'Even you must have had doubt over how easily those charges of treason were dropped against your husband?'

'You're not suggesting...'

'I'm not suggesting anything, other than you think about what lengths Vivius will go to for you. Think about it.'

She was aware he was watching her carefully to see if his words had sunk in.

'And thirdly,' he continued. 'My sources inform me Sejanus has been making enquiries about the woman I took over to Capri. If he thinks Vivius contacts you with information to pass on to the emperor then...' Felix splayed his hands. 'Shall I go on?'

'You mean there's more?'

'Only that you've just helped get valuable information to the emperor from one of his staunchest allies, Julie Antonia Minor. If Sejanus has even an inkling of what you've been up to, he'll have you in Mamertine Prison before he's even figured out the charges.' Felix paused. 'In fact, if I'd known what you were up to, I'd have had you locked up myself.'

She patted his hand consolingly. 'No you wouldn't, Felix, and I'm still not leaving Rome.'

Concern flickered across Felix's face. 'You must. I insist. Sejanus has just had another senator arrested. As far as we know, he's in Mamertine Prison but he's elderly and the gods alone know how long he'll last in there. I'm not meaning to scare you, my love, but you can see how important it is that you leave the city.'

'Then I shall stay on my brother Dorio's estate.'

Felix shook his head. 'The stables? That's far too obvious. No one would think of my summer villa. It's too far out of Rome.'

Aurelia folded her hands neatly in her lap. 'I could stay with Phaedo.'

Felix frowned. 'Who's Phaedo?'

'He's Vivius's Greek slave. He manages his olive grove,'

'A slave? My dear Aurelia, you can't stay with slaves,' Felix was incredulous. 'Besides, if Sejanus finds you there, he's likely to burn the whole estate down. No, it has to be my summer villa.'

Aurelia dropped her head, pursed her lips and focused on forming a plait with the fringe on the cushion. Felix wasn't listening to what *she* was saying she thought angrily. He's squashed every idea I've had. He was a dear man, a kind man, but the fact is... she didn't want to be miles away when Vivius returned. She wanted... a slow smile materialized.

'I won't be putting you in danger if I stay with you, will I Felix?'

Felix's eyes twinkled mischievously. 'Only from Vivius.'

'One favour though. I want Phaedo to accompany us, and of course I want Ruth with me.'

'Of course.' Felix squeezed Aurelia's fingers affectionately. 'Leave it to me. I'll arrange it. We'll leave tomorrow night.'

* * *

'I don't know, which one do you think I should take?' Aurelia picked the two idols off the shelf looking affectionately from one to the other. 'Venus is my favourite, but lately I've been drawn to Minerva, the goddess of wisdom.' She weighed each idol indecisively.

'Mistress, why don't you let me bring them all to you in a few days?' Ruth said patiently. 'The bag is heavy enough and we must go.' Ruth gently took the idols out of her hands wiping a thin layer of dust off the top of their wooden heads before placing them back on the shelf. 'Besides, I will be praying to my God. We don't need an idol for that and I promise you he will answer our prayers.'

'Your god?' Aurelia looked at her in surprise. 'I didn't know you had one?'

'The God of the Jews, mistress.

'Really? Hmm.' Aurelia lightly touched the wooden head of her idols as if bidding them farewell. 'I suppose it won't harm to use another god, for a while.'

The sharp rap on the door startled them both despite the fact they had been waiting for it. Ruth answered, returning almost immediately with Felix.

Felix took Aurelia's hands. 'Are you ready?'

She nodded. 'I'm grateful to you, Felix.'

'I'm so sorry, my love. Change of plan. I can't accompany you all the way there. The Senate is in an uproar. Sejanus has arrested three more senators, and I've received word from the emperor that he intends travelling to Rome. He has ordered I attend him.'

As he spoke, Ruth blew out the single oil lamp standing on table leaving them in virtual darkness. Aurelia was glad Felix couldn't see the relief on her face, but she said, 'It's all right, Felix, really. I shall be in good hands with Ruth, and Phaedo is reliable. He'll look after me.' Wrapping the scarf around her mouth and pulling her hood over her head, she nodded to Ruth who opened the door at the rear of the house.

The cold, damp night air caught her throat as she stepped outside. She coughed. A thick mist swirled around her. She coughed again, her feet slithering on the wet moss. Felix adjusted the bags so he could take her hand.

With Ruth a few paces behind them, they stumbled along in silence. Aurelia found she had to strain her eyes through the mist to see more than a couple of paces in front of her. There were no lights at the back of the houses, and this particular stretch was marshy and the paving was cracked from constant flooding. But uncomfortable though it was, she knew it was safer than taking the main road.

'Shush!' Felix gripped her hand. They stopped abruptly, and listened.

Aurelia tried to stop her teeth from chattering. She heard dull footsteps hurrying towards them. Her eyes strained through the mist and as the footsteps drew closer she saw a familiar shadowy figure emerge from the darkness.

'Hello, Phaedo.' She smiled up at Vivius's slave even though she knew he wouldn't be able to see her mouth because of the scarf covering it.

'Senator. Mistress.' Phaedo greeted them in a low voice as he relieved Felix of the bags. 'The cart is around the corner, Senator, a short distance. Can you manage, little miss?'

Aurelia warmed to Phaedo's reassuring childhood greeting of her.

'Yes, Phaedo.'

Phaedo led them through the dark, dank alley between a clothes shop and a butcher. It brought them out near the warehouses and docks. There were always carts and wagons lined up along this stretch waiting for curfew to lift, although most of them had left by now.

'Over there.' Phaedo pointed to a small cart and an even smaller donkey. 'Not the type of transport you're used to, my lady, but I thought it would be safer if it was assumed this was my usual weekly trip.' He threw their bags into the rear of the cart. 'I hope you don't mind riding in the back with the empty pots.'

'You can't expect the lady...' Felix was indignant.

Aurelia placed her hand on his arm. 'It's all right, Felix. When I was little, Phaedo used to let me ride in the back of the cart. It's quite comfortable, honestly.'

'You're not a little girl now, Aurelia.' Felix's pursed lips indicated he was not pleased with the arrangement. Nevertheless, picking her up, he swung her gently into the cart with the empty pots of oil. Aurelia noticed that Phaedo had placed a pile of blankets in the corner for her.

Felix handed the slave a map. 'If you decide to stay the rest of the night on the Marcianus estate, be sure you leave before sunrise. It'll take another full day to my summer villa; these are the directions.'

'Felix,' Aurelia grabbed his arm before he stepped back from the cart. 'What about Vivius? I know it's asking a lot but...' her eyes pleaded with him.

Felix patted her hand reassuringly. 'The difficulty is knowing when he's arriving, my love, but I'll do my best.'

She tightened her grip on his arm. 'Will you?'

He squeezed her hand. 'I might not want Vivius back in Rome for personal reasons,' he said in a low voice. 'But believe me, I welcome anything he brings back against Sejanus.' He glanced at Phaedo who had climbed up to the front of the cart and was pretending not to listen. 'Take care of the Lady Aurelia.'

Phaedo reached out a hand to help Ruth clamber on the seat beside him. 'I will, Senator, sir,' he said soberly. 'And if I don't, it will be Senator Marcianus I shall have to answer to.'

Aurelia curled up in one of the blankets and Ruth flung the other blanket over her as the cart pulled away.

'Best keep down, little miss,' Phaedo whispered. 'It wouldn't do to be spotted now.'

Aurelia coughed as she pulled the blanket over her shoulders. She raised her head briefly to give Felix a wave. He looked a lonely figure, standing there watching them. Her heart warmed to him and she wondered guiltily whether she had done the right thing in using him like this, and whether she was doing the right thing in changing his well-laid plans for those of her own.

CHAPTER FIFTEEN

(Jerusalem)

'Lucanus, I need that...that...' Vivius pointed at the physician's shabby cloth travelling bag lying in a crumpled heap in the corner of their quarters.

'You do, Senator?' Lucanus's voice rose in surprise. 'Why?'

'For the bookkeeper's ledgers. No one will think of searching in that...thing.'

Banging his bag on the table, Lucanus snatched the ledgers from Vivius's hands but curiosity overcame his bruised feelings. 'When did you get these?'

'The ledgers? The clerk brought them last night.'

'How did he get them?'

Vivius watched Lucanus wrap his clothes neatly around the ledgers and pack them into his shabby bag in an orderly fashion.

'No idea, although I appear to have stumbled on to some religious Jewish sect who seem more concerned with getting justice than killing off Romans. The clerk is one of them, so is Nikolaos.'

'There!' Lucanus stood back and surveyed his shabby, cloth travelling bag, and other than it looking bulkier and being considerably heavier, no one would have guessed its contents.

'And these,' Vivius held up the parchments. 'Can you put them in your medical bag but keep them away from those phials, will you? I can hardly hand them to the emperor smelling of whatever foul concoction you keep in there.'

Lucanus glared at him, opened his medical bag, and pushed it across the table for him to do it. The fractious atmosphere was interrupted by a rap on the door.

'That'll be the clerk.' Vivius dropped the parchments on

the table, but when he opened the door he started in surprise. 'Claudia?'

Her face was flushed, her hair hung loosely over her rust cloak, a button was undone on her pink dress and she was bereft of jewellery. She swept past him without waiting for an invitation, bringing with her a whiff of roses that was rapidly becoming too familiar for his liking. 'You were leaving without saying goodbye?'

With a look of alarm, Lucanus moved swiftly into the bedroom to join Dorio, closing the door softly behind him.

'No. I intended to call before I left Jerusalem.'

'Did you, Vivius?' She drifted over to the table littered with bags, clothing and...Vivius glanced uneasily towards the parchments and Sejanus's new policies.

'Yes, I did,' he said. Deftly moving in front of her he perched on the edge of the table and took her hand. 'There were one or two things I wanted to ask you.'

'Were there? What?' Her eyelashes flickered, her finger lightly touched the bandage on his shoulder.

'We were ambushed and only two people knew where we were going, Claudia.' He spoke tenderly, not accusingly.

Pulling her fingers out of his hands she wandered over to the window and gazed outside, but Vivius could see she wasn't really looking at the grey clouds or the activities taking place in the courtyard. Taking advantage of her turned back, he quickly slipped the parchments into the medical bag and draped a tunic over the top.

'I come from an influential Roman family, Senator. I'm not used to having accusations thrown at me.' Her neatly rounded chin jutted out but he could see she was nervous by the way she twisted the ribbon on the bodice of her dress around her finger as if it were a bobbin. 'And for your information I had nothing to do with your ambush. A random attack, that's all.' The ribbon twisting stopped as her finger reached the end of the ribbon and the wrinkled object spiralled back down her dress. She half turned and pouted. 'Anyway, I don't know why you wanted the bookkeeper's address in the first place. He was an annoying little man, always had his head in his records, forever questioning every coin spent. He infuriated Pilate, especially when he had the audacity to accuse him of misappropriating tax monies.'

'And was he?'

'Of course not,' she said hotly and to Vivius her denial seemed genuine enough. 'Don't tell me you actually believed that silly little man's accusations. You didn't, did you?'

Vivius ignored the question. 'Only you knew where I was going, Claudia,' he repeated.

Claudia rubbed her arms under her cloak as if she was cold and turned back to the open window and the grey and overcast skies. 'If you want an explanation it's quite simple. I heard you ask the clerk for the bookkeeper's address. I was curious. Why would you want his address if, as you had led us to believe, your visit to Palestine was purely personal? I knew Pilate hated the bookkeeper, and so I told him what I'd overheard. But you can't possibly think my husband had anything to do with your ambush. As I said, it was a random attack. It happens all the time in Jerusalem. You were unlucky, that's all.'

'He didn't send Rico after us?'

'Rico? I don't know what makes you think Rico would come after you.'

'It was Rico.'

'If you're sure then...then perhaps Pilate ordered him to keep an eye on you and he misunderstood his orders or ... Oh, I don't know.' She waved her hand dismissively in the air. 'Whatever happened, I'm sorry you were injured, but it wasn't my fault.' She was still pouting as she came over to where he perched on the desk. She stroked the graze on his knuckles; her silken gown tickled his bare leg. 'You're angry.'

Vivius gently took her hand as he stood up. He found the closeness of her body disturbing. 'Do you blame me?'

'What are you going to do?'

'I'm going back to Rome.'

'And what will you say to the emperor?'

His eyes narrowed. 'Why should I say anything to the emperor?'

Her face reddened.

'You think the emperor sent me to Palestine?' He shook his head as he moved towards the door. 'I don't know what gave you that idea, Claudia,' he said, but then halfway across the room his shoulders sagged and he turned to face her.

'I don't want us to part enemies, Claudia. Do you? I shall never forget our day at the olive grove, and...' his voice dropped. 'I don't believe all of it was a lie, was it?'

She moved over to him shaking her head. 'No, not all of it,' she said quietly. 'There were...special moments...weren't there?'

Vivius took her hands in his. Her skin was cool and soft and the perfume of roses alluring. 'Yes,' he said softly. 'There were special moments.' He kissed her lightly on the forehead but she lifted her head as though expecting more. When it didn't materialise, she drew back and viewed him steadily.

'Goodbye, Senator Marcianus,' she said, and despite the winning smile there was an air of sadness about her. 'I doubt we'll meet again, unless it's in Rome.' And then sweeping out of his quarters she brushed her body seductively against him, almost as a reminder of what he would be missing.

He closed the door after her thoughtfully, thoughts that were shattered by Lucanus bursting out of the bedroom.

'I couldn't help hearing what was said, Senator, and I must say, that was extremely well handled.'

Vivius flared his nostrils. 'Do you always have to air your opinion, Lucanus?'

The physician flushed up. 'Drat! I'm doing it again, aren't

I? I'm sorry, Senator. I do tend to be a bit outspoken at times. I really must learn to curb my...'

Vivius was saved having to listen to the confessions and failures of his physician by a second knock on the door. This time he found it was the clerk.

'Good morning, Senator.' He spoke in a whisper, his owlish eyes flitting nervously behind him. 'Sorry about this last-minute information but as you can imagine, working out Nikolaos's departure at such short notice took some planning.'

Vivius indicated the clerk enter their quarters which he did so by sliding around the door with another apprehensive glance behind him. Vivius closed the door.

'He's to be transferred to your trap between here and the city gates.'

'Trap?' Dorio was standing at the bedroom door listening to the conversation.

'Yes, Decurion. It was hoped you would ride inside the trap...'

'Like an invalid, you mean?' Dorio said flatly.

'Yes sir, exactly sir. No one's likely to stop a wounded Roman.' The clerk turned back to Vivius. 'Pilate has given orders for everyone leaving Jerusalem to be questioned. It's Nikolaos and his files he's after. But I doubt he'll risk using his auxiliaries to stop a senator from Rome, and once you're through the gates you'll have an escort—of sorts—to...well, I'm not sure where they'll leave you.'

'Escort?'

'Yes, Senator...sort of. They'll help you get through the city gates.' He paused. 'Which port are you leaving from?'

Not wanting to give too much away, Vivius hesitated. But then, realising the clerk was as anxious for him to reach Rome as he was of getting there, said, 'Joppa. Although I've informed Pilate I'll be sailing from Caesarea. But Joppa is closer; a longer sea voyage but less overland travelling for the Decurion.'

The clerk nodded, his owlish eyes blinking rapidly as he

digested the information. 'Your escort will support you for as long as they can. So it's, er...been extremely interesting meeting you, Senator, extremely interesting. May God go with you.'

Deciding now was not the time to enquire which god he was talking about, Vivius gave the clerk a brief nod of thank-you. It was only as he closed the door behind him that he realised he still hadn't asked the man's name.

Fifteen minutes later, Vivius found a small trap with a tired-looking donkey hitched to the front waiting for them at the stables. Alongside it stood a tall, sturdy army horse.

Vivius could almost feel the bristles of indignation from Dorio. 'Yesterday I was fighting for the glory of Rome, today I'm being treated like a useless invalid,' he muttered allowing Lucanus to take his good arm and help him into the trap.

'Stop complaining, act wounded and show your arm—the missing one,' he ordered. 'If we're being watched you need to look as though you're in a bad way.' Throwing their luggage on to the trap and a blanket over Dorio's legs, Lucanus climbed on to the trap and picked up the reins.

As he mounted the horse Vivius looked carefully around. If Pilate was keeping them under observation, it was impossible to tell. Digging his heels into his mount, and with the trap following closely behind, he made his way out of the fort and into the steady stream of traffic.

Wagons converged all around him, with red-faced tradesmen laden with carts of fresh produce, local farmers bullying complaining asses, merchants from far and wide entering Jerusalem overloaded with goods on snorting camels, grumpy travellers wiping the sweat off their foreheads. Vivius clicked his tongue in annoyance and found his body breaking out in a sweat with the crush of traffic. This was not what he had expected at the start of their journey; it was caused no doubt by the searches taking place at the gate.

The traffic soon brought them to a standstill.

Vivius raised himself in the saddle to see how far they had to go. Not far. He could see beggars gathered around the gate crying for alms, and harassed Roman sentries trying to move them out of the way so they could question the travellers leaving the city. Vivius ran his hand down his face, concerned that they were so close to the gates and there was still no sign of Nikolaos.

And then, without warning, a beefy, big shouldered man, with a butterfly of sweat under the arms of his tunic, pushed in front of Vivius's mount, grasped the reins of the donkey pulling the trap, and to Lucanus's alarm began dragging them and the complaining donkey to the side of the road.

'Make way there! Make way!' the beefy man bellowed, but far from making way a heavily laden wagon of apples appeared to be trying to overtake them.

'Whoa! Whoa!' Vivius was about to steer his mount between the wagon and the trap when a rough, wiry-looking man with unsettling black eyes, and a jagged white scar from the corner of the eye to his chin grabbed his horse's rein and hissed, 'Don't interfere, Senator.'

And before Vivius had a chance to respond, the side of the overtaking wagon fell away and tons of apples rolled on to the highway. Vivius's mount snorted and backed away, alarmed by the angry cries, the waving arms and abuse in all languages around them. But then, in the midst of the confusion, Vivius caught sight of Simon. He had picked up a small figure in a long grey tunic and was hurling him from the apple wagon into the trap. Dorio recoiled. But recovering quickly, helped Simon pile their luggage and his blanket on top of the bookkeeper. The whole transaction was performed with such speed that Vivius barely had time to register what had taken place.

The beefy, big-shouldered man was now pulling at the donkey's reins, leading him back into the stream of traffic as though nothing had happened. Lucanus, having lost control of the steering, was gripping the sides of the trap completely mesmerised by this unexpected turn of events.

Vivius glanced down at the man with the scar. He still had hold of the rein. 'And how do you suggest we get through the gate,' he murmured.

'You're a senator; use your authority. We'll do the rest.'

Vivius tried not to contemplate too hard on what the rest entailed but as his guide clung on to the reins and led him up to the gates, Vivius threw his cloak back revealing his senator's toga. The sentries, surprised to see a Roman senator approaching, and assuming the man walking alongside him was his servant, waved him through.

But halfway through Vivius stopped. Turning in his saddle he saw Dorio was giving a first-class performance of a wounded Decurion by holding the stump of his arm and groaning. The beefy, big-shouldered chap was pulling the trap up to the gate. 'You!' Vivius bellowed. 'Are you going to take all day with my wounded Decurion?' Addressing the sentries he snapped, 'Let them through. I want to reach Emmaus by midday, not tomorrow.' Then urging his mount forward Vivius rode through the gates. Once out of the city he glanced back. The sentries, clearly not wanting to stop a wounded Decurion, and conscious they were being watched by a senator from Rome, were saved the embarrassment of having to make a decision by an angry cry from one of the beggars. A moment later, half-a-dozen beggars were pounding at each other on the ground, screaming abuse and disrupting incoming traffic. The Roman sentries hurried forward to stop the fight. Taking advantage of the chaos the beefy, big -houldered guy pulled the trap through the gate.

Vivius's scar-faced guide waited until the trap was alongside them before giving a shrill whistle. The beggars glanced towards the trap and before the Roman guards had a chance to arrest them, they had fled. Vivius, the trap and their new travelling companions moved swiftly on, but not before Vivius had glanced back to see the driver of the half-empty apple wagon had pulled up and blocked the gate completely. He gave a half smile and glanced down at the man with the scar. 'Your diversion?' he asked.

The man grinned and nodded. 'Pretty good, eh?'

'Who are you?'

'Nathan.'

'And you're from the sect of the Nazarenes?'

Nathan gave a course laugh. 'What? Me? Not likely!' He looked up; his eyes narrowed. 'Is it true; you have information that can get the likes of young Zachary justice and maybe even have Pilate recalled to Rome?'

Vivius raised his eyebrows. 'How do you know this?'

'Is it?'

Vivius hesitated, but only while he contemplated how he was going to explain to the emperor how half of Palestine seemed to have found out what he was up to. 'Yes.'

'And you really are a senator?'

'I am, and now that my identity's sorted, I'll ask you again. Who are you? If you don't belong to this sect of the Nazarenes then...' Vivius pursed his lips as he came to the conclusion himself. What other Palestinian group would have the expertise to get him out of Jerusalem? Not the Pharisees or Sadducees, their concerns were purely religious. The ruling council, the Sanhedrin, with the exception of Joseph, wouldn't align themselves with the affairs of a Roman senator but...'You're Zealots?' he asked quietly and glanced cautiously over to Dorio in the trap and the beefy, big-shouldered Zealot still leading it. Yes, the roughness of their ways, their talk, the carefully planned operation had the markings of the Zealots. 'I'm being escorted out of Palestine by Zealots,' he murmured.

The edges of Nathan's mouth quivered. 'That's exactly what I said to Simon. "What, escort Romans out of Palestine?" I asked, and he said, "You're always working out ways of getting rid of them, now here's your chance to do it, and get something back at the end of it."'

Vivius gave a short chuckle then glanced around. 'Where is Simon?'

Nathan nodded ahead. 'He's in front.' He jerked his head behind, 'I've a couple more following; two left early this morning for Emmaus and the rest...well, you saw the chaos back there.'

'Impressive,' Vivius murmured.

The reply was a nod. 'I know.' Nathan stepped back and beckoning to his beefy, big-shouldered comrade, who now sported an even bigger patch of sweat, both men took up positions to their rear leaving a good distance between them and the trap.

Vivius took a deep breath, and rolling his shoulders to ease the tension glanced up at the dark grey clouds looming above them. They were heavy, but they should get to Emmaus before it rained, he decided. He raised himself in the saddle to get a good look at the road ahead. It was busy. There were legions heading towards Jerusalem, a few small parties of Jews returning home after the Passover celebrations and the usual loaded camels, wagons, tradesmen and businessmen. In the middle of them, walking alone, a good distance ahead was Simon.

Glancing back at the trap Vivius noticed Lucanus was still sitting bolt upright, gripping the reins, his eyes scanning every bush and passer-by with suspicion.

'Relax,' Vivius said dropping back to join them. 'The Zealots are keeping their eyes open. Besides, the road's too busy for an ambush.'

'Relax? Senator, how can I relax?' the physician said heatedly. 'It's been one incident after the other since...Zealots! Our escorts are Zealots?' Lucanus snorted through his nose. 'I'd rather keep watch if you don't mind.'

Vivius shrugged. 'Suit yourself, but I don't know why you think that's going to help.' He edged up to the side of the trap. 'Nikolaos, we're out of Jerusalem. Why don't you come out from under those blankets and sit up front with Lucanus?'

There was no movement from the back of the trap. Vivius guessed Nikolaos was thinking about it, possibly deterred from showing himself by the physician's ill-timed remarks on being ambushed and escorted by Zealots. But then the bags and blankets rolled to one side and a red and bruised-faced, dishevelled and decidedly nervous bookkeeper emerged.

'Yes, thank you, Senator. Thank you, yes I will,' he muttered.

Lucanus drew the trap to a standstill to allow Nikolaos to scramble up beside him. Vivius edged his mount up to the side of the trap.

'I could do with stretching my legs, Dorio. Do you want to ride?'

'Stupid question.'

Vivius dismounted.

'Did I hear you right?' Dorio asked climbing from the cart on to the animal's back. 'We have Zealots escorting us?'

Vivius noted the edge in his voice. 'Yes.' He handed him the reins. 'We wouldn't have made it out of Jerusalem without them and we may still need them,' he added pointedly. He strode ahead leaving the trap and Dorio to follow at their own pace.

It took a few minutes of brisk walking before Vivius was able to catch up with Simon. He had debated whether he should bother but then, deciding he could hardly ignore the man after all he had done for them, he increased his pace until he fell into step with him. Simon didn't even turn to acknowledge him. His face was grim and his stance hostile.

Vivius glanced behind. Lucanus and Nikolaos were babbling in Greek in the trap; behind them rode Dorio. Vivius chewed the inside of his lip hoping there'd be no trouble given the Decurion blamed the Zealots for the loss of his arm.

It was curiosity over the rhythmic march of his and Simon's boots on the dusty road that caused Vivius to break the silence. 'You're a trained soldier?' He could tell the Jew was not as well trained as a Roman by the way he had fought, but he could also tell he'd been trained by someone who knew what they were doing.

'Yes,' came the sullen reply.

A cohort of Roman soldiers approached on their way to Jerusalem, their feet stirring up the dust on the road. It took a while for them to pass, and even when they had the dust didn't settle straight away but took time drifting down on to their legs and feet.

'You better make sure them Romans what killed Zachary are punished.'

The demand was unexpected and argumentative so Vivius decided to give it thoughtful consideration before answering. 'The legionaries won't, no, all they did was to obey orders. Zachary was a Zealot, an enemy of Rome...'

'And he wouldn't have been with them Zealots if you Romans hadn't massacred his family!' The response was aggressive. 'The same Zealots what have just got you out of Jerusalem by the way.'

Vivius pursed his lips and for a while focused on the rhythmic pounding of their feet on the road, the babble of Greek voices behind them, and the squeak of the cart's wheel as the donkey pulled the precious load to safety. They reached an overgrown clump of bushes with long spikes reaching out into the road, and as if by unspoken consent they made a detour around it.

'That ambush we were in,' Vivius said breaking the silence. 'If you hate the Romans so much, why did you come to our aid?'

Simon snorted through his nose. 'Don't kid yourself, Roman. I almost thrust my dagger into your back myself.'

Vivius decided silence was the best tactic after a comment like that but clearly Simon didn't.

'Aren't you curious to know why?'

'Not particularly, but I suspect you're going to tell me?'

'I am. It's quite simple. I hate Romans.'

'Really,' Vivius said dryly. 'I would never have guessed.'

Simon either decided to ignore the sarcasm or it fell on deaf ears. 'I hate being under Roman rule, but what to me is unforgivable is the way you Romans massacred over two hundred of my people,' he said vehemently. 'Zachary's father and his brothers; my father, brothers; we was all in a peaceful demonstration over Pilate using our holy money to build an aqueduct. Then, without warning he turned on us. Our family, they was…butchered…there's no other word for it…butchered, by you Romans.'

Vivius allowed the information to settle before saying, 'Which makes my question even more poignant. Why did you come to help us?'

Simon gave a snore of contempt. 'I've asked myself that same question a million times, Roman. I've no idea. Perhaps it was 'cos Joseph of Arimathea was convinced you would get justice for Zachary, and all Jews like him who was crucified without a trial. He was the one what asked me to follow you, see what you was up to.' Simon dropped his head and concentrated on the steady rhythm of his boots. When he spoke again the anger had gone out of his voice. 'I should have stopped Zachary from joining the Zealots, and from getting involved with that thug Barabbas, but if Joseph's right and you succeed, I can at least get justice for him.'

A Roman Decurion galloped by on his way to Emmaus, a messenger judging from his speed. Vivius watched the dust rise from his horses hooves and when he was well past asked, 'You're with the Zealots?'

Simon shook his head. 'Used to be.'

'Why did you leave?'

'I joined Jesus of Nazareth.'

'I thought they were a peaceful sect?'

'They are. We follow his teachings.'

'Which are?'

Simon pursed his lips. 'He says we're supposed to forgive. But forgiving's not easy when you've watched your family being massacred. Cruelty breeds hatred, Roman. And the hatred I have for your race is...' He left the sentence unfinished. 'But...' Simon furrowed his brow as if trying to find the right words. 'Speaking bluntly...'

Vivius wondered when he had ever done any other.

'I found it...odd...when you said you wanted justice, for Zachary. I asked myself, why and couldn't come up with an answer. Then I saw the risks what you took to get the Greek bookkeeper and his ledgers out of Jerusalem. That was when it dawned on me that, perhaps, you want what I want. To put wrongs right.' He glanced at him sideways. 'Am I right?'

'Yes, you are.'

'Knew I was.' Simon rubbed his scruffy beard fiercely. 'It chokes me to say it but...' He cleared his throat. 'The teaching what Jesus gave us is right. There comes a point in every man's life, whether Roman, Jew, Greek or...whatever, when you decide you've got to stop burning up with hatred every time you relive the past. You've got to stop carrying bitterness around with you.'

Vivius found his own childhood injustices blowing in like a cold north wind. He cleared his throat.

A team of covered wagons approached, swaying over the road and forcing him and Simon to either side of it.

'What will you do with the information you have, Roman?' Simon asked when they were walking alongside each other again. Vivius noticed he had tried to inject a lightness in his question giving Vivius the impression he had even embarrassed himself by his speech.

'Give it to the Emperor Tiberius.'

'The emperor?' Simon appeared impressed. 'Will he do something about it?

'You have my word on it; that is, if you'll take the word of this Roman. I'll be presenting Zachary's case in a Roman court.'

Vivius chose his words carefully before adding, 'And I'm sorry he wasn't. Zealots may be the enemy of Rome but even enemies are entitled to a fair hearing, regardless if the sentence is crucifixion.' He cleared his throat. 'That, er…that massacre; it was against Roman policy, you know. It should never have happened.' He cleared his throat again. 'And as a Roman, I'm… I'm ashamed that it did.'

The small Roman garrison in Emmaus came into sight.

'Thank you for saying that, Roman,' the Jew said gruffly.

'The name's Vivius. Vivius Marcianus.'

They continued their walk in silence.

CHAPTER SIXTEEN

(Jerusalem)

Pilate waited until his wife had flung her cloak across the back of a chair, herself across the couch and bellowed, 'Rico! Breakfast!' before speaking.

'Well?' he demanded. 'What did the senator say?'

She drew the back of her hand across her forehead as though she had a headache. 'Nothing.'

'Nothing? What do you mean, nothing' he snapped. 'You've been away for over an hour. He must have said something.'

'He didn't. When I entered his quarters they were packing, but there were parchments on the table.'

Pilate twirled his ring around his stubby finger. 'Did you get a look at them?'

'A glimpse, that's all.' She ran her fingers through her mass of tangled curls. 'Rico! Curse the man. Where's my breakfast?'

Pilate smirked down at his wife. 'Huh! Well you've certainly come back in a bad mood. Reject you, did he? And there's no point bellowing for Rico. I've sent him after your senator. You'll have to get one of the other servants, and personally I wouldn't bother. It'll soon be lunchtime.'

Claudia sat up abruptly. 'What do you mean, you've sent him after *my* senator.'

'Exactly what I said. Vivius Marcianus is likely to be in possession of information that could have me—and I hasten to add, you—recalled back to Rome.'

He found a certain satisfaction in watching the colour drain from her face.

'Those parchments,'

'Yes, those parchments, Claudia.'

The rap on the door was sharp and Pilate barely had time to

shout 'Come!' before Rico had entered.

'Well?'

Rico bowed. 'The Decurion and physician left in a trap and the senator rode an army mount. They didn't appear to have the bookkeeper with them, but the gates were busy. He could have sneaked on to the trap without me seeing.'

Claudia stood up. Her face was still pale. 'What are you going to do?'

'Don't worry. It's the ledgers and the bookkeeper I'm after, Claudia, not your senator. At least I know where they're headed.'

'Where?'

'Caesarea.'

Claudia's eyes flickered nervously and there was a moment of hesitation before she said, 'I thought they would have been sailing from Joppa.'

'Joppa?' Pilate narrowed his eyes suspiciously. 'What makes you say that? '

She tossed her head at his insinuation that she was trying to protect her senator and her expression was scornful when she said, 'Didn't it occur to you that he would say he was sailing from Caesarea just to get you off his trail?'

Pilate twiddled his ring around his finger, stared uncertainly at his wife then glared at his slave. 'Take those men you hired the other day and go after him. Hire more men if you have to. I don't want any mistakes this time. You're to head for Joppa.'

* * *

Leaving his newly acquired escort in the centre of Emmaus, Vivius marched into the Roman garrison, confident that as a senator from Rome he would receive privileged treatment. Minutes later he marched out again disgusted to find he didn't. He had found the garrison overcrowded, noisy, and its overworked staff unimpressed at having a visiting senator demanding sleeping quarters for four when they were already full to capacity.

'Then you'll have to find us somewhere else and quickly, Senator.' Lucanus demanded. 'Dorio needs rest and treatment— now.'

The physician's nagging did nothing to improve Vivius's frustration. Storming across the road, he headed for the nearest inn. From the outside it looked clean enough so he ordered a meal and beds for the night. But once inside they found the meal tasteless, the mattresses coarse and lumpy and Vivius scratched all night with bedbugs. To add to his discomfort a stiff breeze blew through the town and whistled through the rafters making his room draughty and cold. He awoke the following morning stiff, tired, itching from head to toe and discovered his companions had fared no better. His only consolation was to discover Nathan and the big-shouldered, beefy Zealot had been sleeping downstairs guarding them all night.

Vivius examined his map over breakfast. His next stop was Lydda, twenty-five miles from Jerusalem. He felt slightly more confident they would have a comfortable night in the garrison at Lydda. He had pleasant memories of staying there many years ago. He was less confident the Zealots would provide protection that far from Jerusalem. But after securing the three extra horses from the garrison, Vivius was surprised to find they had planned to accompany them, but at a distance, on this next leg of their journey.

It was still grey and overcast when they left Emmaus but the highway ahead was flat, smooth and well maintained by Romans for the constant stream of legions, travellers and commerce. The only downside to their journey was that every few miles Lucanus insisted they stop and let Dorio rest. Vivius curbed his frustration, knowing that on his own he would be travelling at twice the pace. On more than one occasion, he was tempted to scare them into flight by suggesting the longer they took, the more chance Pilate's thugs had of catching up with them but he decided to keep those fears to himself.

As Vivius had predicted, when they reached the garrison at Lydda he was treated with more respect and provided with a decent meal and a comfortable bed. That was when Nathan and the beefy, big-shouldered Zealot left them. There was no formal departure, simply a nod from Nathan as he and the beefy Zealot left them outside the garrison.

The following day Vivius and his companions left for Joppa. That was when it rained.

It rained solidly all the way to Joppa. And then the stiff breeze which had blown into Emmaus, turned into a squall, whipping through their sodden clothes, and to Vivius's dismay delaying their progress even further.

By the time they trailed into the ancient port of Joppa it was dark. They were drenched and cold and Vivius was concerned that Dorio had been shivering uncontrollably for the last hour and even struggling to stay astride his mount. It didn't take a physician to see he needed food and he needed rest, and although he never uttered a word of complaint, Lucanus was well able to do that for him.

As they rode towards the harbour Vivius noticed there were three vessels secured to the pier.

'Which one of these is bound for Rome?' he called to a drenched harbour master.

'All of them,' the man called back. 'But there'll be nothing sailing in these waters till the wind changes.'

Vivius had already guessed that much. All we have to do now is wait out the storm, he thought, and pray to the gods that Pilate's men don't catch up with them. He swivelled around on his mount to inspect their surroundings. With the exception of a welcoming lantern outside a tired old inn, the driving rain made it difficult to see what other accommodation Joppa had to offer. However, one glance at Dorio was enough to convince him the Decurion had gone as far as he could go. The tired old inn would have to do.

Their rooms he viewed with a curled lip; tolerable was all that could be said about them. And tolerable they remained for three whole days and nights while the gale battered at the doors and windows, and high seas rocked the vessels against the pier with a persistent thudding that kept them awake all night. They stayed indoors, for their own safety as much as for the atrocious weather. The only positive side to this enforced rest was it gave Dorio valuable recovery time.

On the morning of the fourth day, Vivius woke to a blissful silence. The wind had dropped, the rain had stopped beating against their inn and when he went downstairs for breakfast he was relieved to be told they could board the first vessel bound for Rome, a cargo vessel.

As they climbed aboard with their luggage, Vivius examined their fellow passengers carefully. A Syrian judging from his tongue, a dozen or more merchants, a family with six children, a Roman centurion on crutches and a handful of unarmed travellers. Vivius decided he was satisfied, partially. All he had to get through now was the sea journey. He grimaced at the thought of days at sea. This voyage in particular he expected to be particularly arduous with the swell left on the seas by the recent storms.

He was right. The first setback occurred when their captain spotted a pirate vessel not far from the island of Crete. The cries of alarm from passengers and crew alike were sufficient to drag him up from his seasick bed in the hold to investigate. He watched the vessel approach with a set jaw. The centurion on crutches joined him at the rail.

'It's all very well for Roman propaganda to claim they've made the seas safer,' the centurion complained. 'But it's a bit disconcerting watching a pirate vessel heading straight for you and knowing there's very little you can do in the way of combat.'

Vivius glanced at his companion and realised that, discounting his seasickness, he was about the only passenger on board in a physically good enough condition to make a stand. But then he clutched the rail with both hands as their vessel heaved alarmingly as it changed direction. Vivius blew softly through his pursed lips, relieved their captain was playing it safe and had decided to scuttle to the nearest port. Unfortunately, the sudden change of direction knocked his stomach off balance and he was forced to retch over the side—and he keep on retching until they reached the port.

The second setback occurred when a heavy fog settled on the port forcing them to stay in harbour for the next two days. Vivius booked himself and his travelling companions into an overcrowded inn that smelt of fish and stale wine, and where the average guests were of such dubious character that Vivius slept with his sword by his side.

He noticed that the only advantage to these two days in port was to the captain who took the opportunity of loading his already overloaded vessel with extra cargo. Good news for him financially but not for his passengers, Vivius brooded. As he had predicted, when the fog lifted and they set sail again, the swell in the sea had their vessel rolling perilously low in the water with the extra cargo. On this final leg of their journey Vivius was so sick that he lost track of the days and resigned himself to curling up in his dark corner of the hold to wallow in his misery.

He realised they had reached calmer waters when he woke to discover their vessel had stopped rolling. Rising groggily to his feet he cautiously made his way up on deck only to find the glare of the early morning sun so intense he was forced to stand with his hand over his eyes until he had accustomed himself to its brilliance. Then holding on to ropes, rails or cargo he attempted to walk in a straight line across the wet deck to join his companions. Fortunately, they refrained from commenting on either his prolonged bout of seasickness or his unkempt appearance.

Leaning heavily on the rail he closed his eyes and breathed in the early morning air like a baby taking its first breath after nine months in the womb. The gentle breeze ruffled his hair. The sun warmed his back and there was a smell of salt, fresh air and fruit from the captain's cargo. Squinting through one eye, he saw the longed-for sight of land on either side of them. Their vessel was sailing smoothly towards the port of Ostia at the mouth of the river Tiber; and theirs wasn't the only boat. As they made their way up river, Vivius noticed that vessels that had been delayed by the Mediterranean storms were either searching for docking bays or, having found one, were unloading wheat, olive oil and wine from Rome's many colonies.

Vivius's heart lifted. Rome!

* * *

(Jerusalem)

Pilate was sitting at his desk, his head in his hands as Rico delivered his report.

'Gone, you say?'

'Yes, excellency,' Rico kept his eyes fixed to his feet. 'I waited four whole days and when the weather did clear and the boats did set sail, he wasn't on any of them.' The black eyes flickered nervously towards his master. 'I made enquiries and the senator never arrived in Caesarea. Perhaps...perhaps the Lady Claudia was right. Perhaps he did sail from Joppa after all.'

Pilate sniffed; his upper lip curled.

'The...the bookkeeper, excellency? Do you want me to search Jerusalem?'

'Get out, Rico!'

Being familiar with his master's foul moods, Rico moved smartly out of the room closing the door softly behind him.

Pilate rubbed the heels of his hands into the sockets of his eyes so hard it brought white dots floating in front of them.

After a while he stopped rubbing and dragged himself over to the table of wine. The heavy rhythmic stomp of the legionaries' boots from the courtyard echoed through the open window pounding through his head. Claudia's tuneless hum drifted irritatingly through from the bedroom, along with an over-powerful aroma of roses. Nothing had gone right on this trip, he brooded snatching up the wine jug. Nothing! Not since... His jug hovered over his goblet... Not since the arrival of the senator. He filled the goblet to the top pondering on Claudia's obvious attachment to the man, then he gulped a few mouthfuls down as if he was drinking water. The wine was strong and had a bite to it. He licked his lips and then slammed the wine jug down. Damn the woman! He'd been convinced she'd been misleading him when she'd suggested the senator would sail from Joppa. That's why he'd sent Rico off to Caesarea. Pilate sniffed; his upper lip staying in a curled position. The whole thing was a shambles. Well, she'd only herself to blame if he ended up back in Rome without a position. But if the senator had made it back to Rome...then the problem was now in Sejanus's hands. After all, he had more to lose than him or Claudia.

CHAPTER SEVENTEEN

(The Port of Ostia – approximately 15 miles from Rome)

Vivius rested his arm on the rail of the boat as it meandered up the sun-bathed River Tiber in search of a docking bay. With the other he scratched at the dark grey stubble on his chin. He yawned, exhausted from lack of sleep and days of seasickness. His thoughts kept straying towards Aurelia and it was taking a conscious effort of will for him to put her to one side. His first priority was getting Nikolaos and the ledgers to safety, he decided firmly. Only under the emperor's protection would they all be safe.

The emperor! Vivius transferred the scratching of his chin to rubbing at the streak of vomit down his clothes. He grimaced, and wondered how in the name of all the gods he was supposed to present himself to the emperor looking like this. He was unshaven, unwashed and presumably smelled foul as he was wearing the same clothes he'd been vomiting in for days—and due to the storms he was late. The emperor would have expected him back before now.

Deciding his appearance was a minor problem compared to all the others, he picked up his luggage and made his way unsteadily across the deck to join the queue of passengers waiting to disembark. He found Dorio, Lucanus and Nikolaos leaning over the side of the boat discussing the complications of finding a docking bay with so many vessels arriving in port after the storms.

Vivius squinted down at the dockhands waiting for the boats to dock so they could unload their cargo. But after spending so long in the hold all he saw was a blur of figures. His eye travelled along the blurred figures then stopped, drawn to a mass of red and black. He narrowed his eyes further in an attempt to clear his vision. When it did he breathed in sharply. Praetorian Guards! At least ten of them he reckoned, and they were scrutinizing each incoming vessel as it docked.

Vivius rested his hand uneasily on his dagger, his thumb rubbing the ruby inset in the handle, but his eye never left the high-ranking officer who was watching the line of passengers on their boat. His bearing reminded Vivius of a strong man he had seen in the circus, tall, broad, cleft chin, wide forehead, strong facial features The only difference being this Praetorian carried an air of intimidation. Vivius saw his gaze come to a standstill — on him — on his senator's toga. They made eye contact. The officer began ambling alongside their boat, waiting for their captain to find a docking bay. His men followed.

'I think we might have a problem,' Vivius murmured.

Lucanus's shoulders sagged. 'Not more trouble, Senator. Please don't tell me there's more trouble.'

'We're being watched, so turn away from me, all of you. But listen.' He waited until they had their backs to him before saying, 'Dorio, pull your cloak over your missing arm. I don't want those guards knowing you're the wounded Decurion I've brought back from Rome. I want you to take the ledgers in that... that...shabby bag of Lucanus's and lose yourself.'

'Lose myself?'

'Anywhere on the docks, but keep me in sight. If I'm arrested, get those ledgers and the policy parchment to the emperor. The material in the medical case I'll keep with me. If the guards take me to Sejanus I don't want him thinking I've come away from Palestine with nothing. Can you carry the bag?' Vivius knew he'd said the wrong thing by the unspoken bristles of indignation aimed in his direction.

'Lucanus, I want you to get Nikolaos to Dorio's estate in the hills.'

'Dorio's estate? But...'

Vivius addressed the worried-looking bookkeeper. 'You'll be safe there until I return.'

Vivius realised the captain had spotted a docking bay when he found the vessel shuddering towards the dock with its overload of cargo. He grasped the rail when he saw the captain was attempting to out-manoeuvre another approaching vessel.

'I have a problem, Senator,' Lucanus began.

'I'm not interested in your problems right now, Lucanus?'

'Yes, but…'

'Just give me your medical case.' Vivius turned his head. 'None of you know me, understand?'

There was a thud as the medical case fell at Vivius's feet. 'Take care of that case, Senator. It was given to me by…'

'You understand what you have to do?'

'Yes, senator. Swap luggage, we're strangers and I'm to go to Dorio's estate with Nikolaos. But as I've been trying to tell you, I don't know where Dorio's estate is.'

There was a shout as the sailors jumped on to the dock to secure their vessel.

Vivius pinched between his eyes. 'Ask any blacksmith in Rome for directions to the Suranus stables,' he said with forced patience. 'It's in the hills; a two-hour brisk walk northwest of the city. It adjoins my olive grove. Understood?'

'Understood, Senator.'

There was a clatter as the sailors secured the gangplank. Not wanting to be seen near his companions, Vivius sauntered towards the centurion on crutches, and as the passenger began disembarking, he followed him closely down the gangplank. When he reached solid ground, the high-ranking Praetorian officer moved towards him with slow, sure steps.

'I had expected you back before now, Senator Marcianus. Good journey?'

'Dreadful!' He examined the officer intently. 'You're here to meet me?'

The Praetorian officer ignored the question, too engrossed in studying the disembarking passengers. 'I understood you were travelling with your brother-in-law; wounded wasn't he?' His eyes flickered towards the centurion on crutches.

'*Decurion* Suranus?' Vivius made a point of emphasising Dorio's rank. The centurion had served his purpose in being the focus of attention to allow the others to disembark unnoticed. 'Unfortunately, he was too ill to travel. I repeat, are you here to meet me?'

The officer lost interest in the centurion who, with his bag over his shoulder and crutches under his arms was struggling towards the barges that would take them from the Port of Ostia into the city of Rome. 'I am, Senator. I have a boat to take you up river to Rome.'

'Rome?'

'Sejanus wishes to examine your findings for himself.' The officer hesitated when he saw Vivius's raised eyebrow. 'The emperor informed him of your investigation and as you know the Prefect deals with all Rome's administrative matters.'

Vivius set his jaw. 'I'm sorry, but my orders were to report directly to the emperor.' His eyes drifted over the shoulder of a Praetorian Guard to where Lucanus and Nikolaos were walking briskly towards the barges. Of Dorio, there was no sign.

'The thing is Senator Marcianus,' the officer said in a low voice. 'Sejanus believes it would be in your own best interests if you speak to him first. There have been, shall we say, developments while you've been away.'

'Developments? What sort of developments?'

'We'll discuss it on the way to Rome.' He signalled to the Praetorian Guard behind to pick up Vivius's luggage.

Vivius showed the approaching guard the flat of his hand; the guard hovered, uncertain.

'What sort of developments?' Vivius repeated.

'Good ones if you support Sejanus.'

'Really? Then please tell Sejanus I shall be pleased to call on him as soon as I've seen the emperor.'

The officer's face hardened, his upper body moved forward in an intimidating manner. 'I think you will find it is to Sejanus, not the emperor, you will have to answer to if the charges of treason being brought against you are true, Senator.'

Vivius was not intimidated. He had used these same tactics when he was with the Praetorians, but he was uneasy by the accusation. 'Treason?'

'I understand you presided over the case against the Lady Aurelia's former husband. The case that was dropped for lack of evidence.'

'What are you insinuating?'

The officer stepped forward. He was so close Vivius could smell the garlic on his breath. 'I have been instructed to inform you that Sejanus will soon be in a position to make you a very rich and influential man, Senator. And as you know, loyalty to him does not go unrewarded. He can clear you of these charges. But any resistance to his orders...'

'Senator Marcianus?'

Vivius spun around. Senator Felix Seneca was marching briskly towards them with six Vigils in tow. Vivius tried not to look relieved to see him.

'Ah! Good day, officer,' Felix greeted the officer of the Praetorian Guards with his usual wide smile and winning charm but his only response was an angry glare. Unperturbed Felix turned to Vivius. 'And good day to you as well, Vivius. You're late; but nonetheless I'm here to take you to the emperor,'

In the distance Vivius heard the clatter of a gangplank. A moment later he was relieved to see the barge drifting away from the pier with Lucanus and Nikolaos safely on board. He glanced casually around the busy dock. There was still no sign of Dorio.

The Praetorian officer's lips formed into a thin, straight line as he addressed Felix. 'You've had a wasted journey, I'm afraid.

Sejanus wants him in Rome.'

Vivius was aware that the Vigils had fanned out behind them; but they were edgy, nervous. His fingers drifted through his cloak to the dagger in the folds of his toga. The last thing he wanted was Rome's police and firefighters forced into action for him. Knowing they'd be no match against the emperor's Praetorian Guards he forced his tired brain into action. Inclining his head to Felix, he said, 'Thank you for your concern, Felix. But I must confess I find myself in a predicament here. The emperor will be disappointed with what I've brought back from Palestine. A few meaningless reports from embittered Jews and that's about it. I don't think he was...feeling himself when he gave me this assignment.' He gave a forced laugh. 'Sejanus was right about that at least. On top of which, I gather there's a charge of treason being levelled at me so I'm likely to find myself in Mamertine Prison before the end of the day.' He cleared his throat. 'However, Prefect Sejanus has promised me these charges will be dropped if I give him my support. That's my dilemma; Sejanus in Rome or the emperor on Capri?'

Vivius realised Felix was studying him closely, a frown across his brow. But then his face cleared. Addressing the Praetorian officer in a low voice, he said, 'There seems to be some misunderstanding here. I too am taking Senator Marcianus to Rome because that's where the emperor is. He sailed over from Capri earlier today. I thought you knew that?'

A glimmer of uncertainty crossed the Praetorian officer's face. 'Why wasn't I told?'

'I've no idea. How old are your orders? Given the significance of the emperor's arrival on the mainland I would assume Sejanus will want you in Rome with him. I doubt he'll be bothered about a failed mission by Senator Marcianus, not today anyway.' He paused a beat. And especially not tomorrow. Perhaps you need fresh orders?' My orders are clear. I'm to assemble all senators for an important announcement in the Senate tomorrow. As for Senator Marcianus, as a senator he has no option but to be present.' Turning to Vivius he scanned him up and down, his mouth gradually drooping at the corners. 'But we can't have you looking as though you've been ravaged by wolves, Vivius. By all the gods, what have you been up to? Perhaps we ought to get you cleaned up before we head into Rome. Sejanus will not be too pleased you arriving for his big occasion looking like that.'

The Praetorian officer looked unsure of these new developments. 'You're taking the next barge into Rome?'

Felix shook his head. 'Not the next one, no. I think it will take more than an hour for the senator to clean himself up, don't you?'

The grim-faced officer stepped back, but slowly. Vivius licked his lips with relief; they tasted of salt. Picking up his bags he gave him a curt nod and without further comment followed Felix and the six Vigils along the docks and away from the barges.

Felix whistled softly through his lips. 'That was close.'

'The emperor sent you?'

'He did, and he suggested I take the Vigils with me in case of trouble. We've been waiting for you for over a week now.'

'Waiting for me? And he sent the Vigils? Where are his own Praetorian Guards?'

'Some are with him, others...' he shrugged. 'There have been...developments.' Felix indicated a boat a few yards away and after a glance behind headed towards it.

'Vivius's heart sank. 'I thought you said the emperor was on the mainland?'

'I lied.'

There was a clatter of boots behind them. 'I think we have company, Senators,' the Vigil officer warned.

The whole party swung around, hands on swords, to find a one-armed Decurion staggering after them, dragging a shabby cloth travelling bag.

'Your ledgers,' Dorio dropped them at Vivius's feet.

Vivius gave him a brief nod of approval, but that's all it was, a brief nod. His mind was already one step ahead. 'Dorio I want you to get the next barge into Rome. I need you to keep Lucanus and the bookkeeper safe until I return.'

The senior Vigil glanced down at Dorio's disability. 'I could muster more men if...'

Vivius shook his head. 'He'll manage fine, won't you?'

Dorio nodded. 'What about you?'

Vivius's mouth quivered at the edges. 'I always manage fine.'

'Right then.' With a salute to Felix and the Vigil officer, Dorio picked up his own bag and with an unsteady but purposeful gait, made his way back along the docks.

'Oh, there's one other thing,' Felix said as he stepped on to the boat. 'It concerns Aurelia.'

Vivius eyed his fellow senator uneasily as he followed him aboard. 'What about her?'

'I've sent her to my summer villa for safety.' He nodded to the captain of the vessel to set sail.

'You have Aurelia in your summer villa?' Vivius repeated it simply because he was unsure what to make of it.

'Your slave, what's his name, Phaedo, took her. I was tied up with affairs on Capri, and as Sejanus was keeping your estate and the Suranus stables under observation...'

'Observation?' The vessel shuddered as the sailors pushed it away from the docks. 'Why would Sejanus have the Suranus stables under observation?' Vivius clung on to the rail.

'Everyone you know is under observation, Vivius. That's why I sent Aurelia away. She...well, let's just say she got herself... involved.'

'Involved?' Vivius swallowed hard. 'How involved. No!' he raised his hand. 'Don't tell me. As long as she's safe, that's the main thing. But if what you say about the Suranus stables being under observation is true Felix, then I've just sent my prime witness for the prosecution, and the two men with him, straight into the hands of Sejanus.'

* * *

Vivius knew Felix was right when he said there was little he could do about that now. But as he took yet another sea voyage, although to his relief a considerably shorter one, he couldn't tear his thoughts away from the trouble his friends and companions had been left in because of this one assignment.

'I can send men over to the Suranus stables first thing in the morning,' Felix offered.

'Yes, do that.' Vivius rubbed the bristles on his chin. 'So, is it true? Is the emperor coming to Rome? Is he well enough?'

Felix ran his hand through his hair as the sea breezes picked up. 'He's well enough. Signs are he's going through a period of sanity, but how long that will last is anyone's guess. As for whether he will be well enough to come to Rome, I've no idea. sure. It was the first thing I could think of to get you away. There have been developments while you've been in Palestine though.'

'Developments? I keep being told there have been developments but no one cares to enlighten me.'

'The emperor will do that.' Felix settled himself in the stern clearly unperturbed by the choppy waters. 'But the most important thing to ask is, do you have proof of illegalities against Sejanus?'

It was at that moment Vivius realised they had left the harbour and the waves had begun pounding up against the side of the boat tossing it, and him, from side to side. Although he would have enjoyed going into details with a fellow senator, a brief nod of the head was all he could manage. Fortunately, Felix appeared comfortable enough with that and content to continue the rest of the journey in silence.

By the time they reached the Isle of Capri, Vivius found the sea voyage followed by a steep walk up the cliffs had done nothing to help his exhaustion or the pains in his stomach. But both were forgotten when he saw it was Vigils guarding the palace, and not the emperor's own Praetorian Guards.

'What in the name of all the gods is going on?' he murmured.

'You'll find out soon enough.' Felix answered. He led him up to the main entrance and through the same double doors he had entered some weeks previously. They thudded shut behind him. Vivius raised an eyebrow, taken aback by the sizeable gathering of senior Praetorian Guards, Senators, the consul, magistrates and members of the equestrian order in the hall.

'You got back just in time, Senator.' Macro, Prefect of the Vigils, stepped forward, saluted and stepped back to let them pass.

'Time for what?' Vivius murmured as Felix ushered him through the crowded rooms.

'The emperor will tell you.'

Vivius realised that whispered conversations were breaking off as they passed to stare at his unkempt appearance, and he became uncomfortably conscious of the fresh streaks of vomit down his clothes. Although he was comforted by fact that the colleagues whose integrity and judgement he respected acknowledged him in a more friendly manner.

A moment later, he was admitted into a room designed for comfort rather than show. The emperor was seated in a high backed chair; his fingers drummed impatiently on the wooden scrolled armrests. A low marble table sat in front of him. The Vigil who had been following with the luggage dropped it at Vivius's feet and departed.

'See you later,' Felix murmured and closed the door behind him.

'You're late! I expected you days ago,' Tiberius snapped.

Vivius noticed the emperor was pale but the vagueness he had exhibited at their last meeting appeared to be less obvious. 'I realise that, Caesar; the weather...' Vivius dropped his eyes aware that the emperor was scrutinizing him from head to foot with a look of disgust on his face.

'By all the gods, Senator. You look as though you've been dragged out of a pit.' He snorted a chuckle.

Vivius breathed a sigh of relief, finding it small comfort that if nothing else his unseemly appearance had put the emperor in a good mood. 'I apologize, Caesar. The journey...'

Tiberius waved his hand dismissively. 'Quite! Quite! You've got what I want?'

'Yes, Excellency.' Vivius knelt down and opened Lucanus's shabby cloth travelling bag. He grimaced as a smell of damp clothes emerged. Pulling out the ledgers, he dropped them on the table and snapped the bag shut. Then, opening the medical case he pulled out the parchments and couldn't resist spreading his work across the table with a sense of satisfaction. The amount of material he had accumulated in so short a time gave the impression he had been hard at work.

'Can I suggest you take a look at this one first, Caesar?' Vivius handed the emperor the parchment of policies with Sejanus's signature at the bottom.

Tiberius pointed over to the window. 'Sit over there, Senator. I may have questions for you while I read.'

Vivius made his way over to the window, sat down in a heavily embroidered chair, and for a while he was left with nothing to do but listen to his stomach grumbling from lack of food. It occurred to him that what morsel of food he had managed to force down during his journey over the Mediterranean had promptly ended up over the side of the boat again.

He glanced out of the window. A beautiful, semi-naked statue of Venus stood in the middle of the garden. He found his thoughts drifting towards Aurelia. Why in the name of all the gods had she gone to Felix's summer villa? Why Felix? He and Aurelia were no more than acquaintances, weren't they? *Weren't they?* He took a deep breath as the first trickle of doubts filtered into his head. But if Aurelia had been getting pressure from Sejanus he reasoned, perhaps she felt Felix was the only person she could turn to?

He jumped as Tiberius banged on the marble table.

'Pilate has been executing *Sejanus's* policies in Palestine? *Sejanus's* policies?'

'Yes, Caesar. Pilate is a strong supporter of Sejanus.' Vivius stood up as the emperor moved silently across the room towards him; silent that is, except for a slight squeak of his sandal. He stared into the garden, and Vivius thought he detected a look of sadness in his eyes.

'And, if I may say, Caesar, judging from the way Sejanus has been replacing your army commanders and governors over the last year I suspect Rome's colonies will have similar policies; although that has yet to be proved,' he added.

'Proof? You've given me all the proof I need, Senator.' The emperor continued staring out of the window. Eventually he said, 'A letter was smuggled into me from my sister-in-law, Julia Antonia Minor. She's a sound woman. I trust her judgement. She believes Sejanus has been plotting a revolt for months. The reason he's been replacing my army commanders and governors is so that when he takes over in Rome he's not met with opposition. Of course, Julia Antonia had no proof but...' Tiberius waved the parchment of policies with Sejanus's signature at the bottom. 'You have given me that.'

Turning away from the window, Tiberius made his way back to the marble table and picked up another parchment.

'I was told there have been developments while I've been away, Caesar?' Vivius ventured.

'Hmm? Developments? Ah, yes!' Tiberius dropped the parchment back on the table. 'I received a visit from Apicata, Sejanus's former wife. She tells me that my son Drusus...' The emperor's voice shook and he turned his head away.

Vivius waited.

When the emperor turned back, his voice was steadier. 'She makes claims against Lavilla, the wife of my dear son. She tells me Lavilla and Sejanus were lovers. She alleges they poisoned Drusus so they could marry. At first I dismissed her accusations as those of an embittered woman, but then a second letter from Julia Antonia declares there are witnesses to prove it.' His voice broke again but only momentarily. 'I don't believe Sejanus was interested in Lavilla. Sejanus is more interested in being a member of the Imperial family and my heir.' He paced across the room and back again before adding, 'And now Sejanus has turned my Praetorian Guards against me. That's why the Vigils are here.' He folded his arms against his chest. 'I can't say any of this is a surprise to me, Senator. I think I've had my suspicions about Sejanus for some time, but I've been...ill. I haven't wanted trouble. Life on Capri suited me. It was...convenient having Sejanus handle affairs in Rome. I trusted him. I believed him to be a dear friend when all the time...' Tiberius turned away and returning to the table began reading the parchment from Joseph of Arimathea.

Vivius sat down again and listened to a Vigil officer barking out orders. There was a stamping of feet, salutes and uneven marching of guards, none of which resembled a Praetorian Guards' efficiency, but judging from the emperor's comments they were doing their best in difficult circumstances.

He waited, aware that the sun would be setting soon and his body was aching from the effort of vomiting and lack of food. He glanced across at the emperor engrossed in his reading and wondered how time always seemed to move with such incredible slowness when there were so many other important issues to deal with.

Eventually Tiberius said, 'So, Sejanus has been responsible for the deaths of prominent Jewish businessmen and for no other reason than he hates the Jews, eh?' His eyes dropped down to the bottom of the page. 'And it would seem from his signature that once again, Pilate is following Sejanus's policies; no trials before a crucifixion.' Tiberius stabbed at the parchment the clerk had sent from the tribune at the fort in Jerusalem. 'I haven't read all of this, but it puts a completely different slant on the deaths of those two hundred Jews; a massacre, the tribune calls it.'

'Yes, Caesar.'

Tiberius opened the second ledger. Once again there was silence, not so prolonged this time.

'I don't understand all these figures, but I suspect it indicates that taxes from Palestine are going in the pockets of Sejanus and Pontius Pilate?'

'Yes, Caesar.' Vivius paused a beat. 'I brought the Greek bookkeeper back with me as a witness for the prosecution against Sejanus and Pilate. Sejanus needs money for his revolt against you and this is how he's raising it. The bookkeeper risked his life bringing this information back to Rome for you.'

Tiberius looked up sharply. 'But you have him safe?'

Vivius bit his lip. 'I'm hoping so, Caesar. Senator Felix Seneca will be sending in legionaries first thing in the morning to guard the house where he's staying.'

'Good.' Tiberius continued his reading.

'Unfortunately, Fabius, the man who brought these indiscretions to your attention in the first place was murdered,' Vivius added.

Tiberius looked up again. 'Murdered?'

'Yes, Caesar. His home was ransacked and his family threatened.'

'By who?'

'I have no proof but I have my suspicions, and with your permission, Caesar, I'd like to instigate enquiries.'

'Yes! Yes! Yes!' The emperor dropped his head to examine the records again.

Unobserved, Vivius scrutinized his emperor. The sagging flesh under his jaws showed him to be aging, his eyes looked tired but it was apparent his speech and actions were not those of a mad man, at least not today.

'Your Praetorian Guards, Caesar. Will they support you?'

Tiberius dragged his eyes away from the records and his mouth hardened. 'When Sejanus is arrested tomorrow, Macro will be Prefect of the Praetorian Guards. All I've been waiting for is proof, solid evidence, not rumours instigated by ambitious men and scheming women whose only interest is who I will name as my heir.' Slamming the ledger shut, Tiberius clasped his hands behind his back and paced across the room.

'I gather Sejanus is not aware of what's going on, Caesar?'

'I hope not. I've gone to great lengths to mislead him.' Tiberius gave a chuckle. 'I've had coins minted with his head on, statues erected in his honour, and rumours circulated that I'm announcing my heir tomorrow.' Tiberius lost his smile as he turned to him. 'Which is why your late arrival was causing such concern, Senator. I wanted Sejanus to think he was safe until I had sufficient evidence against him—now I have.' Tiberius furrowed his brow. 'But that's not my only problem. Which governors and army commanders in my colonies is still loyal to me? I'm in a power struggle, Senator Marcianus. What I need are trustworthy men who would be prepared to investigate these colonies.' The emperor examined him warily before adding, 'Men like you.'

Vivius licked his lips; they still tasted of salt. 'As, er...a senator, my place is in Rome, Caesar. I have plans to marry. I...'

'You refuse!'

Vivius sent his brain ticking rapidly over his escape routes—it found one.

'Yes, Caesar, I refuse but...if you would hear my reasons for the refusal.'

'I was under the impression you'd given them. Some notion about getting married and at the very time Rome needs you.' Tiberius pouted.

'There are other reasons, sire. They concern...your safety.'

'Oh?' Tiberius's attention had been caught.

'You gave me an assignment, but in my opinion I haven't completed it yet.'

'Go on?'

'As a magistrate I'd best be used in accumulating evidence and preparing a case against Sejanus and his supporters, his governors and Army commanders in the colonies, men disloyal to you, Caesar. Even as we speak, your supporters are gathering around you. I would like to be part of that group. The danger lies here, in Rome.' He paused a beat. 'Your relationship with the Senate has not always been, er...easy, shall we say. As a senator of Rome I can do something about that.' Vivius allowed his words to sink in before adding, 'It would be my privilege to find a suitable, and younger man for you to send to the colonies, if you wish. I...I'm a bad sailor.'

Tiberius examined Vivius with an amused curl on his lip. 'I can see that, Senator.'

'You need me in Rome, Caesar.' Vivius persisted.

'Do I?'

'Yes, Caesar.

'And you would rather be in Rome, which is why you've put your argument so well, Senator Marcianus,' Tiberius said dryly. His eyes flickered over the reports on his desk but Vivius could see he wasn't really reading them. 'As usual, what you say makes sense.'

In the ensuing silence, Vivius wondered how much longer he could stand this interview. He shuffled uncomfortably.

'Are you anxious to be away, Senator?'

'No, Caesar. But I imagine you would prefer a more delicate aroma around you.'

Tiberius threw his head back and laughed. 'I like you, Senator Marcianus.' He closed the ledger on his desk with a thump. 'But if you want to unite the Senate behind their emperor, you may need promoting.' He smiled slyly at him. 'Is that what this is all about?'

Vivius's chin jutted out. Two offers of promotion in one day? The corner of his mouth quivered at the honour of being sought after. Yes, of course he wanted promotion, he thought. Of course, he wanted respect and financial gain. Who didn't? But what he wanted above all else was a far greater voice in Rome than his father had ever...he flinched. This had nothing to do with his father; this was *his* promotion; *his* decision...

The emperor was watching him shrewdly, as though he sensed an inner struggle taking place. But being a man familiar with inner struggles he didn't interrupt, he waited.

'No, Caesar, I'm not after promotion,' Vivius said quietly. 'The key issue for me is the integrity of the Senate. What I would like to see is power taken from Sejanus, Pilate brought back to Rome to answer these charges, and Fabius's killer brought to justice.'

Tiberius rubbed his chin with his index finger. 'Well said, Senator.' He paused a beat. 'Tomorrow morning power will be taken from Sejanus. I'd like you to be there.'

'Yes, Caesar. As you wish.'

CHAPTER EIGHTEEN

(Rome)

Knowing that within the hour there would be momentous changes taking place in the government, Vivius was surprised to arrive in Rome and find life carrying on as normal. The citizens of Rome were enjoying the morning sunshine, stall-holders were vying loudly with each other for business, slaves were being sold in the market square and there was the usual bustle of activity in the streets. As far as the people of Rome were concerned, Tiberius was still on Capri preparing to name his successor, and as far as Sejanus was concerned — that was him, Vivius mused.

When he, Felix and the senators who had been on the Isle of Capri with the emperor reached the Senate House he noticed that most of his colleagues headed for the front benches. They were clearly anxious to get an unobstructed view of unfolding events. Vivius, conscious of his unkempt appearance, crept towards the back. Felix, unfazed by how his companion looked, joined him.

'Any better?' he murmured as they sat down.

Vivius pulled the corners of his mouth down. He still felt acutely embarrassed over his bout of seasickness on the early morning journey over from Capri. 'If I never see another boat again I'll not view it as a hardship,' he said quietly. 'Two hours' sleep, that's all the emperor left me with…two hours. Fortunately he fed me but he had me up talking till the early hours of the morning. Not even a chance to clean up.' He rubbed his eyes. They still stung with sea spray and tiredness. Folding his arms across his chest he gazed down at the balding heads of his fellow senators. A thought occurred to him.

'Felix; yesterday you said Aurelia had got…involved? Involved in what?' He spoke quietly, the circular benches and high ceiling in the Senate House was a great medium for voices to carry.

Felix brought his hand up to his mouth to hide his moving lips. 'She hid Apicata from Sejanus and got vital information to the emperor on the death of his son.'

'She...she did what?'

'Shh! Keep your voice down.' Felix glanced around but the arrival of curious senators with their noisy greetings drowned out their conversation. 'She hid poor Apicata under her couch, then lay on it while Sejanus searched the house.' He gave a chuckle. 'After that she had the guts to meet up with a courier belonging to Julie Antonia Minor and smuggle her letter to Tiberius.' Felix hedged a grin. 'You have quite a lady there, Vivius. If she was mine, I wouldn't have left her to... Whoa!' Felix sat forward. 'Sejanus! And he's early.'

Vivius ran his hand down his face trying to make sense of what he had just heard. Admittedly, Aurelia had always been lively, he thought, but what in the name of Jupiter had possessed her to get involved in...? He sat forward; his thoughts distracted by an immaculate Sejanus strutting across the marble floor in his Praetorian Prefect's uniform, his armour shining, his face glowing with anticipation. Deciding that pondering the bizarre actions of his betrothed would have to be postponed, he sat back in his chair and waited for proceedings to begin.

He glanced around. The Senate House was full. Sejanus was being greeted warmly by fawning supporters. Most of whom, Vivius judged from their excited faces, appeared to be under the same expectations as Sejanus himself. The only sober faces came from the senators who had travelled over from the Isle of Capri with them, and a few puzzled by this extraordinary meeting of the Senate.

Vivius watched Sejanus carefully. He was laughing in an affected manner at a comment made by a fat-faced, over-jewelled senator. But Vivius could see by his glazed expression that he wasn't really listening to what was being said. Whether Sejanus actually felt the intensity of Vivius's stare was hard to say, but he suddenly glanced up the tiered benches to the back of the Senate House, and by the way his laughter faded and his brow knitted, Vivius knew he'd been spotted.

'This could be awkward,' he murmured.

Felix shuffled uncomfortably. 'He's heading this way,' he muttered. 'Keep it together, keep him talking...'

Sejanus gave Felix a nod of acknowledgment as he approached. 'Huh! Senator Marcianus. Here for the big event I see.' Sejanus examined his unkempt appearance in a manner that reminded Vivius of the way he chose his new slaves, with a look of contempt. 'You've been to see the emperor?'

Vivius kept his arms folded across his chest. Whatever happened, he decided. There was no way on this earth he could fawn, bow and scrape to this overbearing son of a...he clenched his fists under his armpits. 'I have.'

In the distance he heard the rhythmic tread of the legionaries' boots.

'And, er...has he arrived in Rome yet?'

There was something almost pathetic in the way he asked the question, like a schoolboy waiting for a crumb of praise from his tutor. Vivius had an overwhelming desire to blurt out the truth and make the arrest himself, but realising the stupidity of such an action kept a firm grip on his tongue. 'I have no idea, Prefect Sejanus,' he said coldly.

'And when you saw him did he...'

The rhythmic tread was now the heavy stomp of approaching legionaries.

'...did he mention the time of his arrival? All I received was a message...'

There was a loud clomp outside the building as boots came to an abrupt halt.

'...that I had to be at the Senate House midday. I assume...'

There was a thud as the doors were flung open. Voices

dropped. Sejanus lifted his head, his face lightened and his eyes gleamed with greedy anticipation. 'Yes, that sounds like his arrival now. If you'll excuse me I shall go and welcome...' His face clouded over in confusion as a grim faced Macro entered the Senate House wearing the uniform of the Prefect of the Praetorian Guards. Behind him were four Praetorian Guards. Behind them a small detachment of the emperor's loyal Pretorian Guards who spread out quickly around the circular floor.

'What in the name of...?' Sejanus hastily made his way down to the centre of the Senate House. 'What in the name of all the gods are you playing at, Macro? Where...?'

Vivius leant forward as Prefect Macro's voice carried around the benches. 'Lucius Aelius Sejanus, by order of the Emperor Tiberius I am arresting you...'

Sejanus's ruddy face drained of colour. A roar echoed around the building, a mixture of cheers, shock and objections as senators rose to their feet, their arms waving like a display of white and purple flags. Four Praetorian Guards stepped forward, positioning themselves on either side of Sejanus. His eyes widened with shock.

'What is this?' he demanded.

His supporters had moved forward in his defence, but as the Praetorian Guards drew their swords they stepped back, uncertainty written across their faces.

'I'll have you hung for this, Macro,' Sejanus bellowed. 'I'll make sure...' He lunged forward. His remaining words lost as the emperor's Praetorian Guards restrained him.

Macro never flinched. Withdrawing a parchment from the belt of his tunic, he unrolled it and read, 'I am also placing under arrest...' His voice carried clearly around the House, only to be drowned out a moment later by the stomping boots of a further detachment of Praetorian Guards, these ones to arrest the supporters of Sejanus.

Vivius stood up, his arms still folded across his chest, a sense of satisfaction hovering over him, waiting for a convenient time to be wallowed in. His eyes scanned the room as the abusive cries towards Sejanus grew louder. Some of them he noticed, included those who had proposed to be his most ardent followers. Others cringed on their benches, waiting for their names to be called, waiting for the inevitable arrival of Praetorian Guards at their side to drag them off to Mamertine Prison.

And then a captain in the Praetorian Guards arrived at the trot. Macro paused in his reading of the list to listen to what the captain had to say. Then Macro's head turned, and with an expression of alarm he pointed the captain in their direction.

Felix breathed in sharply. 'Something's wrong.'

The captain was panting when he arrived at their bench. 'Senator Felix Seneca?'

Felix nodded.

'Sejanus's children...there's been an order...Sejanus must have no heirs.'

Felix grabbed the captain's shoulder. His face was grim. 'Where are they?'

'In Prefect Sejanus's house, Senator. But there's a unit of Praetorian Guards already on their way there.'

'What? Who sent them?'

The captain looked uncertain. 'I...I'm not sure, Senator. But Prefect Macro's ordered we get them, take them to their mother, the Lady Apicata.'

'Right. Get two of your men.' He turned to Vivius. 'Are you armed?'

Vivius patted his short sword under his toga. He could already feel the adrenalin pulsating through his body, fighting off the tiredness.

'Come on then.'

But to Vivius's frustration, getting out of the Senate House was considerably harder than it had been to get it. They were forced to push their way through irate senators who had gathered in the aisles to give full vent to their bruised feelings at being under the rule of Sejanus for so long. Once outside they then had to fight their way through the curious citizens of Rome who had congregated to find out why Praetorian Guards had descended on the House of Senators.

It took longer than Vivius had expected to get through them, but when they had he, Felix, the captain and his two men ran all the way to Sejanus's town house. It wasn't far, a matter of streets that was all. But Vivius slowed down when he caught sight of the house.

'We're too late,' he panted and pointed ahead.

A unit of Praetorian Guards, led by the high-ranking officer who had met him off the boat the previous day, were coming out of the house. The officer was wiping blood off his sword. He watched them approach, his lips pursed, his cleft chin jutting out.

'You're too late. It's done! The emperor need have no fears that heirs of Sejanus will be claiming his empire.'

'Why you ... You're on the emperor's orders?' Felix demanded incredulously.

The captain and his two guards ran inside the house.

'Yesterday you supported Sejanus,' Vivius challenged.

The officer shrugged. Ignoring Felix's question he turned smugly to Vivius. 'You're the politicians. I simply obey the orders of whoever is in charge at the time.'

'And who ordered you kill these children?' Felix insisted.

The officer slid his sword into its sheath. His men, hearing the raised voices, gathered around their commanding officer. Vivius caught sight of the captain at the door. When he caught Vivius's eye, he pushed his helmet back off his forehead and shook his head.

Leaving Felix to deal with the Praetorian Guards, Vivius made his way deliberately up to the front door. It was gloomy inside, barely any light coming through the partially closed shutters. At what point he asked himself why he needed to see this slaughter for himself he wasn't sure. But once inside he knew there was no going back. He wandered through to the living quarters and instantly spotted the smooth leg of a child protruding from behind the couch. It was the boy. Vivius grimaced. He was used to death, he'd seen plenty of it in his time, but he had never been able to reconcile himself with the unnecessary cruelty or death of children. Perhaps it had something to do with his own experience of childhood, he mused, and was surprised that that thought had never occurred to him before.

He looked down at the boy; he was young; hadn't even reached puberty, and there were four, five, no six sword stabs in the skinny young body. Vivius examined the scene of the murder. There was blood on the walls, furniture overturned and a sword still in the boy's hand. At least the lad had put up a good fight, Vivius thought. His mother could be proud of him for that. He glanced around. Two children the captain had said.

Vivius made his way back across the hall and into the bedroom. He knew what he would find before he got there. Pushing back the door he found himself staring down at a pathetic little figure, barely into womanhood, lying on the bed. Her long, brown hair was spread across the pillow as if she was sleeping. But the open eyes and terrified expression was not one of a young girl's innocent sleep. Her bodice had been slashed to expose barely formed breasts and her dress had been ripped up to her waist leaving her purity sullied, exposed and bloody. A dagger had sliced her throat. Snatching up a sheet from the floor, Vivius covered the naked body. He wasn't revolted; he'd seen it before. It was common practice. No Roman would kill a virgin and offend the gods, he knew that. But...

'It was on the emperor's orders.'

Vivius turned. Felix was standing at the door staring down at the girl's foot protruding out of the sheet.

'By Jupiter, Vivius. Do you think we're simply replacing one monster for another?' He spoke quietly, confidentially.

Vivius shook his head. 'I don't know. I'm too tired to think straight.'

They stood in a heavy silence; the euphoria of victory over Sejanus lost in this tragedy.

Eventually Vivius took a deep breath. 'I'm going home,' he said. He looked purposefully at Felix. 'And then I'm going to get Aurelia.'

* * *

It was a combination of the uphill climb in the hot afternoon sunshine, an aching stomach and tiredness that slowed Vivius down. Common sense told him his bags should be lighter without the ledgers and reports, but it didn't feel that way.

After an hour he stopped and ran his tongue around the inside of his mouth. It was thick and tasted foul. Making his way over to the high arched aqueduct which brought water into the city, he cupped his hands under the trickle seeping through a crack and drank deeply. Then splashing cold water over his head and face he rubbed his hand around the back of his neck and rolled his shoulders. His head was pounding as though the boots of an entire legion was marching through it.

Flinging himself and his luggage under the shade of a tree he brought out the small loaf and slab of cheese he had bought on his way through the city. As he still had well over an hour of brisk walking ahead of him, he decided he would rest for no longer than ten minutes.

It wasn't a restful ten minutes. He found the bread tasteless, the cheese too strong for his upset stomach, and he spent the entire time brooding over Aurelia—*and Felix*. His thumb searched out the smooth red ruby in the handle of his dagger as his bruised ego ruminated on the relationship between them. After five minutes he poked his teeth with his tongue to clear the crumbs and cheese, then tossing what remained of his meagre meal in the undergrowth he staggered to his feet again.

An hour later he turned off the main highway and followed the track to the left, towards the prosperous Suranus stables Dorio had inherited from his father. The track was rough in places, gouged out by carts from his olive grove and horses from the Suranus stables.

He paused behind a tree, scanning the green terrain for any sharp reds, silvers or blacks of the Praetorian Guards who hadn't yet been informed of Sejanus's arrest, but the estate was quiet. True to his word, Felix had recalled the Praetorian Guards keeping the Suranus stables under observation.

Vivius was debating whether to check on his prime witness, when a small, bandy-legged man emerged from the villa laughing. Dorio was behind him. The breath going through Vivius's nostrils let out a faint whistle of relief at the sight of them.

Deciding he'd had enough of playing nursemaid and he was in no mood to talk to anyone, he waited until they had gone inside before moving back on to the track again. As he followed the boundary around the fields towards his olive grove, the horses from the Suranus estate raised their heads from their grazing. They made no attempt to canter up to investigate; he was after all a familiar figure. A few minutes later, Vivius gave a sigh of pleasure at the most beautiful sight in the world, his olive grove.

A welcoming whine and the cantering of hooves told him his horse had sensed his approach, as she always did. He clicked his tongue at her, although he knew she was too far away to hear him. But sure enough, she was at the fence when he came over the rise, her ears up, her tail swishing away the flies, her nose blowing fiercely in greeting. Vivius dropped his bags by the fence and rested his head on the animal's silky muzzle. She was warm, the touch of her flesh familiar, she smelled of horse feed and had flies buzzing around her but he didn't mind. He reckoned he didn't smell too good himself.

He stroked her ears. 'I can't live without her, you know that?' he whispered. 'I have to get her back.'

The animal snorted into his neck as though she understood the comment was not directed towards her but the other woman in his life, Aurelia.

'Why did I never tell her that?'

The horse nudged him. He continued stroking her silky neck.

'Vivius!'

Vivius felt his heart lurch, then it moved into a steady gallop.

'Vivius?'

He could hear the swish of her feet on the grass. He turned slowly and watched her approach as though he was seeing her for the first time. He noticed that she didn't have the voluptuous figure of Claudia; Aurelia was thin, painfully thin. Nor did she possess the strong sexual attraction that had drawn him to the Procurator's wife in the first place but...

'You're beautiful,' he said, and to his embarrassment his voice cracked. 'You're the most beautiful woman I...' He was surprised at how easily those words had come out of his mouth.

She raised her eyebrows, equally surprised, and then she was by his side, her small hand tucked into his, her expression questioning this unexpected openness in him. He buried his head in her shoulder and for the first time in his life, Vivius Marcianus wept—not out loud, not so that she would notice, but silently and deep within himself. If Aurelia was confused by his behaviour she didn't show it, but held him close, rubbing his back, her breath warm in his ear as she whispered how much she loved him.

Vivius never imagined he had the capacity to love someone as much as he did at that moment. Nor did he imagine his heart could be open enough to receive so much love back. All he wanted to do was soak in it, so he took the risk, and did. Only when he believed he was sufficiently in control of his emotions again did he lift his head.

'When I got your letter... I...I would do anything for you, anything... But...you and Felix...' Confused by his inability to string a sentence together, he rested his lips on the top of her head so she wouldn't see his face. Her hair was soft and silky. Aurelia stepped back.

'Anything Vivius?' she asked. Taking his face into her hands she regarded him steadily. 'Does that include compromising your integrity?' She didn't speak accusingly but gently. 'I need to know, Vivius. Sejanus said you had concealed evidence from Julius's trial.'

Vivius didn't answer, not at first and when he did, he said, 'Once. I did it once, to save you being arrested alongside Julius.' He paused. 'You...and Felix?'

She shook her head. 'I went to him because I was afraid Sejanus would arrest me.' She paused. 'Felix wanted me to go to his summer villa but...I couldn't bear to be so far away from you, my love. So I persuaded Phaedo to bring me here, not that he needed much persuading. I've been staying with him. As for me and Felix, it was a long time ago and...' A teasing smile played across her lips. 'Don't tell me you're jealous, Vivius?'

He gave a crooked smile. She laughed up at him, running her fingers through his hair.

The horse nudged them to remind them she was there, but they ignored her.

But then Aurelia knitted her brow and examined her fingers. Stepping back she looked him up and down.

'I love you, Vivius,' she said tenderly. 'I love you dearly, but...' Her eyes twinkled mischievously and she wrinkled her nose. 'But you're all crumpled and dirty, and my dearest senator, you smell disgusting!'

* * *

After a brief inspection of his new and completed villa, and a relaxing sampling of his new sophisticated bathing facilities with its underfloor heating, Vivius and Aurelia made their way to the Suranus villa. Vivius to check on his witness for the prosecution and Aurelia to see her brother. The only difference was, after their evening meal together, Vivius made his way home alone. Aurelia insisted on staying with her wounded brother, who angrily told her to stop fussing, insisting that he wasn't wounded, he had simply lost an arm in Palestine.

After an evening of continual chatter, Vivius was relieved to be alone. He needed time to think, which was why he didn't go directly to his new villa but stopped by the long flat rock at the edge of his olive grove.

Sitting down he lifted his face to the cold night air, took a deep breath, then closing his eyes lost himself in the vastness of the heavens. Only his ears picked up the chirp of crickets, rustle of one animal stalking another, and the whisper of leaves from his olive trees.

For the first time in weeks, Vivius rested.

When he opened his eyes again, he found they landed on a blaze of lights stretching the length and breadth of the city of Rome. Somewhere down there the position of power was shifting, he mused. Sejanus and his supporters would be in prison. Tiberius would be in control. There'd be court cases he would be asked to judge, but...that was for another day.

Swivelling around he viewed the single lamp burning in the kitchen of his new villa; young wispy bushes waving around a patio, and from this angle... Vivius's gaze drifted towards the old farmhouse. Half demolished it was barely recognizable. Once it was completely demolished he would never need to think of his father or his childhood...or....

The silence around him seemed loud. Loud enough for him not to feel awkward in breaking through that stillness. He ran his tongue around his mouth. Each word he spoke was stilted, clipped.

'Fact; my…father…never…loved…me.'

It was a shock to hear the truth spoken from his own lips.

'Nothing…I…did…ever pleased him.'

The trees in his olive grove seemed to rustle their leaves in a whispered understanding; the way they always had.

'My father was a harsh and unforgiving man.'

Vivius found he was getting used to the sound of his own voice. It seemed to him like…speaking out crimes and facts, the way he spoke them out in his courtroom.

'Fact; my father only loved himself.'

The crickets chirped nearby, their musical notes urgent before the night settled down to wait for dawn. Vivius rested his arms on his knees as a thought occurred to him.

'So why do I still search for his approval?'

This time he murmured because he wasn't stating a fact, he was asking a question of himself.

'Why do I still wish that he'll love me, even from his grave? Why do I still need to prove I'm a better man than he was?'

Vivius waited, as though expecting an answer. But the night was still.

It was an impulse that drove him to his feet. Vivius found that strange because, unlike Aurelia, he wasn't given to impulsive actions. Yet as he made his way towards what remained of the old farmhouse he sensed this impulse was different. There seemed to be a reason, even logic behind it, although he couldn't quite figure out what that was—yet.

The moon gave little light so he had to pick his way carefully through the wood piled up outside waiting for the builders to dispose of. He viewed the old kitchen dispassionately. All that remained were a few shelves, chairs, a dismantled cupboard and… His eye fell on a familiar object in the corner, a basin. He picked it up. Bad memories of the morning Fabiana had whipped the clothes off him and left him stark naked in front of Aurelia surged back. Pursing his lips, he threw the basin outside as if he was flinging away an unwanted relic from the past.

He paused. He wasn't sure what made him heave a cupboard door on to his shoulders and stagger outside with it. He was already exhausted so his knees buckled under the weight and he stumbled over the builders' debris. But he found a deep sense of satisfaction in hurling the door on to the pile of rotten wood stacked for burning.

He stared at the dry timber.

Then moving briskly towards his new villa he marched into the kitchen and snatched up one of the lanterns. His housekeeper threw him a puzzled look but he had no intention of enlightening her. In fact, Vivius realised he wasn't too sure what he was doing himself. For the first time in his life he was following his instincts rather than logic or reason, and it felt good.

The lantern lit his way back to the old farmhouse. He stopped by the woodpile, stared at it momentarily, and then hurled the lantern on to the rotten wood. The oil dripped through the rotten beams and on to the old kitchen door. A tongue of flame caught the oil, flared and then lapped it up. Vivius gave a grunt of satisfaction and marched back into the old farmhouse kitchen feeling like a man who had been given an assignment.

But an assignment of his choosing.

Every broken chair, kitchen shelf, rotten floorboard and useless beam was dragged out of the old farmhouse, across the grass and hurled onto the fire. Splinters of wood caught his hands but he barely noticed; his clean tunic was soon filthy but he wasn't aware of that or his tiredness.

Eventually, exhausted by his actions, he stopped. His body sagged as he stared into the flames. His eyes drifted up to the heavens, up to that place of the dead, wherever that was. He didn't know and he didn't care. 'Father!' He shouted. 'These things were my childhood. I give them back.' He paused. 'I give you back...the...the physical and...and mental pain you inflicted on me — *me*, your son.' Picking up a stool he hurled it into the fire.

Sparks flew into the air, hissing, spitting, cracking. The flames grew higher.

The table was next.

'Father, you can take my bitter disappointment that...I was never good enough for you.'

The basin.

'Father, I give you back the sting of those...whippings... beatings...'

Chairs, benches, floorboards.

'Father, you called me a liar...but I never lied... Take it back.'

Vivius was intelligent enough to know that what he was doing was symbolic, yet he was finding in these symbolic actions a sense of freedom. Naming his demons out loud and watching them burn in the fire reminded him of a comment Simon the Jew had made.

Forgiving is all about deciding not to carry bitterness and hatred around with you anymore.

That's what I'm doing, Vivius thought. I'm getting rid of bitterness and hatred. I'm getting rid of the rot inside *me*.

And as the moon rose higher into the sky, Vivius continued feeding the fire outside the old farmhouse until there was no more wood to burn and all of his demons had been cremated. Only then did he slump against the wall in exhaustion and stare unblinking into the flames soaring into the night sky.

At what point he noticed Phaedo he wasn't sure.

'How long have you been there, Phaedo?'

'Long enough, young master.'

'I'm getting rid of the rot, Phaedo.'

'Aye, it needed getting rid of, especially with a new mistress about to take up residence. We don't want old ghosts upsetting things, do we?'

There was silence between them, a comfortable silence. There had always been that between them.

'Fire's beginning to dwindle down. Would you like me to keep watch on it, master?'

'No. I'll do it.'

'Only if you want to, but seems to me you might need to attend to your guest.'

'What?'

'The new mistress, sir.' Phaedo moved towards the fire and they viewed each other through the flames. 'She must have seen the flames and come to make sure you're all right.'

Vivius turned around. Aurelia was standing outside the villa. 'Well, I am all right.'

'I know that,' Phaedo said quietly. 'I made sure of that, but the little mistress needs to see that for herself.'

Turning his back on the old farmhouse, Vivius made his way over to the villa wondering how in the name of all the gods he was going to explain not only his unkempt appearance—again— but having a fire in the middle of the night.

'I saw the fire,' Aurelia said hesitantly.

Vivius nodded. 'I've been fighting a battle,' he said. It was all he wanted to say. It was all he had the energy to say. And he knew that with Aurelia, it was all he needed to say.

'Did you win?' she asked softly.

'Yes,' Vivius said quietly. 'I won.'

Footnote:

Charged with conspiracy against Tiberius, Prefect Lucius Aelius Sejanus was arrested and executed, along with his followers.

The Emperor Tiberius recalled Pontius Pilate to Rome after the murder of the Samaritans, but before he reached Rome, the Emperor Tiberius died.

**TOP HAT
BOOKS**

Top Hat Books

Historical fiction that lives

We publish fiction that captures the contrasts, the achievements, the optimism and the radicalism of ordinary and extraordinary times across the world.

We're open to all time periods and we strive to go beyond the narrow, foggy slums of Victorian London. Where are the tales of the people of fifteenth century Australasia? The stories of eighth century India? The voices from Africa, Arabia, cities and forests, deserts and towns? Our books thrill, excite, delight and inspire.

The genres will be broad but clear. Whether we're publishing romance, thrillers, crime, or something else entirely, the unifying themes are timescale and enthusiasm. These books will be a celebration of the chaotic power of the human spirit in difficult times. The reader, when they finish, will snap the book closed with a satisfied smile.
If you have enjoyed this book, why not tell other readers by posting a review on your preferred book site.

Recent bestsellers from Top Hat Books are:

Grendel's Mother
The Saga of the Wyrd-Wife

Susan Signe Morrison

Grendel's mother, a queen from Beowulf, threatens the fragile
political stability on this windswept land.

Paperback: 978-1-78535-009-2 ebook: 978-1-78535-010-8

Queen of Sparta
A Novel of Ancient Greece

T.S. Chaudhry

History has relegated her to the role of bystander, what if Gorgo,
Queen of Sparta, had played a central role in the Greek resistance
to the Persian invasion?

Paperback: 978-1-78279-750-0 ebook: 978-1-78279-749-4

Mercenary
R.J. Connor

Richard Longsword is a mercenary, but this time it's not for
money, this time it's for revenge…

Paperback: 978-1-78279-236-9 ebook: 978-1-78279-198-0

Black Tom
Terror on the Hudson

Ron Semple

A tale of sabotage, subterfuge and political shenanigans
in Jersey City in 1916; America is on the cusp of war and the fate of
the nation hinges on the decision of one young policeman.

Paperback: 978-1-78535-110-5 ebook: 978-1-78535-111-2

Destiny Between Two Worlds
A Novel about Okinawa
Jacques L. Fuqua, Jr.
A fateful October 1944 morning offered no inkling that the lives of
thousands of Okinawans would be profoundly changed—forever.
Paperback: 978-1-78279-892-7 ebook: 978-1-78279-893-4

Cowards
Trent Portigal
A family's life falls into turmoil when the parents' timid political
dissidence is discovered by their far more enterprising children.
Paperback: 978-1-78535-070-2 ebook: 978-1-78535-071-9

Godwine Kingmaker
Part One of The Last Great Saxon Earls
Mercedes Rochelle
The life of Earl Godwine is one of the enduring enigmas of English
history. Who was this Godwine, first Earl of Wessex;
unscrupulous schemer or protector of the English? The answer
depends on whom you ask...
Paperback: 978-1-78279-801-9 ebook: 978-1-78279-800-2

The Last Stork Summer
Mary Brigid Surber
Eva, a young Polish child, battles to survive the designation of
"racially worthless" under Hitler's Germanization Program.
Paperback: 978-1-78279-934-4 ebook: 978-1-78279-935-1 $4.99 £2.99

Messiah Love
Music and Malice at a Time of Handel
Sheena Vernon
The tale of Harry Walsh's faltering steps on his journey to success
and happiness, performing in the playhouses of Georgian London.
Paperback: 978-1-78279-768-5 ebook: 978-1-78279-761-6

A Terrible Unrest
Philip Duke
A young immigrant family must confront the horrors of the
Colorado Coalfield War to live the American Dream.
Paperback: 978-1-78279-437-0 ebook: 978-1-78279-436-3